Since leaving Oxford, Kate ████ ████ publishing and television. She re████ ████ for her poetry in 1996 and Seren published her first collection, *Cohabitation*, in 1998. Her first novel, *Mummy's Legs*, was published by Virago Press the same year. She lives in London with her husband and daughter, Eve.

Praise for *Mummy's Legs*:

'Elegant and powerful – her eye for the infinitive capacity of human beings to cause one another pain is developed to a fine degree' *The Times*

'Bingham bursts the bonds of the dysfunctional mother-daughter paradigm while at the same time perfectly capturing its dark heart' *New York Times*

'The mother and daughter roles are reversed and Bingham shows us the messy difficulties of this relationship with perception and empathy' *Daily Express*

Readers won't be surprised to learn that Bingham is a poet . . . nor are they soon likely to encounter such a sensitive rendering of a painful, if memorable childhood' *Washington Post*

Also by Kate Bingham

COHABITATION
MUMMY'S LEGS

S l i p s t r e a m

KATE BINGHAM

For their patience, support, and sound advice, I would
like to thank Imogen, Maggie and Richard.

A *Virago* Book

First published by Virago Press in 2000
This edition published by Virago Press in 2001

A CIP catalogue record for this book
is available from the British Library.

ISBN 1 86049 779 9

Typeset in Bembo by M Rules
Printed and bound in Great Britain by
Clays Ltd, St Ives plc

Virago
A Division of
Little, Brown and Company (UK)
Brettenham House
Lancaster Place
London WC2E 7EN

Slipstream

Philip barred the Staff-Room door. He stood against it, crucified, reciting the same bland teacherly assurance, smiley and anaesthetised with shock. A pale hair curled at the knot of his grey silk tie and, underneath, the sleeves of his one and only plain white shirt were shadowy with sweat. The girls at the front stared up at him, wide-eyed and pleading for the latest news. 'Stand back. There's nothing to see,' he muttered automatically. Wasn't it time they went to bed? Had no one been listening to the Head when she appealed for calm? Why couldn't they, for once, just do as they were told?

Nina wedged her foot in the hinge, brushing his sleeve as she twisted for a better view. I can remember smelling her hair, thinking *I knew it, she's borrowed my shampoo again*, and vowing there and then to keep it locked up in future. 'Sorry, but I ran out,' she said, as though she'd read my mind, and we looked at each other and actually laughed, and the mistresses, thirty feet away, by the window, turned as one, glaring at us as though we'd interrupted the most important part of some incredibly complicated lesson.

Philip blinked. 'Go to bed, Beth,' he said to me.

Dr Slime snapped the catch on his briefcase, nodding at Mrs Greene. 'She'll be all right. Watch out for signs of concussion.' Mr Greene stuck out his hand like the host at a cocktail party saying his first goodbye, and Philip waved us aside. Fourths and Fifths nudged forwards, straining for a better view, and Nina squinted at them, pursed her lips. They were older than us, but sometimes age is not the only privilege, even at school.

'Did you ever smell such rank BO?' she muttered, shuddering as the doctor left the room. I looked at Philip. *Not you*, I wanted to say, in case he'd heard. The stains were fading now, they smelled of heat and salt and man's deodorant after the musk's rubbed off.

'There's nothing to see,' he said in the same blank voice, as Mr and Mrs Greene took an elbow each, lifting their daughter to her feet. The dress uncrumpled. All of a sudden it looked too big. Inside it, she sagged. Slowly the trio limped towards the door. Mrs Greene's cheeks were blotchy with dabbed-away tears and Mr Greene's mouth twisted as though he thought he ought to smile. The tips of his fingers were a mouldy white, his shoulder shook.

Sophie followed, cradling the violin. She whispered to Nina and me, 'We're taking her home,' but the other girls heard anyway.

'Send her our love,' I said. 'Tell her to come back soon.'

Everyone left quickly after that. Philip waited until he was sure the Greenes must have driven away, then disappeared in the same direction. Someone closed the

Staff-Room door. The Dining Hall was bolted shut. Nina wandered into the Quad, staring as the last few visitors faltered along creaky aisles and down the Changing-Room steps. Out through the double glass doors into a balmy, disbelieving night where friends and classmates huddled beneath the apple trees. Families drifted towards their cars. A knot of sympathisers lingered curiously in the passage way. The jukebox had been unplugged. Shadowy pyramids of Mars bars, Kit Kats, crisps and penny chews glinted behind the Tuck-Shop grille. Upstairs, where the Sixths slept, swing doors huffed and bedroom slippers squeaked along the lino. Louis Armstrong crooned from the nearest dorm. We drifted across the polished concrete, listening. We watched our feet. Nina stood before the podium, turning a slow pirouette. 'Budge up,' she said at last, crouching beside me on its lip. Shoe-prints dusted the tatty felt. We rested our chins on our knees and stared at the empty banks of seats ahead. Programmes lay scattered in the aisles and no one had remembered to turn off the stage lights.

'I wish we could stay here all holidays,' I said at last, 'and rearrange the dorms so we could be in with who we liked, and all the mistresses would go away and leave us in charge instead.'

Nina blinked at the ceiling. 'Swimming would be fun I suppose,' she allowed. Behind us an invisible orchestra performed its own, inaudible, repertoire. Never-heard notes burned black spaghetti into the faces of the music stands. 'They will be able to mend it, won't they?' she whispered, thinking of the violin.

'Maybe.' I was remembering the sound of the applause, the way each particle of noise is really the sound of a feeling, the sound of hundreds and hundreds of simultaneous tingly slaps, and it occurred to me that clapping is a kind of physical addiction, like scratching a mosquito bite, or smoking, or craving a single kiss.

We sat there for a long, long time, not saying anything, thinking too fast for the words to get a grip. The podium pressed into our bones. Nina checked her watch. She nudged me, tilting the face, and slowly we both stood up. We'd never been out that late before. The lights would be off in all the dorms on House. We could stay up until dawn and no one would know. Nobody cared about us tonight. Where was our spirit of adventure?

Nina yawned, sliding her arm through mine. It was a kind of promise. Next year, she smiled.

The taxi dips over a hump-backed bridge, pulls in at the edge of the tarmac, slides to a stop. The engine cuts and we fall silent in the back. Rain taps loudly at the dismal glass. It twists and streams along the windscreen-wipers, beads the water-meadow to a thousand silver pearls.

'You'll have to get out here and walk the rest. I told you we'd had flooding. This is as far as I can go.' The driver looks at us over his shoulder, half apologetic, half defiant. 'That'll be six pounds.'

Nina shuffles through her pockets, rummaging for change as I hand over a greasy ten pound note. Lou climbs out. She stretches and yawns, tipping her face flat-on to the sky. Her milk-blue eyelids flicker and she opens her mouth, extending her tongue to taste the rain.

The driver unlocks the boot and passes us our rucksacks one by one. 'You do know where you're going?' he asks with a resentful kind of fatherly concern. Nina looks at Lou.

'Of course we do.'

He shrugs, folds himself behind the steering-wheel once more and drives away. Lou waves stupidly, she gazes into

the empty space where the car has been. Already its intri-
cate, muddy tracks begin to shine. I grin at Nina and
shudder. Ahead of us the flood-plain shimmers and
twitches. Seagulls bob in the water. Blackbirds hop along
the tattered shore, fishing for worms. A cluster of glum-
looking ponies stands on an island of scrubby high ground
nearby, waiting to be rescued.

Coming up, there have been plenty of jokes about the
weather, as though expecting it to rain all week we can't
be disappointed, as though avoiding disappointment is the
most important thing. Lou and I stared through the window, chain-smoking. Raindrops raced silently from one
end of the glass to the other, shivering inside their gleamy
trails as the train jogged west across Berkshire and Nina
congratulated herself for having thought to bring a pack
of cards. 'Let's face it, there isn't going to be anything else
to do,' she muttered, propping her feet against the free seat
opposite. It would take four or five days to get the boat to
Lou's house. Four or five days of cheese on toast and
whist and soggy anoraks. Nina sighed. They were 18, not
45 for fuck's sake. They should've booked to go Club
Med.

'Is there a tape machine?' she asks.

'Unless she's taken it with her.' Lou loosens her
shoelaces. They've snapped so many times the ends aren't
long enough to knot, let alone tie in a bow. The grimy
nylon is beginning to unplait. She pockets her socks and
pushes her 501s to the knee. Mud squeezes into the gaps
between her long white toes. She wiggles them deliciously

and shivers as the soggy earth sinks, and puddles well slowly up the sides of her feet. 'Ahh.'

Nina fakes horror. 'Are you completely mad?' Water ripples into the distant tree-line. Willows at the edge of the meadow seem suspended in mid air. Behind them the black outlines of roof-tops and chimneys saw into a pewter sky. 'No way am I paddling through that.' She climbs the stile, curls her fingers into binoculars and swings round, scanning the horizon. 'Boatyard ahoy,' she points. Lou squints in approximately the right direction, stoops to gather the last three carrier bags. She hoists her rucksack, struggling to click the buckle around her waist.

'This way.' Nina follows a gravel path up the bank to the edge of the canal and disappears, momentarily, behind a bramble bush.

'I have been here before, you know,' Lou grumbles cheerfully. '*I* should be in charge.'

'And so you would, if you weren't so inept.' Up on the towpath Nina has stopped by a hawthorn tree for shelter. She's looking back at us, blinking in the rain. Her eyelashes have stuck together and her jacket clings, dark and tight across the shoulders. When she takes off her rucksack there will be a dry blue stripe around each arm. The muddy canal sweeps under a footbridge, out of sight. Dinghy masts poke up between the trees on the opposite bank. Far away we can hear people talking, and deeper than that the mutter of the river itself.

Lou picks her way along the grass at the edge of the gravel, trying not to wince. Raindrops well at the slicked-together ends of her elfish hair, trickle down the nape of her neck and seep into the collar of her shirt. One of her trouser legs has slipped, it drags in the mud. 'My fingers,' she wails, cheeks pink with effort. She slumps a carrier bag to the ground, sighs, turns her throbbing palms skyward and pulls a face. Raspberry creases zigzag furiously across her finger joints. The bag shifts, bottles clink and a matchbox wrapped in tin-foil topples out into a puddle.

'What the fuck—' Nina stares.

Something rattles inside as Lou pats it dry on her cuff. 'Homoeopathic asthma pills. Mum put them in for me.'

'I thought it was—'

'*You* should be so lucky!' Lou pauses. 'Isn't this wonderful.' They link arms, backpacks jostling for space on the path. It's raining harder now. Dockleaves by the side of the towpath flicker beneath the heavy drops, and the canal dances with light. Nina allows herself a grim little nod. 'It better not rain all sodding week.'

'Who cares?'

'I do, I want a tan.'

'I thought too much sun was meant to be as bad for you as cigarettes.'

Nina looks smug. 'Depends on your colouring.'

Lou bows to her superior scientific knowledge, dropping back as the path gives way to a narrow footbridge. From the top of it you can see across the opposite bank, right through to the far side of the river and the red-brick walls of an ancient brewery, crumbling between the trees.

'Where's the boat?'

'Down yonder.' Lou waves vaguely. Punts have been hauled up the stony beach to the side of the boatyard. Narrowboats jut from the pontoon in parallel red and green stripes. The rain makes everything seem soft and clean and luminous and suddenly I wish I could hold it like that for ever – photograph the temperature, the taste of the air, the moment-to-moment lace of each small watery explosion. Staring into the distance, Lou and Nina – my best friends – are warm and solid and larger than life. There is a lump at the back of my throat. Upstream the canal is rippling and oozing at its broken banks, the river pours itself across the towpath and the waters merge.

'We're stuck.' I nod at where land should have been. A row of tree stumps and saplings points the way.

'I told you we should go across the water-meadow.' Lou is triumphant.

'I'd rather wade through this.'

'Looks dangerous.'

'Looks fun.' Nina shrugs deeper into her rucksack. She lifts her carrier bag, steps into murky water.

'Take off your shoes!' calls Lou.

'Who cares, they're drenched already.' It's cold, then wet and cold. Very slowly she begins to walk. After fifteen steps her feet go numb. Halfway along she stops to look back at us, waiting on the bridge.

'Come on. It's perfectly safe,' she waves. It looks like a miracle. I wait for Lou to cross. Next to them, inches away, the river seethes.

★

By the time we reach the pontoon we're wet to the skin. My basketball boots wheeze as the air sucks through the foam in the heel, and my jeans stretch tighter at the knee with every step. We stand on the slippery platform, shivering as the ends of our fingers crinkle, trying to avoid any movement that might bring our goose-pimpled skin in contact with the stiff, unpleasant touch of our clothes.

'Which is it, then?' says Nina, inspecting the boats. Close-up they seem improbably long, heavy, precarious somehow – as though at any moment one might simply topple and sink, dragging the flimsy pontoon and all the other boats after it, one by one. A cobweb of mooring-lines sags like perished elastic. The water at our feet is black. A generator hums and smoke trails doggedly from a thin metal chimney, four or five boats down. These are the only signs of life.

Lou points left. 'It was on this side, I remember. And red. And the hatch thing you go in through hadn't been painted yet. Sophie kept praying it wasn't going to rot.' She dumps her rucksack, opens it and rummages inside. 'I'd recognise the name.'

Nina sets off down the pontoon, reading out loud. '*Mayfair, Shining Horizon, Chardonnay, Lady of the Lake*.' She pauses. 'Please God let it not be *Lady of the Lake*.' Larger than life *trompe-l'oeil* tabby cats and pink geraniums decorate its sides and a lawn grows fine and spiky on the roof. Crocheted curtains twitch as we pass and she resumes her litany.

'*Jolly Gem, Otterburn, Blenheim, Tuscarora*. I can't believe

I'm doing this. Only you could forget the name of your own sister's boat.'

'Piss off—'

'Didn't you ever write to her?'

'Post went straight to the college.' Lou jangles something noisy and orange – a bunch of keys and four corks threaded onto a sort of nylon bracelet – in Nina's face. 'Not such an air-head after all!' She marches to the end of the pontoon and back again, stops at the rail of a 47-footer with a white-washed hatch and peeling body-work. Riotous mint and dandelion quiver in a washing-up tub on the roof.

'Are you sure you've got the right boat?' I wonder. I don't care how much Sophie may have changed at university, I can't imagine her ever living here. Rust seeps into the window frames at every screw, the paint is chipped, and a greasy green tidemark slurps against the hull. The platform creaks as Lou steps aboard, keys first, in a gesture of good faith.

'They can only have us arrested for attempted burglary,' Nina says, thrusting her hands in her pockets. She turns her back.

It's dark inside. The windows glow in two wide ruby strips, then Lou flicks a curtain and the afternoon pours in. In silence we examine the room. Faded curtains, rugs and scraps of tapestry drape the walls like the inside of a Bedouin tent. Sand-stained scarves hang from the posts of the bunk, and a jumble of cushions and pillows makes the third bed a kind of settee. A small gold moth flutters into the light.

Lou sneezes twice, curses her allergies. She opens the inside door and we follow her along a narrow passage, where the shower room is, and through to the saloon, ducking our heads and drawing in our shoulders and arms. Nina wrinkles her nose. A teabag grows penicillin in the sink and, later, she finds a coffee mug where the mould has collapsed and re-seeded itself. Breadcrumbs litter the draining board and crunch beneath our feet on the lino. Cobwebs in every corner gather dust. We sniff the dank, almost edible smell of rotting wood. Lou lifts her T-shirt over her face and points to where a pudding basin stands in the middle of the table, thirty or forty sickly white tentacles hanging limp and twisted from its rim. Some have broken off, gnarling into dun-coloured aerial roots, while others nudge their way towards the window, fat stems kinking randomly this way and that. At the tip of one, a pair of tiny withered leaves forks out like a tongue. The bottom of the bowl bubbles with thick brown glue.

'Bean sprouts.' As Nina waves the empty packet, I step back for air and a small black shadow darts along the wall below the sink.

'I think I'm going to puke.' Lou fixes her eyes to the spot where the mouse has disappeared.

'Sit down then. Put your head between your legs,' says Nina, taking a deep breath. She grasps the bowl and rushes outside with it held firmly at arm's length. We hear a brief, wet, fluttery sound like a rush of air.

There's nothing so melancholy as the moment after an

arrival when the travelling is done and whatever you see is what you know you must enjoy and grow fond of, no matter how it contradicts expectation, when everything is cold and unfamiliar but, somehow, *yours*. Nina washes the table while I pull up the blinds and Lou loses patience with the fire controls, clicking the automatic sparker ineffectively as gas exhales. I throw her my Zippo and she opens and lights it with one hand. The middle bar whooshes into flame, ticking, glinting, warming up. Our backs begin to steam. The windows fug. Nina makes tea — strong, hot, almost too bitter to drink without milk, and the smell of it washes into every shadow of the room. Lou wriggles out of her trousers, unbuttons her shirt and huddles as close to the fire as she can without catching alight and soon we are all undressing, stamping and shuddering in the little pools of rainwater our clothes have dribbled onto the lino. We wrap ourselves in blankets stripped from the bottom bunk, drape our shoulders in scratchy cloaks of wool. The goose pimples go down. Our faces flush in the glow of the fire. The air is thick with the scent of tea, dissolving sugar, cigarette smoke, an echo of gas.

'Here we are then.' Nina yawns, breaking the silence. Sat there, cross-legged, Lou's head resting in her lap, she is thinking about her love-life. I can tell from the way her fingers stroke through Lou's hair, combing it, sweeping it from side to side.

Lou opens her eyes and stretches her fingers to the fire. 'Bliss,' she murmurs sleepily. 'Let's have a drink.'

We keep our mugs as hand-warmers and pass round

tumblers for the wine. Nina rests a cushion on her lap in the place where Lou's head has been.

'My granny embroidered that when she was twelve,' says Lou. A golden bird with a long fan tail and a lacy black crest above its eye sits in the branches of a lemon tree. Two of the corners have been chewed. The *Otterburn* is furnished with bits and pieces scavenged from the attic at home. 'She did it from memory. From a painting in Prague.'

'Your gran went to Czechoslovakia?' I ask.

'Born there.'

'I never knew that.'

Lou shrugs. 'It's not very interesting. Why should you?'

'I don't know. Shit, I can't open this.'

Nina takes possession of the bottle, rethreading the screw. She stands and pulls out the cork with a flat little pop.

'Did you know Lou had a Czech granny?' I ask.

'Lou's family remains eternally mysterious to me.'

Lou stares into the fire. 'Is anyone hungry?'

'Starving.' Nina fills each glass to exactly an inch below the rim and hands them round. 'To freedom,' she says. A curtain of hair swings loose as she lowers her head to sip. It's kinked in the rain. Like that she almost looks fourteen again.

She walked in as I was swapping the names on the beds in C Dorm. Stood in the doorway, quietly watching me turn pink. 'What are you doing?' she said.

'Nothing much.' I sneaked a look at the sticker I'd half managed to hide in my hand. 'Are you Anna?' She wore a mini-skirt and a long green baggy top. Her basketball boots were exactly my favourite shade of blue.

'No, Nina. I'm in the room next door. I heard you through the wall.'

'Have you come from the airport?'

She shook her head. When she smiled you could see the train-tracks through her taut upper lip. 'I live in Froxton. About ten miles away. Mum and Dad had to drop me off early, the bastards. They've got Surgery this afternoon. Mum says it's an attack on working women to have term start on a Tuesday.' She paused, as though considering the argument. 'She's thinking of writing to the Head to voice her disappointment. Girls schools ought to take particular care about things like that. They send out dangerous sub-conscious messages. What's in your hand?'

'Swear you won't tell?' I showed her the label. 'You could swap yours too if you like, only don't go by the window, that's too obvious.' There was a pecking order: Fifths got windows and radiators, Thirds were always closest to the door and Fourths went anywhere in between. Hawkley didn't believe in prefects. Its philosophy was mixing girls up to make a happier, friendlier sort of school. Even so, the Sixths slept over the Dining Hall and didn't have to be On Flat until ten. 'Go on, everyone does it.'

'Are you sure?'

I nodded. 'Compensation for arriving first.'

'How do you know? Are you in the fourth form?'

'A *Fourth*?' I corrected gently. 'No, I've come up from Lockhurst – the junior school.' There had been twenty-one of us. Thirteen boarders and eight days. Except when there was no one to go to breakfast with, or when I needed to scrounge a fag, I never much spoke to any of them again. At the end of the summer term we'd had a farewell barbeque, with jumbo sausages, chips and fruit punch. Everyone went round writing telephone numbers in their Snoopy address books, promising to meet up in the holidays. My number ran over two full lines. I didn't think anyone would ring, but they liked having it there, under P for Porter. The length of it made them feel jet-set and cosmopolitan, though Brussels seemed a fairly ordinary place to live to me. Afterwards, Caroline Price and I held a celebratory midnight feast. We sat wrapped in duvets on the grass outside the science room, eating pepperoni and crisps. We took a solemn vow never to set foot in the place again.

Nina frowned. 'I didn't know Lockhurst was Hawkley's junior school. We thrashed you at tennis last year.'

'Probably—'

'Definitely. I remember it. We didn't get Tea.'

I shrugged. We never got Tea at Lockhurst, just squash and biscuits half an hour before bed. There wouldn't have been time between lunch and supper for another meal. The teachers would have had to get us queued up orderly before and Mrs Hodgson would have had to check our fingernails. The sandwiches would have had to be arranged the way they were arranged for parents' meetings – crustless triangles of egg and cheese in spiralling brown and white chrysanthemums. Mummies and daddies used to smuggle them out of Hall in handkerchiefs. Caroline and I would share, she'd send her mum back in for seconds of ham. At Hawkley we were allowed to eat what we liked. No one had the authority to make us finish our plates. Mealtimes were staggered. The Dining Hall couldn't seat everyone at once. Sometimes we had to queue for twenty minutes just to get through the doors to the canteen. A Sixth or a mistress would stand there with a metre rule, letting us through in bursts of ten.

At Tea the serving-stands were empty and clean, the hot-lamps off. We could hear the kitchen staff chattering in Spanish. At the end of the counter Pablo stood guard over three huge tubs of sandwiches. On Tuesdays, after Orchestra, we got Chelsea buns or doughnuts or red and yellow jam tarts instead and Pablo would watch us carefully, one by one, as we filed past.

I followed Nina next door to a smaller, darker room where there were only four beds. She had already rolled out her duvet and a pillow from home. *Imogen*, by Jilly Cooper, lay face down on a bashed-up navy-blue trunk.

'Have you unpacked yet?'

'No.' She flopped on her bed. 'I didn't know which chest to take.'

'They're all the same.' I opened the top right drawer of the nearest one and read the graffiti. *Sarah, Mione, Rachel and Cathy T. Spring '82. Cool riots*, it said. 'Have you brought a padlock?'

'Yeah.'

'That's good, I've forgotten mine. Très chic curtains.' I pinched the end of one and billowed it in and out slowly. Sunlight twisted through wreaths of huge, splayed red and purple daffodils. Outside, a footpath led through orchards up to a hill where the Church of St Peter stood buffeted by the wind. I knew it was St Peter's because we'd walked there on a nature trail last year and that's what Mrs Hodgson said.

'Are your parents doctors, then?' I asked.

Nina concentrated on peeling her name sticker off the enamel bar at the foot of her bed. 'Yeah, how about yours?'

'Dad's in the Foreign Office, Mum does teaching every now and then. Have you got any brothers or sisters?'

We swapped the usual family information. She had a nine-year-old brother called William, I had a nine-year-old brother called William and that was enough. Seemed like we had to be friends.

'I wish I could have short hair.'

'You can,' says Lou as if she were my fairy god-mother. She pulls at her fringe, rolling her eyes to try and catch a glimpse of the sharp mousey ends.

'I can't, you know, I haven't got the face for it.'

'Stop fishing.' Nina squints at us through the side of her glass.

'I'm not. It's true. I don't.' I finish my wine and light a cigarette. But for the orange glow of the fire, it's dark in the cabin now, shadows flicker with the fading match. A paraffin lamp hangs from a nail above the sideboard. 'Shall I light it?'

'Might as well,' Lou shrugs. I pull off the glass and adjust the wick a fraction, guessing what's right.

Nina flares her nostrils. 'Smells like a petrol station.'

'Smells like Olden Days.'

'You're so fucking nostalgic.'

'I've just got a vivid historical imagination.' I replace the guard. Thick tongues of smoke lick up the sides, blotting out half the light.

'I'm getting cold.'

'So put on some clothes.' Lou folds her long legs into the armchair.

Nina stands, padding through the passage way where we dumped our bags. 'I can't, they're all wet,' she wails.

Lou stretches out an arm to feel her trousers. 'We'll have to unpack everything.' The fag in her mouth shakes violently and a chunk of ash breaks off, dusting her blanket. 'Come on, Beth. Get up, you lazy slag.'

We smother every available surface, corner, ledge and nail with a layer of cotton, rushing back to the fire for warmth. Damp T-shirts halve themselves over the backs of chairs. Sun-dresses and bras dangle from the edges of open cupboard doors.

'Hasn't your sister got something we could borrow?'

Lou tugs at her fringe again. 'Not sure – She's probably taken them to London.'

'She won't have taken everything—'

'Hey, Nina, do you remember that purple cardigan she had that everyone kept borrowing?'

'Heather Allen's cardigan, you mean?'

'No, *Sophie's*. It passed round the whole bloody school and never got washed. God, it stank. They just kept spraying on more and more perfume – all different kinds.'

Lou's brow wrinkles with disbelief.

'Before your time,' Nina says airily, waving her hand. 'Oh go on, she won't mind.'

'She doesn't like me borrowing her stuff—'

'She's let you borrow her boat.'

'That's different.'

'Anyway, she'll never know.' Nina stands up, letting her blanket fall. All she has on is a pair of black Calvin Kleins and a running vest. The hairs on her forearms bristle as she waits in the sudden chill. Her nipples bump. We look away.

Lou breaks the silence. 'Oh OK, then, but promise not to say.'

We swear on our life, then shift the table, watching as she lifts the seat of the inside bench and rests it easily against the wall. Inside, a flame-red cocktail-dress shimmers, crushed, at the top of the pile. Nina strokes the chiffon greedily. The seams and neckline have been stitched by hand. She picks it up, holding it to Lou's shoulders as though she were one of those cut-out paper dolls you hang with cut-out paper clothes. 'Beautiful!'

Lou pulls a face. 'There's warm stuff further down,' she murmurs, holding the dress.

Nina slips into a kimono-style dressing-gown, then takes it off again when the next layer reveals an evening coat. It shimmies in the firelight. The droopy cuffs pout softly, pocketing her small neat hand in pearl-grey velvet. All these clothes will be too big. 'Where did your sister find this stuff?'

'Junk shops mostly – she's been collecting it for years.'

'It's like a dressing-up box.' I find a suit and push my arms through the charcoal chalk-striped jacket sleeves, hunching my shoulders. The trousers are loose at the waist, they sag in a shallow smile across my hips and wrinkle at the ankles. I flick up the collar, tip an imaginary Trilby, wink. 'Do I look like a gangster?'

Nina laughs. 'You look like a clown.' Her quick fingers slot the final button through its hand-stitched loop. She ruffles her hair and goes in search of a mirror.

'Your turn, Lou.'

She shakes her head. 'I'm warm enough.' She picks up Nina's discarded blanket, throws it across her shoulders and goes to the cabin door. Unhooking it, wanders out. Lamplight slithers across the deck and glitters in the rain-drops on the rail. She shudders. The fresh air takes her breath away. She opens her lungs. The pissy smell of flow-ering nettles floats across the canal. A fleet of thin clouds skims the moon, and the water is calm and black. A mist is rising and she lets herself drift with it, further and further from the end of the pontoon, into the basin, across the towpath, through the willow and hawthorn trees on the bank and right out into the middle of the water-meadow once again. Minnows shoal across the footpaths, flashing in the unsteady moonlight. Sticklebacks hide in caves of grass. Eel-fry wriggle curiously between the corpses of drowned worms and an empty snail-shell floats on invisible currents this way and that, a galleon lost at sea. Nina tiptoes across the shining deck. Lou feels a warm hand on her shoulder.

'Are you OK?'

Silently she nods. There seems to be fishing-line knotted round the inside of her chest. It squeezes the breath right out of her.

'Lou-Lou, don't cry. What's wrong?'

'Nothing. Isn't it beautiful?' She wipes her face on a corner of blanket, shakes herself and smiles.

I was a child when I arrived at Hawkley. There had been no great argument, yet, with Mum or Dad. The clothes I shook from my suitcase were the same clothes – mended, washed and ironed – I'd worn the term before.

Nina came in and went away again several times, charging from dorm to dorm while I arranged my sweater drawer. She hovered in the doorway, filling me in. 'There's a bathroom with *four* baths in it!' 'I've found the Coke machine.' 'Someone called Natasha's arrived upstairs. A Fourth.' Everything was new and *marvellous*. Natasha had the *prettiest* eyes.

'Coming for a walk?' she said, and the two of us followed her along the path between the French and English Blocks, up past the Music School and the Beech Trees and over a gate behind a hedge where bullocks had trampled the grass to mush. Sticky mud seeped into the blue of Nina's basketball boots. 'Should be safe here.' Reaching into the pocket of her overcoat, Natasha took out a packet of cigarettes and offered them round.

'No thanks,' Nina smiled. I smiled too, remembering how much I'd looked forward to Mrs Hodgson's educational documentaries at Lockhurst, how in *The Truth About Tobacco* there had been an actual cankered lung from a real dead person and a clip from an advert with a girl who lay on the floor as clotted tar trickled down her naked, prepubescent chest. The tar had looked so black against her skin. Natasha struck a match, lit up, breathed in.

'First of the day,' she sighed deliciously, changing my mind.

Smoking at Hawkley was like a kind of wonderful, elaborate war – a clash between conflicting ideologies – fought with all the passion and ingenuity you would expect to see watching a gang of six-year-olds play cops and robbers in the park. It went on every day, all term, from year to year. Sometimes the mistresses lost heart and there would be a lull for weeks on end with chicken-shits and scroungers creeping into the fields at Tea and fair-weather tobacconists ousting the hard-core from their danger zones. Dare-devils would light up behind the Art Block after dark, or lean from dorm windows. Butts could be found at the foot of the Changing-Room steps. Then somebody would go too far. A thundery quietness heralded the start of each new major staff offensive. It was the adrenalin we got addicted to.

Though Nina never touched a cigarette herself, she seemed quite happy for others to die of heart disease and came with me whenever I asked. There was always a crowd at the Beech Trees. Nina and I would stand at the periphery and learn to imitate the way the older girls spoke, soaking up their phrases and exaggerations into an approximate, precocious language of our own. We relished the loose, hysterical camaraderie of those lunchtime gatherings, the joking, the scares, the way the older girls could listen to a twig snap and know whether or not to run away. Standing out there, day after day, we saw the seasons change, picked up the logic of cloud and temperature, observed a little more of nature every term. Almost in spite of ourselves, we came to love the place.

Sometimes, when she wanted to piss me off, Nina would say I only smoked because it was against the rules. She fancied herself as a scientist of human behaviour and had this supercilious way of describing us all as *adolescents*. 'Every *adolescent*,' she'd say, 'should have a cause, a secret, something no one in their family can interfere with. *Mine* is wanting to be a doctor. *Yours* is cigarettes.'

She had a point. The well-mannered child my parents had kissed goodbye at passport control back in September stepped onto the plane and never returned. The Christmas holidays, and then the Easter holidays – the holidays before Lou came – crackled with live domestic confrontation. What started out as trivial bickering became less trivial. I answered back. Doors slammed. Dinner plates clogged the fridge, untouched, and after a while I only had to look at Mum and she'd freak. Dad recited the Riot Act so many times I knew it by heart. I listened and sighed and smiled, imagining the Beech Trees and the naked girl with tar on her chest. Now *that* would give them something serious to complain about, I thought. If only they knew.

I rang them from the pay-phone by Dr Goodman's flat. It was the first day of the Summer Term. Dad picked up.

'So you've arrived.'

'Yeah.'

'Everything all right?'

'Yeah.'

'Hang on, then. I'll fetch your mother . . .' The receiver thudded and his footsteps dimmed. I listened for the squeaky floorboard by the kitchen door, then voices –

Where are you?

In Beth's room, changing the sheets.

She's on the phone. Reverse charges. Hurry up.

More footsteps, then Mum, out of breath, asking her usual stupid questions. 'Was the plane on time? And Mr Clarke was there to meet you? Have you got a nice dorm? I'll speak to you Sunday, then. Have a good week. Work hard . . .'

It's funny, I thought, so long as there's at least 100 miles between us Mum and I seem to get on fine. Staring past the bicycle sheds, deep into the branches of a giant oak, I savoured a moment of homesickness. There wasn't much else to do. Drizzle spat across the scrubbed glass and the corridors were quiet. Nina should be here by now. Our dorms were at opposite ends of the building. This was the second time the housemistresses had ignored our request. Still, N Dorm would be OK. Harriet and Kate were cool and at least we had a room with a sink. The windows opened properly. Someone had scribbled a limerick behind the wallpaper at the head of my bed: *There was a housemistress called Goodman, who fell pash in lurve with a woodsman. As he chopped off her head, he shuddered and said, serves you right, you ugly old battleaxe.*

The face-mirror behind the door was screwed in askew. I blew myself a kiss, and then another, watching my face go slant and sexy as the lips creased, puckering into a gorgeous, pouty bow. I liked my lips, they were my strongest attribute, and Nina and I believed in attributes. No one should love themselves too much, that would be vain, but it was OK to have just one or two features you particularly admired. Nina's was the colour of her eyes. Sometimes she lay awake at night worrying the blue would fade.

A car horn tooted three times in the forecourt below and someone shrieked as the front wheels rolled against what sounded like a very heavy trunk, shunting it across the tarmac. The beginning of term was always mad like this. In half an hour the driveway would be jammed with cars, the corridors thundering with cheery collision as dragged bags veered off course and dads apologised, smiling at each other bashfully.

Leaning at the windowsill, I watched for Nina's car. She was going to be so envious of my new clothes. Mum had said she couldn't face another scene like the one in Galerie Agora at Christmas. She'd sent me off to the rue Neuve with 2,000 francs and strict instructions to keep the receipts. That summer everything had to be pale blue or white.

'I saw it in C&A,' Nina said when I showed her my knitted cotton top.

'Liar,' I laughed. The grumpier she pretended to be the more I knew she wanted it. She paced from mirror to sink and back again, inspecting her spots. 'It's by *Chic-Chic* and you can only get them on the Continent.'

'Well C&A are selling one just the same.'

'You won't be wanting to borrow it then.'

She shrugged. 'So who's this new Louisa girl?'

'I don't know. Stop there a minute. Close your eyes.' She swayed obediently at the end of the bed, cupped her hands. 'Just because I bought you a present last term,' I teased. The begging bowl flashed a double V.

'I think it's what I hope it is,' she beamed, folding her fingers over the five-pack. You couldn't get Hollywood over here. Lemon was the best. She opened a packet and we stood there, sucking, blissed on flavourings. Nina's eyes were watering. She cleared her throat as though about to make a speech.

'The thing about gum is you think you're so cool chewing it, but really you just look a total prat,' she said.

'It's worth it, though. Stops you getting a double chin.'

'Makes you hungry – gets your gastric juices all excited.'

'Bollocks!'

'It's true, I swear.' She wandered back to the mirror, pulling a face as I snickered the shrink from a pack of 20

Marlboro Lights. You couldn't get them in England either.

'Come on, then.' I grabbed my violin.

'It's raining.'

'So?' I borrowed her my coat and we drifted out into the April afternoon, dodging between parked cars, across House Lawn, towards the classrooms. A fountain sprouted from the pond outside the Admin Block, sputtering feebly over the hiss of the rain. Goldfish nuzzled the murky weeds. Someone in kitchen-whites – Pablo – hurried away towards the Quad. The Library windows glimmered. Nina sighed.

'Glad to be back?'

'Not particularly. I was thinking how depressing it looks, all empty and dark.' She tucked her arm through mine and we swished across the Orchard, past the Gym and up to the Music School. Philip was in. We passed his car. Unhooking herself, she stepped back, shook her head at me as I stared in. Newspapers and sheets of music covered the whole back seat. Coke cans and crisp packets littered the floor. He'd left his key in the ignition. His jacket – a second-hand suede thing with a fake fur collar and loose threads dangling from every seam – curled into the passenger seat like a mangy fox. Although he never played or taught in it, it followed him everywhere, and every week I staggered from our lesson clouded by its leathery, old-aftershave and tobacco stink.

'What is it with you and older men?' said Nina, quiffing her fringe.

'Piss off!' I pushed ahead, leaving her to read the notice-board while I dumped my fiddle in the store.

'What did you get in your Grade Six?' she shouted after me.

'Merit. Why?' My basketball boots squeaked back along the polished corridor. Low Merit. Borderline. 'Why?'

'Anna Birdwood got Distinction.' She looked at me, try-ing not to smile. Carrying bad news to a close friend is one of the few thrills freely available to the average 14-year-old. I shrugged it off. Some girls were coy about using the word 'hate'. 'I don't hate anyone,' they'd say. Not me – I hated Anna Birdwood, Anna Birdwood hated me, and we didn't care who knew it. We'd shared a dorm in the Autumn – the longest – Term and hated from experience. Now she would take precedence in Orchestra.

We trailed out, back past Philip's car and round along the track behind the long-jump pit, the discus patch, the chalked-in tennis courts. The posts were up already, soaked nets drooping black and miserable in between. A cluster of seagulls circled the hockey pitch for grass-seed. Everything looked green and ready

'When does term time actually begin?' I wondered, thinking of lighting up right there. The place was deserted, for God's sake, no one would see. 'I mean, there must be a definition. A moment when the rules kick in.'

Nina side-stepped a puddle, pulling me into the water as she tried to balance. 'Why must there? When does blue turn into red?' She paused, watching me climb the wet gate. 'When does a bud become a flower? When does day turn into night? When does spring turn into summer?'

I struck a match. First cigarette of term. First cigarette for nearly a month and God I'd been looking forward to it. 'OK, OK. You can shut up now, I think I see your point.'

'Nina! Beth!' A woman's voice yelled after us as we meandered towards the Quad. Nina turned round and blushed. Sophie Greene was leaning from her study-unit window. 'Come here,' she waved. 'Come up, I want to talk to you.'

If a fairy godmother could have magicked us into the shape and intelligence of any other girl in the school, Nina and I would both have chosen to be Sophie Greene. We lurched uncertainly up narrow stairs to a landing, right above Miss Dudley's Biology Lab. Even from here you could smell the formaldehyde.

'Do we just go in?' I mouthed.

'I don't know.' Nina knocked, peeped through the half-open door. Sophie sat on her desk cross-legged, sipping Cup a soup, surrounded by paper, exercise books and files. She wore her sleeves rolled and her long hair fastened in a diligent plait. Silver bangles glittered and chimed approvingly whenever she moved. 'Come in, sit down,' she said, 'I want to ask a favour.'

We steadied ourselves against the wall and nodded, ready to agree to anything, while Sophie blew softly into her steaming mug. Her upper lip gleamed above the chipped china rim and her cheeks had flushed a moist and delicate pretty-girl pink. I still couldn't believe she actually knew my name.

'My sister's coming. She's going to be in your year. Keep an eye on her, will you? Make sure she's fitting in.' She gave us an almost innocent look, as though she didn't understand perfectly well that, thanks to her, the girl was guaranteed instant popularity. Even the mistresses would creep.

Nina blinked and a postcard fell off the wall behind her head, fluttering picture side up to the scratch-streaked lino. 'What's she called?' she muttered, picking it up.

'Louisa. Lou.'

'She's in—' I started.

Sophie interrupted with a smile. 'Be nice to her – she's had a rough time recently.'

'How come?'

'Ask her yourself when she arrives.'

'When's that?'

Nina glowered, shutting me up. With Sixths it didn't do to show too much curiosity. Questions could be taken as evidence of potentially subversive cockiness and no one wanted to encourage that.

Sophie Greene observed our mute exchange with an indulgent smile. 'Next week I think.'

The first we saw of Lou was a silver trunk abandoned at the foot of the stairs. The bell had just gone for end of Break and the corridors clattered and buzzed with girls. Lights flicked, windows banged. Aretha Franklin, Annie Lennox and the boys from Wham broke into silence. Dorm doors slammed and opened and slammed again as the forgetful ran back for exercise books and a laughing crowd queued for the full-length mirror. The landing clogged and someone at the back began to push as the girls at the bottom of the stairs stepped one by one around the obstacle. Nina rushed off to Double Chemistry. We had been put in separate streams for Science, even though I was just as good as her at Maths. I wandered after her the basement way to see if there was any post. A tall girl – taller than me, six foot perhaps – stood by the Surgery door. She fiddled with the scales as sobbing filtered through the frosted glass and, on the far side of it, Matron clucked and patted and shushed.

'Louisa?' I said. 'I'm Beth. We're in a dorm together.' For a moment I thought she was going to shake my hand, or topple as she twisted, leaning into me, the calm of her

moon-face shattering with quick surprise. 'Your sister mentioned you might be coming today. I like your skirt. Très
marvellous—'

'Thank you,' she said, not sure if I was taking the piss. I
wasn't sure either, it looked the sort of thing my mother
might wear – cream linen, expensively pleated to comple-
ment the fuller figure. Lou was as thin as low-fat milk. She
fingered it self-consciously and smiled. Pixie boots shuffled
overhead and Matron's voice murmured through the
Surgery door as the sobbing began again.

'*Come on, Alice. Crying like this will only make you feel
worse.*' There was a stammered pause, a sort of hiccup, then
wailing. The new girl flashed me another quick, embarrassed smile. She rattled her shoulder-bag. 'I've got these
pills to hand in—'

'Sounds like your trunk's a bit in the way up there.'

'Mum said I should do this absolutely first. Anyway, I
can't move it—'

'I can lend a hand.'

She frowned at the ceiling, dithering. 'I warn you, it
weighs a bloody ton.' Upstairs, we grabbed the front handle and heaved. Tin studs scraped across the wooden floor,
snagging horribly on each uneven board. The girls on the
stairs surged forward, stared with curious contempt. 'How
was I to know everyone would come down exactly then?'
she muttered, flopping against the pocket-money table.

'Have you seen our dorm?'

'No. Only just arrived.'

'How come you're so late?'

'I've been in hospital.'

'What's wrong with you?'

'Skin-graft.' Her pronunciation was so matter-of-fact I felt ashamed not to know what that was and didn't like to ask.

'Does it hurt?'

'A bit.' She folded her arms. 'So where's this dorm?'

'I'll show you. Follow me.'

We stopped outside the bogs on the next landing up. It was quieter here. A curly-haired woman in a pale blue overall and pink rubber gloves backed out of one of the cubicles, a bottle of bleach bulging precariously in her front pocket. Louisa winced at the smell of it and turned away. 'Will you be late for lessons?'

'It's only Library.'

'What's that?'

'When we do homework.' We ran up a second flight of stairs, turned left at the end of the passage and pushed through a heavy swing door into the modern part of the building. 'Bathrooms. More dorms.' Her shoes clicked on the lino like a grown-up's shoes. 'All mod cons. A bit stuffy but very popular in winter. There's another row exactly the same upstairs and – who's your housemistress?'

'Dr Goodman.'

'Bad luck. She lives below.'

The passage kinked right and we shouldered through another fire door. The floor was wood again now, the ceiling sloped and daylight flooded in through an open window. We stopped outside N Dorm. I stepped back with a flourish. I was enjoying myself. 'Voilà!'

Louisa's hand hovered above the door-knob. 'This is it?'

I followed her in, watching for expressions of approval or dismay. Harriet's Simon Le Bon poster peeled from the wall in a glossy diamond. The mirror was covered with frosted-pink lip-prints. Smudges of eye-shadow and blusher edged across the wallpaper in a flesh-coloured blur.

'This is you,' I pointed, hurriedly returning an assortment of bath towels, records and magazines to the beds of their respective owners. We stared at the no longer very smooth or very white sheet. Kate, our Fifth, had pinched the pillow yesterday.

'Was I supposed to bring a duvet?' She turned round slowly, looking from bed to bed to bed as though she might burst into tears. Her grey eyes glassed and the start of a flush crept in from ears to nose.

'Didn't your sister say? Don't worry, Matron will find you a spare. Have you boarded before?'

'Not really.'

'I started at nine.'

'God, you must have been homesick.'

'No –' I wondered whether to lie a bit, tell her my mum and dad force-fed me cockroaches kind of thing, but she looked shocked enough already. 'I just pretended to be, every now and then, when Mum got weepy down the phone.'

'Parents –' she shrugged, '– what can you do?'

Oh good, I thought, she's really quite attractive when she smiles.

★

By Lunch the news had spread to every girl in our year. An inquisitive silence flickered along the table as Lou and I squeezed through to the spaces at the end, plonked down our trays. She was embarrassed, I could tell. She'd taken a bowl of rhubarb crumble when everyone else had fruit.

Nina led the interrogation, starting with all the questions we'd been asked when we were new and didn't know it was acceptable to tell the older girls to fuck off and mind their own business. How much pocket money did she get? When did she start her periods? What was the furthest she had been with a boy, and did she kiss with tongues? Fucking hypocrites, I thought, waiting for somebody to mention the skin-graft. It was the same when Miss McKendrick admired the zeugma in Isobel King's essay on *Lord of the Flies*. No one wanted to be the first to admit our ignorance.

'I'm sure I know what it is, I've just forgotten,' Nina said afterwards. She liked to consider herself an expert on the human body in all its frailty. 'I'll ask my parents.'

'Matron would know.'

'She might not want to say.'

'Or we could look it up in a medical dictionary.'

'*What* medical dictionary?' We pulled out the Maths books from our English-Block lockers. Nina's wouldn't shut properly, it had to be wedged with a six-times-folded sheet of paper which would drop to the floor and be thrown away by the cleaners every day. Nina and I were in the top set. We were taking our O level a year in advance. Nina wanted to do as many subjects early as she could.

That way, she said, she would have time to concentrate on A levels and getting into Oxbridge. For nearly a term and a half I thought Oxbridge was an actual place.

'Alice Dickinson's been sent home,' Nina said that night. She'd bought a packet of crisps at the Tuck Shop and wandered in crunching noisily. She occupied her usual position, cross-legged in the middle of Lou's bed. Harriet and her cronies from Fourth sat in a row on the opposite bed with their French books open, learning vocab.

'Why?'

'Anorexia, why do you *think*?'

'Pathetic,' said Millie, who, for a bet, had pierced her left ear with a smoky needle.

Natasha wiped a stray hair from her thick, mascara-ed eyelashes. 'They'll have to pay a whole term's fees for nothing.'

'How do you know, anyway?' asked Harriet. Nina tapped her nose. Because she was so little and pretty, the girls in Sixth had made her baby of the school. They teased her and petted her and cooed across the Dining Hall or from their study-unit windows as we walked by. Nina would smile angelically and wave.

'Fuck off and die,' she'd mutter between clenched teeth, accepting invitations to their rooms for tea. She'd sit on their knees like a doll and let them plait her hair, lapping up gossip in return. They told her our form mistress Miss Dudley was a lesbian and last year she'd tried to kiss a girl so better watch out. She'd found out which girls were bulemic and who was said to have lost her virginity when. She'd learned the names of mistresses we weren't to meet in class for several years – which were good teachers, who marked strictly, who wouldn't mind if your prep was late. She'd heard about the girl who'd had a secret abortion the week before her A levels.

Quicker than most she'd memorised the punishment tariff and the common law of the school with regard to the lesser offences of late-on-House, bunking off and answering back. She knew the precedents and mitigations – a complete run-down of which girls had been caught doing what by whom for the last four years – as well as the circumstances of every bust: that such-and-such an off-licence telephoned the Staff Room if girls went in for alcohol, which nearby restaurants the mistresses visited on Saturday nights, the footpaths where Dr Goodman liked to walk her labrador, Winks.

'You're making it up,' said Harriet scornfully.

'I saw her trunk in the corridor!'

'And how do you know it was hers?'

Nina granted herself permission to smirk. 'It had "Alice Dickinson" painted in large black letters on top.'

That shut them up. I smiled. Valerie lay in bed with her back to the room engrossed in Danielle Steele.

Lou was still unpacking her trunk. She had refolded her sweaters and shirts. Dresses and skirts lay spread out flat across the bed, their hangers already clipped or looped in place.

'That's gorgeous,' said Nina, stroking a long black velvet skirt. Patent leather buttons ran halfway up the back seam.

'Thanks.' Lou twisted a strand of mousey hair and flicked it out of sight. 'I've got a pair of jeans in here somewhere.'

Nina fitted a Hula Hoop to the end of each finger and thumb. She fanned her hands, admiring the effect, and offered one to Lou, who hesitated. 'From the packet, idiot,' she muttered, rolling her eyes. Lou took a crisp, ate it, and carefully wiped her fingers on her hand towel. Nina smirked. 'What records did you bring?'

'I didn't know—'

'What do you like?'

Lou thought. 'The Beatles,' she said at last. It sounded more like a question.

Nina crunched another Hula Hoop. Kate came in.

'Louisa's here,' I said, a bit louder than usual to show who I was speaking to.

'Hello,' she smiled. She had already seen. She leaned against the windowsill, wiping her nails with cotton-wool pads dunked in varnish remover. Her hair swung in a purple veil across her panda eyes.

'Hello,' said Lou.

'Good day?' Nina asked, speaking in the ever-so-casual, vaguely American voice she kept for older, trendier girls.

'Not exactly. Goodman set us another fucking timed essay to do by the weekend and Dudley says we're all going to fail Biology.' She took a bottle of nail polish from her locker top, shaking it until the little glass beads at the bottom tapped.

'I'll do your right hand if you like.' Nina stood behind,

watching intently as the brush streaked nail after nail with a line of black shine, quickly and neatly dipping back to colour the edges of every U. Lou unzipped her sponge-bag and arranged its contents in order of height across the top of her chest of drawers. From the side compartment, wrapped in tissue, she took a silver-edged photograph frame. She polished it on a corner of her towel, leaned it beside a family-sized bottle of conditioner.

'Is that your mum and dad?' They'd smiled right through the camera lens. It was the sort of photograph you'd need to turn face down every now and then.

Lou nodded, lowering herself onto the edge of the mattress. She inched back to the spot where Nina had been, folded her too-long legs and gazed at Kate. She had the nervous, pleading look I'd seen on new girls before – the sort of look that can't think where to put itself but desperately needs to belong. Anyone smiling at her now, I thought, will make themselves a friend for life. Harriet's gang tittered quietly at some private joke as Tina Turner faded and the needle-arm, lifting, squeaked back, dropped to its manacle.

Nina blacked in the wisps of Kate's last fingernail. 'And not a single smudge!' she crowed. 'I must be a genius!'

'Now one of you will have to entertain me while they dry,' Kate said, waving her hands imperiously. 'Louisa, can't you do a belly-dance or something?'

'I can stand on my head,' Lou mumbled, blushing again. 'Sometimes it makes me faint.'

For a moment Kate pretended incredulity. 'Own up,' she softened. 'You can do much more than that.'

Nina stared at Lou's puce forehead. 'What can you do?'

'Nothing – It's not here anyway. It's in the Music School.'

'*What is?*' Even Harriet was listening now. Natasha fixed her with a furious quizzical look.

'My violin.'

The whole dorm sighed with simultaneous disappointment. 'Not another one,' said Millie, twiddling her stud. 'Why can't somebody learn to play something a bit more interesting, like saxophone, or trombone, or the tambourine?'

Matron peeped round the door to check the music was off, nagging us to get ready for bed. Kate picked up her files and headed back to the Study. Slowly, I started to get changed. Nina was throwing meaningful looks.

'Brekky tomorrow?' She drifted towards the door, dropped her empty crisp packet in the bin and beamed at Matron.

'Eight?'

'Yeah – were you going to wear your dungarees?'

I pulled them off. 'Catch.'

'Ta very much.' She disappeared, flicking the light switch as she went. Valerie cursed in the darkness, swung out of bed and thumped across the floor to switch it on again. Harriet rushed off for a last-minute shower. Millie and Natasha drifted back to their own dorms. Lou slipped out of her court shoes very carefully, one by one.

'I play violin too,' I told her. 'That'll be why they've put us in a dorm together.'

'I'm sorry if you wanted to be with Nina,' she said.

'Oh, that's OK. It's not your fault. They don't believe in putting best friends together anyway.' I looked at her. 'Have you met Philip yet, the violin teacher? Mr Gregory, I should say, but the Music Department likes to be a bit informal. He's gorgeous.'

'Love is blind!' Valerie slammed her book shut. 'He's twenty-eight and he still gets spots, for God's sake. He's a total crater-face—'

'He's rugged. Anyway, who asked you, *perve-merchant*?'

'Don't call me that.'

I smiled. Several battered copies of *Lace* had passed from dorm to dorm last term and Valerie had admitted to Anna Birdwood she thought the trick with the goldfish sounded quite nice. Lou glanced nervously from one of us to the other and didn't know what to say. From under her pillow she took a pink and white Viyella nightie. 'Just going to the loo,' she muttered, rolling it into her sleeve and heading for the door.

'Don't worry, she's not a lesbian – it's safe to change in here.'

'I know, it's just—' she paused. 'It's just my burns.'

'Your what?'

'You know, why I've arrived so late – Oh, fuck it.' Now she was blushing all over again, her fingers shook at the thought of what they were about to do and as we stared at her the words broke into clumsy, half-shouted blurts of sense and nonsense. Unbuttoned, her cotton shirt gaped in a long thin V. 'I don't show everyone,' she stammered, trying to laugh as it slipped to the floor. She stood there, shivering in her underwear – knickers and a skin-tight, flesh-coloured vest with sewn-in circles for tits and a high neck reaching an inch or two above her collarbone. Her fingers tore at the Velcro seam. 'Sophie poured hot oil on me when I was five. By accident.'

The thing it reminded me of most was one of those three-dimensional maps you see sometimes in nature reserves, with bumps and hollows to show where the valleys are, and a worn-out look to the mountain-range where every child tall enough has run their finger across the pointiest peaks. Only Lou's map was more a continent than a National Park, or several continents joined together the same way Africa and Europe are. It looked the way Africa and Europe would look if we never had rain again and the forests, farm-lands and savannah blew away and all you could see were the colours of the earth and the shape of the rocks beneath. Below her right breast there was a kind of Mediterranean sea of pale, skin-coloured calm with an island in the middle – a flat, round mole. I pinched my fingers to stop them reaching out to touch the stretches where her breasts were trying to grow. It was a beautiful scar. And I knew from the way she stood there, still with her shoulders back, quite straight, presenting herself, that sometimes she thought it was beautiful too.

A scar is memory preserved, a souvenir that clings to its own importance, rejecting the company of scrap-books, shells and ticket-stubs, the damp bank-holiday nostalgia of attic sales. It is the only part of you that will not thicken, harden, weaken or bruise. There had been something not challenging, exactly, but almost deliberately casual about the way she let us look and look. I'd stared. I'd managed not to flinch.

'Poor you,' I said when she'd already turned, wrapped up. I never mentioned it again, the way I never mentioned Nina's looks. Later she told me she wished I had. I shouldn't have been so sensitive. She had grown tired of always covering it up. Of watching her mum and dad tact-fully look somewhere else whenever her neckline slipped and the terracotta gnarl peeked through. Of trying to ignore her sister's remorse. The scar was there, and now she wanted everyone to know. We laughed, remembering our-selves fourteen again, so deadly serious and wrong – how can it have been possible? – so wrong about practically everything.

The bunk-springs jitter as Lou unrolls her sleeping bag. All I can see of her is a pair of kneecaps – pale skin narrowing into leg-muscle above and below, a shoal of white hairs glinting as she stretches, smoothing the nylon quilt.

'Are you sure you're OK on the bottom?' she says.

'Don't worry. If you're noisy I'll give the mattress a hefty kick.'

Out of sight, in the shower-room, Nina spits peppermint down the sink. The water-pump heaves. Lou hoists herself up to bed and wriggles into her sleeping bag. The mattress sags. 'Remember the time we had a fire alarm and the bell wouldn't stop?' she muses, almost wistfully. 'God, it's quiet. Doesn't feel like we're floating at all.'

'If the boat was sinking and you could save one thing what would it be?'

'If I was saving it for Sophie?'

'Yeah.'

'I don't know – those clothes, I guess. But boats like this don't sink. They're indestructible.'

'Just as well.'

The bunk-frame squeaks as Lou rolls over. 'Sophie's not really into *things* at the moment,' she muses.

'What do you mean?'

'She's gone all buddhisty – you know: *people* are what's important, *belongings* weigh you down. She chants and shit. It's all the rage. Don't you just hate it when people get religion?'

'Buddhism's not a religion.'

'What is it then?'

'I don't know. A philosophy.'

Nina slams the shower-room door, flops into bed, still chewing her toothbrush. 'What are you two on about?'

'Nothing much.' Lou yawns, flicking out the light. 'I'm going to have a hangover tomorrow.'

'Drink some water.'

'Can't be shagged. Anyway, then I'd have to piss in the night and the mouse would get me—'

'Shh a moment.' I can hear something: a gentle, regular, scrabbling sound.

'What?'

'That?' I listen again.

'It's Nina.'

'What *are* you doing?'

The sound stops. 'Polishing my teeth.' She pauses. 'Do you think boarding school will have made us easier to live with in later life? You know – more tolerant. Sharing. Adaptable?'

It's an unanswerable. For a long time no one speaks. I

know I'm going to miss the bustling, taken-for-granted intimacy of life at Hawkley. The everyday emergencies, the private jokes.

'This is the first time we've shared a room, you know, all three of us together,' I tell them. 'Isn't that strange.'

Caroline Price went into the shower a white girl, came out lobster pink. Nina was shivering beside me in the queue, sleepy still and wet with steam. We sat on the edge of an empty bathtub clutching shampoo bottles, tooth-paste, razors and soap, bandaged in dewy towels, waiting our turn. Millions of vapour beads whirled between us, a slow-falling cloud of tiny rain.

'So does she snore?' Nina watched the goose bumps prickle, collapse, then prickle again on her arm.

'Louisa? No.'

'I like her.'

'I like her too.'

She looked at me sideways, tracking the echo of dividing loyalty in my quietness, listening for what I didn't say. Someone else could tell her about the scar. I didn't know why I didn't want it to be me. Another lobster staggered from the shower but already the hot was running out. 'You go first,' I yawned.

Sleepy Fifths stepped from the shadows in twos and threes, dressed and ready for Breakfast. Lights flickered into the chinks beneath closed doors. Radiators ticked and sighed, loos flushed. Forgotten alarm clocks bleeped in empty dorms.

We met again at eight o'clock downstairs. 'Lou's gone up to the Music School,' I told her.

'That's a bit keen. Does my hair look funny?'

'No. Can you see my spot?' In the Dining Hall we helped ourselves to toast and Weetabix. One day, I thought, I will be beautiful. Everyone deserves to be beautiful once in their life. 'She'll never be as pretty as her sister,' I said out loud.

'God, I'm glad I haven't got a sister.'

'Except for borrowing clothes.'

'And boyfriends.'

We were the last to leave Breakfast. Most of the tables were clean already and the canteen door had shut. Pablo heaved half-full tea and coffee urns into the sink, flushed out the dregs with a length of rubber hose. We cleared our trays and dawdled through the empty Quad. Someone had already gutted the Common-Room papers, the horoscope page lay scuffed and torn at the top of the Changing Room steps. Jingles blared full volume from the nearest dorm upstairs.

'Radio One is so naff,' said Nina, shouldering through the double glass doors. Morning mist silvered the Orchard. Up on the hill beyond the Science Block, the Music School was barely visible. A blackbird hopped for bread-crumbs on the tarmac by the kitchen windows. Girls nudged into the Hall for Assembly, late.

Inside it was cold, the radiator seats had all been taken. Miss Dudley stood in the aisle with her arms crossed, glaring. She pursed her lips. 'Shh,' she said again and again, feeling stupid. We slid along a mostly empty pew near the back, shuddering as the wood pressed through our jeans. Nina sat sideways, chatting to Fifths on the bench behind. My dungarees were much too big for her, the shoulder straps kept slipping off. The Head marched in and everyone went quiet. Somebody whistled as Philip stood up and Dudley whipped round, glaring at the back three rows.

'As some of you may know by now, Hawkley has a new music scholar. Arriving in the middle of a year or a term can be difficult, so I hope you will all make an effort to be friendly.' He grinned towards the piano stool, gallantly flourishing his hand, and suddenly Lou was standing up. She walked to the lectern, picked her way between a jumble of feet and legs as Sophie cheered. A titter of applause went round.

Nina leaned into my left ear. 'No wonder she was in the Music School.' There was a cough and a pause, an echoing crack as Lou raised her violin, squeezing it between her chin and shoulder. Just looking at the way she stood there – gawky but confident, relaxed and powerful somehow – I knew she would be better than good. She drew the bow from heel to tip, and a sound that made me shiver streamed sweetness into our astonished ears.

'Why didn't you tell us?' Nina demanded. We were queuing for Morning Break.

Lou shrugged. 'Yes please,' she held out her hand for custard creams. In turn we filled our paper cups with coffee from the black-no-sugar urn and Nina found a space. The mist had burned off. Columns of sunlight leaned through tall, south-facing windows at the far end of the Dining Hall. It hummed with banter. Someone shrieked as an over-enthusiastic nudge sent cold tea flying across the table. Chair legs scraped. We huddled round Lou like bodyguards expecting trouble. Everywhere we looked, girls turned to her and smiled.

'Are you Grade Eight?' I ventured, suddenly shy.

She nodded, dunked her biscuit, watching as the coffee-shadow crept towards her fingers and the sugar melted in a filmy swirl.

'So why the big secret?' Nina stared at her, waiting.

'I don't know,' she mumbled at last. 'I didn't want to boast.'

'Of course you should boast, you idiot.' Nina rolled her eyes. 'How else is anyone supposed to know you're a genius?'

'You should have heard some of the girls at my old school.' Lou fidgeted, pleased but awkward. She had been in a daze of congratulation all morning. 'I practise a lot—'

'Don't give me that modesty bullshit. Beth *practises*.'

I sipped my coffee, wondering why no one had warned me something like this was going to happen. 'What school were you at?'

'The Corelli Music Academy – in London. We didn't get to do much else, that's why I'm so crap at science.'

'Didn't you like it there?'

She sucked her biscuit. 'I don't know. Not really.'

Nina leaned forwards. 'How many hours do you practise a day?'

'Depends.' Lou shrugged.

'Are you a child prodigy?'

'No.' Her custard cream slumped heavily against the rim and plunged to the bottom of her cup. She pushed it away, stood up, crashed straight into Zoe Ross, and ran from the room.

'Highly strung, that proves it,' Nina said when she had gone. She vanished behind the table for a moment, rerolling the leg of my dungarees. 'Come on then, are we going for a cigarette or what?'

I slipped the last biscuit up my sweatshirt sleeve and dropped my half-full paper cup in the bin. Miss Dudley was still on duty. She looked at us suspiciously as we walked out.

One by one Nina and I slid side-saddle down the handrail in the middle of the Changing-Room steps. We drifted out towards the hockey pitches, cutting across where the tennis courts began. Neat grass glittered with dew.

'We should have gone after her,' I thought out loud.

Nina shrugged and flicked her hair. She gave me a look.

We shouldered through a gap in the hedge, tramping over twigs and fallen leaves. I vaulted the gate, unrolled my cigarette from its paper disguise and struck a match. Nina leaned against a tree trunk, peeling a twig, watching my face with lazy condolence.

'I don't know if she's a prodigy,' I said at last. '*Mozart* was a prodigy.'

'You're just envious.'

'Not really.' I smiled, thinking of Anna Birdwood. Nothing beats seeing the ambition of a close enemy well and truly thwarted. She could sit in the Music School all day, every day for all I cared, but she would never, ever, ever catch up with Lou. Lou could have played swinging upside down from a trapeze and made a cleaner, sweeter sound.

Nina let out an affectionate, exasperated little sigh. 'Well that just proves you're mad. *I'm* envious, and I don't even like the violin.' She struck a match, watching the scorched head twist and crack as I stubbed my fag against the nearest tree. The bark was black with layer on layer of ash, the triangle of bald earth at its roots a higgledy-piggledy mosaic of butts. 'I wish I had a talent.' She looked at me. 'Shall we go?'

She went first, checking for mistresses while I smeared my teeth with toothpaste, a policeman tasting drugs. 'At this rate you're more likely to die of fluoride poisoning than lung cancer,' she muttered, squeezing her arm through mine. 'Rub your hands on the grass, get rid of that disgusting smell.'

'Nah, Philip won't notice.' We cut across the tennis courts and round along the Music School, watching our glossy reflections jump from glass to glass. Was anyone there, I wondered, thinking of the mirrors in Nothing-To-Declare at Gatwick, how I was always tempted to go up really close and pick my nose. The sun made shining helmets of our hair. Even wearing my size-12 dungarees, Nina looked skinny and petite. People expected her to be pathetic but she liked that, she liked to challenge their assumptions, it made her feel original. I wished I could have been fragile and ferocious too. I didn't know, then, that bodies like mine could be described as statuesque, that statuesque was just another manifestation of femininity — no better or worse than Nina's type, just different.

Nina's reflection ruffled its hair, stopped to tie its shoelaces, then vanished in a sickening swoop as the window in Philip's room swung open and a girl in a tattered tan overcoat jumped out, hurrying around the front of the building and down towards the Science Block. Nina squinted. 'Who was that?'

It was impossible to tell from the back.

'How very peculiar.'

'Peculiar indeed.' We laughed, then separated, heading in opposite directions, Nina to the Library, me for Violin. Philip's lessons always began the same way. Walking the long, straight corridor to his room, my footsteps would slow, my heart accelerate. Itches would trickle up the backs of my hands. I would remember his instructions from the week before — the tricksy fingering tips, which scales, which bars to concentrate on practising, all those good intentions — and know I had accomplished none. He was too young, too cool to raise his voice, but I could tell I disappointed him from the way his face softened if I did something right, the desperate enthusiasm of his compliments. Easy to say it now, but I might have benefitted from the odd sarcastic jeer.

His door was closed. I knocked and stood back, leaning against the wall, swinging my violin case. Most of the practise rooms were empty this period, but the flute lesson next door had already started and someone somewhere tinkled through the first three bars of the *Moonlight* over and over again. Fluorescent strips flickered the length of the corridor, humming accompaniment. Mintiness faded, the cigarette tasted stale at the back of my mouth. How many did you have to smoke a day to make your fingers go yellow? Philip would notice then, I thought. The handle turned. Miss Walker, the piano teacher, swayed in the doorway, giggling through her nose and waving her floppy fat hands like a rag doll trying to conduct Stravinsky's *Rite of Spring*. I could see Philip in the teaching mirror, laughing with his lips. He nodded me in and Miss Walker tore herself away.

'So what do you think of the music scholar?' he asked when the door was shut at last and we were alone together. He rubbed his fingers, watching me unpack my violin. He always seemed to have cold hands. *Tell him to stick them up your jumper. That should make 'em nice and warm*, Nina used to tease.

I thought of saying we were in a dorm together but that seemed embarrassing, somehow. The same way eating could be embarrassing, or choosing what tape to play. 'She's very good,' I mumbled, tightening my bow so the gap between the hair and the stick was precisely the width of my middle finger. I ran it with resin, six times, up and down from heel to tip. All at once I seemed to care very much about little things like that. Not everyone can have a music scholarship. Not everyone can have a gift.

Philip said, 'You could learn a lot from her.' He shrugged his jacket to the back of a chair. That so many Hawklies fell a bit in love with him was inevitable, I suppose. Apart from Pablo, Dr Slime and Frederick in Woodwork, he was the only man we ever saw. On Valentine's Day his pigeon-hole spilled poems and cards and, once, a broken A string twisted round and round in the shape of a heart. Violinists were a kind of running joke in the school, pitied and envied at the same time. Our weekly 40-minute one-to-ones were subject to predictable winking innuendo and even the most apparently sincere would soon collapse with sniggering at any mention of *position, vibrato, fingering*.

Philip, of course, pretended not to know. We practised our trills. He practised looking innocent, giving us the time-honoured baffled professorish blink. No one could tell for sure how thick he was. He had a Guarneri and a string quartet, a higher degree from the Royal Academy. Singled out for the Elgar solo at their summer graduation concert, he had been praised by all. Freelance teaching, he said, he charged £80 per hour. It was a mystery why on earth he bothered with any of us.

Anna Birdwood barged in at the end of the lesson, just as I

was wrapping up my violin. She had been listening at the door again. She never knocked, never apologised for coming in early. 'Is it true that Louisa Greene's violin is worth three thousand pounds?' she demanded, crashing her case on top of the piano next to mine. Somewhere, rattling about inside the exoskeleton, existed an intelligence of tiny and exquisite nastiness.

Philip smiled. 'I wouldn't be surprised.'

'But that's outrageous – it's cheating, isn't it? Even Beth would sound like a pro if you gave her a Stradivarius to play.'

He stepped back against the radiator. He never stood up for me. I squinted at Anna, curled my lip. 'And what do you know?' I said. It didn't make much sense but the scorn in my voice more than compensated.

'It isn't fair to give a girl an instrument none of the others can afford. No wonder she's got the scholarship.'

'She's got a scholarship because she's brilliant. The violin has nothing to do with it, ask Philip—'

Philip gave an enigmatic shrug.

'Lend us a hand with this, will you? The bloody thing won't go up.' Lou yanked at the music stand. A jagged streak of rust ran down the outside of each leg where the clamps had scraped at the grey enamel. Each one was stiff or dented and marked like that. I hovered a moment by the door. I hadn't meant to disturb her, only to check she wasn't still pissed off from Break.

'You shouldn't be so tall,' I joked. 'Stay there, I'll get you another one.'

She followed me as far as Miss Walker's room. A print of Vermeer's *Lady Seated at a Virginal* hung off-centre below the clock at the end. The cellos were setting up for Orchestra in the Rehearsal Room next door, a sequence of muffled booms rolling along the corridor as Susie Hargreaves tightened the timps. 'What are we playing this term?' She twisted her tongue around the words, self-conscious, like a French Exchange asking for breakfast.

'Rossini Overture. It's rank, but Philip says we've got to play something *Oom-Pah-Pah* for Parents' Day.'

'I had a goldfish called Rossini. Sophie fed him too much and he died. We buried him under a rosebush in the garden but then it died too and Dad made her dig the whole lot up as punishment. It took forever and she got these puffy white blisters where the spade had been.' I tried to picture it but the closest I could get was the Scarlett-O'Hara-sieving-earth scene from *Gone With The Wind*. Lou held out her hands to demonstrate. The tips of her fingers were black with finger-board ink.

We knocked on Miss Walker's door, went in when no one answered. A record player rested slant on the piano stool and the lid of the piano itself could hardly be seen beneath a heap of scores and flute and oboe cases. Keys hung from a row of pegs on the wall behind the door and a cello leaned face-in like the classroom dunce in the furthest, darkest corner of the room. Lou thumbed through a pile of music on the desk, pulling out a part for first violin. She opened it, looked at the notes and hummed the opening bars. I grabbed the stand and we wandered back.

'Have you got perfect pitch?'

She nodded.

'Can I see your violin? Is it really worth three thousand pounds?'

She nodded again. 'More than that now, I should think,' she said, unlocking the case with a cheap-looking silvery key.

'You keep it locked?'

'Have to – insurance. No one's allowed to play it except for me.'

'What if you lose the key?'

'I've got about fifty million spares.' The zips purred open. Inside, the case was lined with thick red velvet, like the coffin of a cabaret queen. A Velcro choker fastened the neck, the lid held space for four bows and a clip for a tube where extra strings awaited their particular emergency uncoiled.

'The sticker inside says it was made by Stradivarius, but lots of violins have that,' she said, unwrapping it from a dusty white square of silk. She tilted it so I could peer in through the f-hole, flipped it over to show the tortoise-shell back. I stroked it the way you might stroke a fierce but exhausted tabby cat, sliding my finger across the left-hand shoulder where there seemed to be a bump in the varnish.

'That's where it was dropped, about twenty years ago,' Lou explained. 'Mum and Dad could never have afforded it otherwise. It barely affects the sound.' The chin-rest was cherrywood. The pegs had ebony pin-heads at the end.

Everything about it seemed hand–made and luxurious compared with mine. Even the strings seemed sleeker, plumper, more silvery. 'Can I hold it?'

She glanced through the window in the door. 'OK, but don't tell anyone. They'll all be wanting a go.'

The kettle hums and the spitting smell of bacon drifts beneath the cabin door. The grill tray clatters as Nina shoves it under again for the meat to crisp. She has been busy. Two washed wine bottles stand together on the table. Plates and glasses twinkle on the draining board, and the ashtrays gleam. The saloon doors are open and a soft through-draught brushes away the stink of cigarettes. The gas-fire chuckles to itself on lowest heat.

Waiting for the water to boil, Nina folds clothes, arranges them on the armchairs in four piles, one for each of us and one for Sophie. By daylight she can see small tears and food-stains in the velvet coat she was wearing last night. Hand-stitching in places where the seams have gone. And now that the air is clear she senses the musty desperation of jumble sales on the collar, and lavender in the lingering scent of the unknown woman who had worn it first. She shudders, imagining a thousand dried-out particles of skin – Sophie's skin, even – trapped in the warp and weft of the cloth, imagining the salt-encrusted fibres at the back of the neck.

'Smells good.' I slump in an armchair, toppling the clothes into a confusion of legs and shoulders on the floor. 'God, I feel rough.'

'Coffee?' Nina passes me a mug. 'And lots of water, I'd say.'

'Doctor's orders?'

'You need to rehydrate.'

'I don't remember packing these.' I refold a pair of blue linen shorts, my favourites, about two sizes too big. Unrolled they reach almost below my knees, Swallow-and-Amazon style.

'Your shorts?' says Nina, not turning round. 'I brought them. I borrowed them at the end of term, remember? Thought you'd want them back.'

'I completely forgot. What else have you got?' I must have boxes of her stuff – paperbacks, earrings, lipstick, cover-up, tapes.

She shrugs. She brushes the hair from her face and smiles. 'It's like the end of a marriage or something, don't you think? Couples fighting over who gets the Lionel Ritchie album.'

I blow at my coffee-foam. 'You can have that.'

Sliding the rashers onto a plate, she pinches the darkest piece between her fingers, crunches the rind at the back of her mouth. Its saltiness fizzes across her tongue. 'Coming outside?'

I nick a slice of bacon and follow her, squinting in the silvery air. The deck-dew soaks my bare feet and the hairs on my forearms prickle. Flattened grass and limp and shadowy leaves on the far bank mark out where the flood is already beginning to recede and in the distance, quiet like the fuzz of atmosphere on a not quite perfectly tuned radio, we hear the roar of the weir. We clamber up onto the slippery coach-roof for a better view and walk the length of it, listening to the creaks. Our toes splay, gripping the camber like the toes of apes. A rusty Post Office bicycle lies chained to the handrail on the roof of the *Singing Swan* next door. Nina hoists our boat-hook, poses like Neptune with his trident, considering the weight of it in her hand.

'Have you ever driven one of these things?' I ask.

'You must be joking. Lou says she knows what to do.'

'That's what I'm worrying about.' We look round as snatches of conversation mingle with the low growl of an engine straining into reverse nearby. Glittering wavelets slap the hull and the *Otterburn* shifts weight.

'Morning,' we call as the *Tuscarora* slips from the pontoon, nosing into the moss-green elbow of the basin. A line of bubbles bobs in its wake, tracing the manoeuvre. The helmsman lifts his straw hat, grunting once by way of reply.

'Ask him the way to Coventry.'

'Ask him yourself.' We watch in silence as the boat completes its turn.

Little by little the wash dies down, the lap and splash of it fading into watery quietness again. Now there are other sounds: the whine of an electric saw in the boatyard, a dog on the towpath, birds and aeroplanes. I close my eyes, dizzy and thoughtless with morning bliss. The sleeve of my T-shirt brushes Nina's arm.

'We'll be able to sunbathe up here,' she says.

'As if you need to.' Nina's skin is olive all year round. She tans the way most people breathe. Lou thinks it must be something to do with the Pill.

As if there aren't enough happy side-effects already, she used to complain. *Why can't I have acne?*

Spots, corrected Nina. *Not acne, hormone spots.*

Same difference. They come and go mysteriously, failing to mar her brutal prettiness. Somehow nothing can do that.

The bacon has gone cold and powdery with bubbled fat. Nina makes a shopping list while Lou crunches through the last three rashers. She lounges in an armchair, toasting her feet on the ledge of the fire. Her matted hair stands up in a half mohican and there are three red welts at the back of her neck where the mosquitoes bit her on deck last night. She licks her fingers, wiping them across the front of her jeans.

'By the way, Mum says we're to use as many of the tins as possible.' She twists back in her chair to catch my eye, nodding for a fag. 'They'll only be thrown away.'

'What tins?' Nina chews her pencil end.

'Down there,' Lou waves vaguely.

I throw her a pack of Marlboro Lights but they slip between her fingers, bouncing off the grille in front of the fire. 'I can't believe they're going to sell it, Lou. Can't you persuade them not to?'

'*Where?*' Nina peers into the cupboard beneath the kitchen sink.

Lou lights her cigarette. She lifts herself from the arm-chair and wanders over, pointing her long white foot at a square cut in the lino. 'There used to be a bit of string poking out. The mouse must have eaten it.' Her fingernails grapple with a sliver of chipboard, slowly easing the cover free as a cool, dank diesel-stench filters across the room and mingles with the cigarettes and the grill tray.

Nina sniffs and squints in. 'I'm not eating anything that's lived in there.' Tentatively she pulls out a tin of custard.

'Sophie got that last time I came,' Lou says, dusting the tin on the front of her T-shirt. 'We were going to make trifle. We were desperate for trifle. Can't think why.' She reaches up to flick her fag ash in the sink. Nina kneels, her head and both arms disappear into the hole. Beside her, Lou constructs a supermarket pyramid of miscellaneous tins. Chickpeas and pineapple chunks. Kidney beans, rice pudding, cream of celery soup.

We drop our trainers in a plastic bag and roll our jeans to our kneecaps, ready for the wet walk into town. Nina hogs the bathroom mirror, curling her eyelashes, prodding them deftly with a black mascara brush, and glossing her lips with cherry balm. She squirts Chanel No 5 at her collarbone and fluffs her hair, running back to the glass to check for smudges or flake as Lou padlocks the saloon door.

'Fucking slag,' we mouth behind her back, and she whips round, glaring. Grins.

'I saw that,' she guesses. Three mallards waddle along the

pontoon in front of us, flopping down into the water one by one as we draw near.

'I'd like to come back as a duck,' Lou says, draping her long arms round our shoulders. 'I'd fly over Mum and Dad's house and shit on their balcony.' She stares at our six feet on the planking, marching in and out of synch. The edges of the wood are gentle and sad with mould.

Where yesterday the towpath seethed, today it lies submerged and peaceful between the swollen river and the still canal, as though some kind of an equilibrium has been achieved. Grass tips, dandelions, and one or two wild barley heads surface below the thorn trees, and the thorn trees themselves look all the better for their long, involuntary drink. Tiny purple seeds float at our ankles as we stagger to the bridge, lurching across sharp invisible stones. Lou hops, stumbling from jag to jag while Nina purses her lips and claws at the air for balance. 'Yowtch' she whispers quietly to herself, determined not to make so much of a bloody fuss.

On the bridge we stop for a cigarette, waiting for our feet to dry. The sun considers the possibility of breaking through the clouds and our earliest footprints warm up and disappear. An ant sniffs over the ghost of one of Lou's big toes. As we set off again, bark crumbs and little stones rattle deep inside our shoes.

On the tarmac the puddles have almost all evaporated. We link arms and walk up the middle of the road towards where Lou thinks she remembers there were shops. No cars come. Red-brick cottages pair up, join into terraced streets.

Uphill, ahead of us, the avenues gather themselves into a
city. Hobbled bicycles lean against front garden walls.
Caught between the branches of a lilac tree, a blue and
white striped carrier bag fills and spills in the breeze like a
crinkly, blown-away lung. Neat net curtains the windows
of every other house, vying with Jimi Hendrix posters,
Gustav Klimt's *Kiss*, and Indian drapes.

'Just think, you'll probably be living in one of these next
year,' says Lou to Nina. A courier swoops by on his racer,
accelerating down the hill, his fingers knotted easily behind
his head. 'You can show us your college.'

'*Sophie's* college. I'm not in yet,' says Nina superstitiously.
Lou rolls her eyes. She's been rolling them ever since Nina's
two-E offer came through, the week before Christmas.

Counting back, I reckon the board will have posted our
results this morning – jammed together in a fat brown A4
envelope, perhaps, with FIRST CLASS written in spiky
biro capitals across the franking stamp. Goodman and
Wilson will see them first, of course, then they'll be pho-
tocopied and compared and the subject mistresses told how
well or badly their classes have performed.

By lunchtime tomorrow the original print-outs will be
sorted, sealed into their very own self-addressed envelopes
and ready to post. For O levels two years ago flamboyant
envelopes had been all the rage. Lou and Nina chose
shocking pink and electric blue respectively, while mine
was white with little red hearts all over the front like a
valentine. We'd journeyed into town for them especially.
This time round, by silent, mutual assent, we have played

the whole thing down. The coolest envelopes are minimal white. In spite of the fact that her stomach lurches like a box of china in the back of a colliding transit van each time she thinks of its inevitable, inexorable and thoroughly predestined approach, Lou even threatened to use a second class stamp on hers. She claimed it was all she had. At the very last minute, and only to avoid the possibility that we might somehow fail to recognise our own handwriting and open the envelopes in public, unawares, Nina drew a pill-sized smiley face in the top left corner of each. For luck, she explained, not once imagining how useful those stick-man grins would be. How else will our families know for sure which envelope they are permitted to open on our behalf?

I give Lou's arm a secret squeeze. She looks away as Nina leads us onto the pavement through the gap between a skip and a parked Sierra. Polythene has been masking-taped over the shattered passenger-seat window as a makeshift guard against rain. We pass a newsagent, an Indian restaurant. The launderette on the corner is closed, according to a sign in the window, for refurbishment. Grass grows in the cracks between the paving stones and a street-light leans crooked above the kerb.

'What shall we get?' I ask out loud, breaking the silence. This is the season of cut-price strawberries and nectarines that take a fortnight to go ripe. One day shopping will be a chore. The novelty even of very large supermarkets with toilets and cafés and nappy-changing facilities will wear away, the exotic allure of kiwi fruit

and pawpaw will dull a little every week. As we manoeuvre cantankerous trolleys away from the delicatessen
counter, the crisp and biscuit aisle, we'll look back on
today and shake our heads.

'Let's see what you got.'
'Bath pearls.'
'Let's have a look.'

Lou reached into her pocket, pulling out a Boots plastic bag, the kind with no handles. She tipped it up, spreading her long hands wide to catch whatever might fall out. Seven shiny balls the size of gob-stoppers rolled slowly across the laminated menu. Nina picked one up and squeezed it. 'Careful.' Lou's fingers hovered.

'I've seen them before, in the Body Shop.' I ripped the shrink-wrap off a pack of ten Silk Cut and pulled out the tongue. 'Let's have a sniff.'

'They're like eyeballs.' Nina tried squashing one into her socket but it wasn't big enough and fell out, thudding with a dull half-bounce against the table. She balanced it on the spout of a vinegar shaker. Squinted at the plasticky sag.

The waitress rushed past, a tray of cups and saucers propped against her chest. 'You're next, ladies,' she called over her shoulder.

I took out two cigarettes, lit one and slipped the other

back, filter up, for luck. Natasha leaned over from the table behind and scrounged a light. Nina peeled off her soaking sweatshirt, pushing up her sleeves. She combed her hand through her hair and shook it dry. The girls at the garden window had drawn hearts and flowers in the condensation and it was hard to tell if the rain had stopped. The corners of the room were dark and airless. Cigarette smoke hung from the black mock-Tudor beams like sediment.

Grammar-school boys in St Columbus uniforms – grey with ruby red piping, button-holes and shield – sat drinking Coke from cans at a table in the corner. They had removed their jackets and loosened their ties into hangman's nooses with the shirts still buttoned up behind. They sat with their knees apart, jiggling. Under the table luminous pink and yellow ski-socks grinned from the gaps between their charcoal flannels and scuffed black shoes. The girls at the next door table swished their hair and sniggered at definition jokes. *What's the definition of a drawing pin? What do you call a man with no arms and no legs who swims the Channel?* Wet coats and cardigans dripped from the backs of every chair and the gum-pocked, fag-singed carpet was littered with satchels and carrier bags. The waitress folded her tray under her arm and flipped her pad.

'Right then, ladies, ready to order?'

'What are you having?' Lou asked, squinting at the menu upside down. This was her first time in the Tea Tray, usually she spent Wednesday afternoons in the Music School.

She practised every day from half past one until tea time at four. She was exempt from Games. She didn't do Art and Design, and gave up French after a week. 'Music is my second language,' she would quip smugly, heading off to Miss Wilson's room for a theory class as we fumbled for our vocab books in the English-Block lockers.

She never hung out in the Quad, or came for walks, or squeezed into the TV Room on Thursday nights for *Top of the Pops*. One minute she'd be right there beside you, feeding 10ps into the Coke machine. Turn your back and she'd be gone the next. Nina was philosophical. After all, she predicted, Lou was going to be a star. Her publicist would send us complimentary tickets to gala performances at the Royal Festival Hall. We'd sit in the stalls and whisper how we'd always known she'd make it big, and strangers in the row in front would turn to stare admiringly at us in spite of themselves. We'd fan our cleavages with the programme and wait by the stage door afterwards, flirting with handsome groupies. Sometimes Lou would be mobbed by autograph hunters and we'd have to come to the rescue. Sometimes she'd walk right by, unrecognised – a tall, thin woman in a second-hand winter coat with perhaps a trace of cold cream on her cheek and dents in her fingertips. She'd hurry down the pavement and we'd all link arms and wander off to find a restaurant or a cab.

Nina had it worked out, right down to the detail of what colour evening dress Lou ought to wear for the televised final rounds of *Young Musician of the Year*. 'I can see it now,' she said. 'Full length, with a slit up the back and no sleeves. A sort of plunging neckline. The judges will love that.'

'It's got to have sleeves,' I pointed out, thinking of the scar. 'She's got to be able to play, remember.' We were lounging in N Dorm, waiting for someone to come and tell us to go to sleep.

'So?' Nina redipped the varnish brush, smearing it against the bottle's neck. Shiny globs of peach-glitter slid back down the sides.

'Her tits might fall out.'

We giggled at the thought of Lou revealing herself on national TV but she refused to be baited. 'I probably won't even enter,' she murmured, peering curiously over Nina's shoulder at her abducted hands. 'I told you they'd look crap.'

'Ta very much. I haven't finished yet.' There was only one to go. Nina shook slightly as the bristles splayed. 'There, what do you think?'

Lou fanned her long straight fingers, trilling the air. She'd been biting her nails as long as she'd had teeth.

Kate came in with a stack of files. 'Time to go, Nina. Matron's premenstrual. God, it stinks in here.' She opened the window and drew back the curtains, flapping them to make a draft, flicked off the light. Slowly, the dorm changed shape. The window glowed, faint at first, then brighter and brighter. 'Lou, why aren't you changed?'

'My nails are wet.'

Kate groaned. 'Not you as well. Where's Harriet?'

'Tanning, in the bath.' It had been Millie's brainwave.

The only question was how many tea bags they should use.

'Looks like you've crapped yourselves,' Nina remarked, inspecting the experiment after an hour. 'Have you changed colour yet?'

Harriet held out a wrinkled hand and waved imperiously at a packet of Skips on the chair at the end of the bathtub. 'Mais oui.'

I climbed into bed. Nina hid herself behind the door, hopping from foot to foot in the semi-dark as we waited for the approaching clip of Matron's sensible shoes to pass. The radiator fluttered. Someone raced along the corridor outside, bare feet slapping the boards. Upstairs Emily Waterhouse rolled over in bed, the sound of rusty springs creaked through the ceiling.

'Nina?' The door swung open. Matron stood in a fan of light, her hands on her hips, looking stern. 'Come on. I know you're there.'

Her eyes weren't used to the dark. We were pulling faces but she couldn't see. Nina shivered, counted to ten, then shuffled out from her hiding place with her hands in the air. 'I surrender. Please don't hit me. Please!'

The shape of Matron's mouth evolved into a reluctant smile. 'Now there's a thought.' She ushered Nina out and closed the door. No one said anything for a while. Silver-edged clouds slipped silently across the windows and the curtain bellied like a lazy sail.

Lou shuffled into her nightie, throwing her day-time clothes at the chair. 'Beth, are you asleep?' she whispered.

'No.' We had rearranged our beds along the wall so the heads were together. That way we could talk all night without disturbing anyone. Valerie sighed pointedly. I lay with my chin on the pillow, staring at the top of Lou's head. Her hair curled out from the crown in a pale brown whorl. It smelled of lavender.

'What would happen if I gave up, do you think?'

'What, violin? I dunno. Why?'

'I dunno . . .' She trailed off, snorted, rolled over onto her stomach so we were eye to eye.

The waitress tapped the order pad with her biro. Its end had been chewed.

'I'm having toast and chocolate,' I said.

Lou looked from me to Nina and back again as if to check we weren't just taking the piss. 'I'll have that too.'

'Three please.' Nina grinned foolishly at the woman's huge chest, her roly-poly chins and heavy-veined cheeks.

'Be about ten minutes, ladies. So many of you here this afternoon. Like bloody bedlam.' She scribbled the order, wagged her finger at the Fourths on the table next door who had been flicking sugar cubes, and waddled into the kitchen.

Nina said, 'Isn't she *marvellous*? She used to be a night-club singer, you know.'

Lou's eyes widened.

'She went to prison – fraud or something – not for long. She tells the most disgusting jokes you've ever heard.'

'Like?'

Nina looked at me. We had decided there was something sweetly idiotic in Lou that seemed to need protection. 'They're obscene,' she said. 'You don't want to know.'

I puckered my mouth for a smoke ring and coughed. Nina hit me on the back and I slapped her off, cursing. One of the St Columbus boys turned, ready to smirk. He had a stud and a tinkly silver cross in his left ear and his hair was spiky on top and shaved at the back so that, running your fingertips up his neck, it would feel like the under-side of a nettle leaf, all soft and prickly at the same time. 'Do teachers ever come in here?' Lou was saying.

'Nope.'

'Never?'

I nodded at the waitress. 'She'd tip us off. It couldn't be safer.' Lou stared at the fag packet, then at my hands and mouth, as though she'd never seen a person smoke before. I tapped the white and purple cardboard. 'Want one?'

'Better not, I promised Mum—'

'She can't hold you to a promise not to do something you've never tried.' I flicked my ash neatly into the ashtray but the St Columbus boy was busy setting up a match trick. Nina had her back to us. She'd twisted in her seat to watch the waitress, the two red hair-clips that sagged lop-sided one at each pink temple. Grey roots glimmered behind the back-combed black. Her bra straps showed through at the back of her nylon shirt and you could see the skin and muscle, I suppose it was muscle, bulging underneath.

'Anyway, so long as you don't go down to the filter it's

OK . That way you can still say you've never smoked a cigarette because you haven't – not literally, not a whole one.'
I rattled the pack at her, flipping up the lid. She pinched a
filter and dragged it free, slotted it elegantly between her
fingers, index and middle, at the very tips. 'Don't inhale
straight away, or you'll be sick. Just suck a bit to get it
going.' The yellow flame bellied, then flared. I shook it out.
Lou studied the ember, squinting at it soberly. Tiny, hushed
explosions fizzed in the ember and one more millimetre
turned to ash.

'Now what?' she said at last.

'Just smoke.' I lit one myself, keeping her company as she
half-lowered her eyelids, lifted the cigarette to her lips and
sort of kissed it, hollowing her cheeks. It glowed for a
count of three. Then she looked up, flaring her nostrils, and
inhaled. Blinked twice. Breathed out slowly and rolled the
tip against the edge of the ashtray, smiling as the food
arrived. The waitress handed down a plate of thick buttered
toast and an aluminium chutney dish, its three compart-
ments dolloped with marmite, honey and jam. A mountain
of whipped cream floated in the chocolate, melting into
bubbles and lakes of fat. Lou sucked in again, exhaling as
Nina turned and snatched the cigarette from her mouth,
crushing it into the ashtray before I had a chance to protest.
'You don't smoke,' she muttered. 'Jesus, Beth. Don't you
know she's got asthma?'

'So? She can if she wants.' I picked it out, examining the
paper for tears and straightening it between my fingers.

'Another convert, eh?' The waitress looked down on us

and laughed. She tore off our bill and folded it beneath the sugar pot. Nina shrugged, spooning what was left of her cream onto the edge of the saucer.

When she had finished eating Lou relit the stubbed-out cigarette and smoked it all the way down to the filter.

Lattice-windowed and pocked with soot-black gar-goyles, Sophie's college – Nina's college-to-be – looks just like all the others, but already the medieval city is beginning to recede. Cars and buses stream over the bridge, speeding up, relieved to be crossing back into a modern world where the roads are straight and wide, the cobbles long gone.

Lou steps into the porter's lodge, abandoning us by a hand-painted sign that prohibits visitors between the hours of two and five p.m. We prop our shopping bags between our feet and Nina rubs her hands, examining her palms with the kind of scrupulous attention usually reserved for tropical skin complaints as, through the polished glass of his stone-vaulted office window, the duty porter stares at us hard.

'Don't look at him,' she whispers, surreptitiously twisting her back to the glass. One of the bags tips sideways and a peach rolls slowly across the cold stone flags, curling to a stop below a noticeboard headed JCR as Lou peers round the office door.

'Nina, he wants to talk to you a mo.'

The bags slump further as she steps away from them, frowning, and a second peach threatens to escape.

'Be sweet,' Lou mouths as they cross in the doorway. She strolls off across the grass, squinting up at the tower. Turns back and smiles at me.

As soon as she's in earshot, I think, *I'll tell her to pick up that peach.* It bothers me, lying there, so bruisable and bright against the stone.

A curly-haired man in tweed swerves off the narrow path, ducks striding under the arch, blinks at me once and shoulders through the office door as Nina comes out. She's sauntering towards me, looking pleased with herself.

'We can go in now. Special dispensation since I'm to be coming up in October. Where's Lou?'

I nod outside. 'Rescue that peach, will you? It's really bugging me,' I say, but Nina doesn't seem to hear. Once more, the tropical skin complaint absorbs her full attention. The curly-haired man is back and he appears to think he knows her from somewhere. Envelopes and a shrink-wrapped magazine rustle under his arm as he stops in front of us and stares. He clears his throat, blinking twice, as though deep in thought. He smiles at me quickly and hurries off into the street.

'Who was that?' I whisper, nudging her to show he's gone.

Nina squints into the traffic after him. She shudders, fluffs her hair. 'Remember when I came for my interview and I snogged an undergraduate?'

'*Him?*'

'Not sure.' She pauses in quick mental comparison. Kissing him, she'd been so impressed by a sense of her own outrageousness she'd managed to forget the mottled cheeks and the large bump, white like a knuckle, at the top of his nose.

'Who is he?'

She shrugs. 'He was showing us round.'

'Who was?' Lou stands in the archway, a lanky shadow, dark before the vivid lawn.

'Oh nothing,' Nina mutters, jiggling on the spot. She has one hand over her mouth, and behind it grins with embarrassment from ear to ear.

Lou disappears into the office, ignoring Nina's stormy looks. Seconds later she returns, brimming with glee. Twinkles at us sideways. 'Before I reveal his true identity I want to know the full extent of your relations with this man,' she taunts.

'Fuck off, I'll go and find out for myself,' says Nina, devil-may-care.

'I wouldn't if I were you.' Lou strolls slowly in front of us, circles the shopping bags. 'Take it from me, the last thing you want to do is draw suspicion.' She saunters towards the fallen peach, stops eye to eye with the Finals list on the noticeboard and scans it idly, just for the thrill of seeing her sister's name, her degree, on paper. Mr and Mrs Greene had been so proud, that First made up for everything.

Lou picks up the peach, feeling it all over. The yellow fur

is soggy where it hit the floor. She turns to the noticeboard again, frowning, combing through the list of names.

'Oh well, I guess I'll just find out in October.' Nina has turned her back on us. She leans beneath the archway, gazing across the lawn. Stumbling from her December interview, flushed and shivering with sudden relief, she had passed through the beam of a floodlight – just there – and thrown a thirty-foot shadow across the chapel's clean bright sandstone wall, so accurate it had embarrassed her. Undergraduate silhouettes watched from lighted windows overhead. Her sensible, ambitious, tied-back hair, her winter coat that hung like a thin box, hovering stiffly just below the knees, her DMs – all the pieces twisted and enlarged into a schoolgirl monster. She hadn't dared stop walking, and looked at herself side-on, at the teasing black outline of her self-motivated chin. For a moment, only a moment, she had been certain she'd get in.

Lou crunches a large chunk from the side of the peach, chews thoughtfully. She's bitten right through to the stone, which glistens with juice and saliva, and a sticky drop wells against her teeth-mark at the edge of the fur. She finishes it. When she speaks, the naked pit rattles solidly against her teeth. 'Sophie's not on this list,' she says at last, swallowing.

'Must be a typo.' Nina glances at us impatiently. 'Come on, then. Are we going in?'

We echo round cloisters, swinging our bags, goose-pimpled in the stony chill. The 400-year-old lawn is cut very short, striped hard and perfect, the sort of lawn you

need to be wearing a straw hat and a floaty chiffon skirt
to appreciate. Roses cluster heavy-flowered below the
spidery wisteria leaves and Nina skips and jiggles with
unexpected pride. She'd known the college would be
old and handsome, but this was like the National Trust.
We should be walking with our hands behind our backs
and speaking Greek or, at the very least, mock-Tudor
couplets.

'How long does it take to get used to this much beauty?'
I wonder, trying to imagine Sophie in her second-hand
gangster suit racing round blind corners, late for a bollocking or some tutorial. Nina prattles happily, charging ahead.
Peeping into the chapel, she marvels at worn, uneven flags,
calls for Lou. They've walked right past the sandwich board
outside, in spite of the poster drawing-pinned to its faded
black paint. I stand in front of it, alone. After a little while,
Nina comes back, creeping up to me, wondering if I'm
OK. She looks at it, reads in an instant what I have taken 60
full seconds to understand.

'Philip Gregory,' she says in a voice of calm, almost mali-
cious, incredulity. Then: 'We've missed it.'

Lou closes the chapel door, quietly turning the handle so
the click of the latch won't echo back along the flags. Her
face is numb. Part of her still can't believe we're allowed to
be here, I suppose. 'We've missed what?'

'A concert – last night.' I feel her hand on my shoulder,
her breath on my neck. Imagine her stiffening behind me,
her eyes not reading so much as rediscovering, line by line
and curve by curve, the letters of his name.

'I used to love the Beethoven Quartets,' she says at last, simply.

Nina counts the dates on her fingers. 'Looks like they're on tour.'

I reach out and tear the poster from its pins, fold it in four and slot it under my arm like a newspaper, Lou and Nina turning on me with slow amazement.

'I wanted it,' I shrug. 'He won't mind.'

Nina grimaces at Lou, tapping her head. 'I can't think what either of you ever saw in him,' she says, remembering the undergraduate, the shape of his shoulder blades, so solid and wide and tentative, somehow, as she had reached up, kissing him.

Lou glances at her hands, shrugging her reply.

I jammed a finger down my throat as far as it would go and vomited pathetically. Pieces of sweetcorn and raw red pepper floated in the bowl, looked almost edible. They didn't even smell too bad. I hurried to the Surgery and knocked on the door. A Fifth came out and sat on the chair by the weighing scales, sucking a thermometer. Matron ushered me in.

'Can I have an Off-Games note, please? I've been sick.' I leaned against the medicine cabinet as though about to faint.

'What did you have for lunch?'

I told her.

'And how do you feel now?' She picked up her pen and clicked the nib.

'Shaky.' Thin blue biro scribbled across the top of the pad in spiky loops.

'What is it this afternoon, hockey?' she guessed wearily, glancing at the fugged-up window. Scots pines shuddered in the wind and drizzle spattered the Surgery glass. In the summer term Thirds only had to play hockey once a week.

'I think so.'

She tore out the note and handed it to me, folded in half. 'I don't want to see you here again next week, Beth. This is becoming repetitious.'

'But I was sick! It's in the loos by K Dorm. You can see for yourself if you don't believe me.'

'How thoughtful of you to have preserved the evidence,' she smiled. 'I suggest you go back, now, and flush the chain.'

Nina was waiting for me, lying on Lou's bed reading the agony column in last week's *Just Seventeen*. 'You won't believe this,' she said, looking up as I came in. 'There's a girl here who thinks her nipples are spots. She's been squeezing and squeezing and wants to know why no pus has come out.'

I waved my note at her gleefully. We shrugged into our overcoats, wrapped Benetton scarfs around our heads like Nastassja Kinski in *Tess* and hurried across to the Changing Room to find Miss Ballard.

'How do you get detention?' asked Nina at the top of the steps. She slid down the bannister, jumped clear at the end with an echoing thud. I side-slipped after.

'I don't know, how do you get detention?'

'Ask a Games mistress to spell her name.' We crashed through the Changing-Room doors. A row of worried-looking girls leaned against the radiator shivering, oblivious to the stench of sweat and bleach. Their heads turned simultaneously as we walked in and there was silence.

'Hockey's cancelled!' said Nina, precipitating the start of what promised to be a very loud cheer. 'Only joking.'

Isobel King stuck out her lengthy foot, which Nina pretended not to have seen, kicking it heartily. In the corner Catherine Scott sniffed the armpit of a rugby shirt she'd dragged through the wire mesh door of the next locker down. She shuddered, wrinkled her nose and slipped it on as Bollard walked in dragging a sack of hockey sticks and whistled for attention. She opened her register and shouted out names, added another red capital 'O' to my Thursday attendance column.

'Hand these out, then you can go. There should be twenty-four.' She kicked the sack in my direction. Nina fastened her laces in double bows and grinned as I went round. Caroline linked arms with Zoe Ross. Hockey sticks clattered, drummed the chilly concrete floor and rattled between the lockers. Thirds streamed out into the damp grey afternoon. I followed them, turned away uphill, dodging the puddles. Shards of drizzle needled my face.

The Music School smelled of floor polish. I wandered along the parquet corridors, past lockers and cupboards and door after door after door. The teaching rooms were all south-facing with radiators and posters and baby grands. The practise rooms opposite were cold and dark. Grey spaghetti sound-proofing tiled the ceilings. Moss-dappled skylights brightened windowless dead-ends.

Lou stood, back to the door, in her usual cubicle. The music was too far away for me to read. A five-bar sequence of diminished thirds modulated through the keys and she repeated it, a little bit faster every time, resetting the metronome on the windowsill at the start of each new tempo. Sometimes she'd hit a wrong note, miss a position shift or get her bowing back to front and have to stop, go back to the beginning and start again. If the key-change was difficult and wouldn't unknot with simple repetition she'd break off altogether, running through it at half, or even quarter time, like a teacher patronising some recalcitrant class. You could hear the frustration in her fingertips as though, reigned in, the music fizzed and only her will to play perfectly kept it at heel. But for her hands and arms she barely moved. Her fingers pressed the strings like a trumpeter's fingers pushing down imaginary stops. Mine would have soon got bored and started showing off but hers were calm and sensible. They knew exactly where to go next.

Anna Birdwood burst from Philip's room at the end of the corridor, bashing the wall with her violin case as she turned. She scowled at me and swung past into the instrument store. Philip followed, listening with his head on one side as he went. I felt him standing there, behind my shoulder. Lou must have heard the footsteps. She stopped, glanced round and then looked down, embarrassed. She tucked the violin under her arm and turned to face us, mouthing something that looked obscene, waving dismissively and opening the door. Philip jingled the coins in his suede jacket pocket.

'Stop spying on me.' She wagged her bow in our faces. The metronome ticked like a heartbeat. Something papery fell to the floor.

'Let's hear it, then.' He leaned in the door frame, folded

his arms and cocked his head. 'Show Beth what she should be aiming for.' He gave me a conspiring wink.

'I saw that,' muttered Lou, lifting her violin. She flicked her hair.

Philip squeezed past me and grabbed the metronome. 'You don't need this,' he said, stopping it. 'Come on now, stand up straight.'

Lou scowled, took a quick breath and launched herself before he could think of anything else to criticise. Her bow bounced easily and her fingers flew, scattering the clean, bright notes so fast it left the tune falling over itself to catch up. The sense of the piece came afterwards, the way the sound of the engine trails an aeroplane.

'Very good,' he mumbled when the music stopped. 'Have another look at the F-sharp section.' He touched his ear, crinkling one side of his face as though he'd bitten a lime.

'Intonation?'

He nodded, turning to me. 'You could play like that too, you know.'

I rolled my eyes at Lou but she looked back steadily and wouldn't tease. I knew I should have been better at the violin. Everyone said so. Everyone said I had potential. If only I would practise properly, learn to bounce the bow, read fifth position and master about one hundred other small technicalities, they said, there was no reason why I shouldn't catch up with Lou in a matter of months. The more I let myself believe them the less I tried.

Philip glanced at his Casio. 'What are you up to now?'

I shrugged as Lou turned back to her étude, fiddling in F-sharp *sotto voce*.

'Come on, then. Get your violin and I'll show you that new bowing again.'

We traipsed down the corridor, into his room. It smelled of aftershave. He leaned against the radiator, watching me open my case. Black paint had started chipping from the fibreglass, and the purple felt lining peeled away from the rosin-box inside. One of the catches in the lid had slipped again, letting the bow knock loose. I had a cotton handkerchief to wrap around the fiddle's neck but there was still a small gouge beside the bridge where the stock kept hitting. I clipped on the chin-rest and shifted it across my shoulder, practised resting my face against the cold black plastic. Lou's cherrywood chin-rest was always the perfect temperature. Violins seemed to float on her shoulder of their own accord. I tightened my bow.

'That's enough rosin. Here, give it to me.' Philip held the stick lightly in one hand and brushed the underside of the hair with his thumb. A cloud of sticky, scented dust puffed into the air between us and drifted slowly to the floor.

He tuned the violin and slotted it between my shoulder and chin once more, stepped back to look at me from a distance. I shuffled my feet. If you had dropped a weighted line from the scroll it would have landed plum on my left big toe. He nodded.

'Let's see how you hold the bow.'

My fingers re-spaced themselves along the stock, waiting uncomfortably. 'Relax your hand. Let it go floppy.' He was standing behind me now, adjusting the arrangement of my right hand with his. 'That's better. Can you feel the difference?' I nodded. It felt all wrong. 'Now balance the bow. Go on.'

I held out my arm and squeezed my thumb and little finger alternately, watching the tip move up and down along the perfect arc of some invisible circle.

'Good,' said Philip, putting his hand on mine once more. 'That's very good. Feel how the weight is evenly distributed? Just one or two millimeters out and this would be impossible. Lean into the stick. Very good.' He held our hands as steady as the point of a compass pinned through the middle pages of an exercise book, and I coloured in three-fifths of an imaginary pie-chart the exact purply blue of his shirt and tried to remember the feel of the extra wide gaps between the fingers on my bowing hand.

Suddenly he let go and walked back round in front of me. The spell broke. 'Now let's see you bounce the bow.'

'It's going to sound horrible,' I warned.

'Come for a roonie?'

Lou was dusting the front of her violin. She packed it away. The ends of her fingers were black and raw. We drifted down the corridor, arm in arm, and out along the track by the tennis courts, towards the Beech Trees. Sky shone in the puddles like a string of silver beads. Low branches drenched the sides of my coat as I stood to one side, letting Lou walk through dry. I reached for my cigarette.

'Philip's so funny,' she shivered. 'He takes it all so seriously, don't you think? He's always coming in, telling me stuff I know already – it's like he can't help interfering.'

'Lucky you.'

Lou laughed. 'He's nice,' she said.

I struck a match and nodded, breathing in its sticky, thick explosive.

'Is he married?'

'Don't think so, he's too young. Why do *you* want to know?'

Lou fluttered her eyelashes. She helped herself to a drag. I wasn't concentrating so I didn't wait for her reply. The branches fluttered overhead, and raindrops gusted, spattering across new leaves. Through the chinks in the hedge we would be able to see if anyone came within a hundred yards. Lou shuddered happily and closed her eyes. We tore the chewing-gum in half, trudged back across the soggy pitch. She opened her arms, a spiky bird about to take off. 'Doesn't all this space just make you want to sing, or scream or leap about or something?' she said, tipping back her head to stare at the clouds. The wind ruffled her jacket, puffing her long skirt into a kind of sail and pushing her off-balance as she tried to tightrope-walk backwards along the wet chalk boundary. I grabbed her arm and suddenly we were holding on with both hands, stamping and sliding on the mud and whirling round faster and faster until it seemed inevitable that one of us must let go.

Can it be true that Nina and Lou and I never once fought at Hawkley? Surely we must have quibbled and bitched a thousand times a week, we must have sulked and snapped and flared with just or unjust accusation, must have been wrong when we thought we were right and hated to admit it. Even by accident, we must have given and certainly taken offence. I can't remember it. I don't remember this stink of irritation floating between us as it floats between us now, sulphurous and short of breath like the lead-in to a thunder storm.

We trudge along the High Street, out of step, Nina grinding between the pedestrians, head down, gritting her teeth. Everything is wrong, she shouldn't be here yet. Somehow, she's nudged ahead of herself, a heavy ghost, visiting the scenes of what will be her brilliant university career. *This is the shop that prints the poster for my Trinity Term production of* Death of a Salesman. *This is the pub I go to, Wednesday nights, for French Club. This is the drain I drop my room key down the night I meet Paul . . .* She stares at the paving stones as though afraid to recognise herself – two years, three years on, to the day – gesticulating in the window of some red-checked tablecloth café. She hopes the city might not notice her, at least not yet, while there are still so many things she'd rather look at, first, alone, for Lou and I are an embarrassment and she wishes she could shake us off. If only her undergraduate would pass again and she could speak to him, frankly, woman to man, in the clear, intelligent voice of her grown-up persona. She doesn't want to be Nina any more. She barely notices the way her old friends lag behind.

Blood-sugar is low and the shopping bags cut into our hands. The afternoon has soured and there are people everywhere, sight-seeing, shopping or simply dawdling through their lunch break. Tourists gawp through college gates. Pensioners totter from second-hand bookshops. Lovers in matching blue wheel a bicycle along the pavement in front, stop suddenly to kiss across the handlebars. Lou steps sideways into the gutter and another cyclist yells as he swerves to avoid her, swinging into the middle of the road. Passers-by turn and stare. She flushes, murderous and wretched, ready to weep as the shopping bags crack into her ankle bones. 'That's it,' she says as Nina walks on. 'We're getting a taxi. Nina, stop. We're getting a taxi.'

Nina hesitates and people surge by, tutting and sighing as they step around her, shaking their heads. *Nobody knows who I am*, she thinks, *nobody guesses who I will be*. 'I haven't got any money left,' she shouts, turning to look at us. A sea of faces intervenes.

Lou picks up her bags again, struggling on. 'I'll pay. Come back will you?' We meet halfway, take shelter beside a Pay and Display stand.

'I want to walk,' says Nina, petulant. She knows we know this is exactly the opposite of what she wants but it's too late to be rational and we're bugging her so badly that right now, more than anything, she needs to fight. She squeezes her aching hands into fists and the shopping bags lift another centimetre from the ground, hang there heavy with unspecified significance. 'Why can't we walk?'

'Why can't we go by taxi?'

'Walking's good for us, and cheap.'

Lou sniffs. 'Saving for your retirement?'

'Fuck off and die.'

'Well, *I'm* going by cab.' Lou pulls her fringe, her voice shifts gear: defiant to wheedling. 'Come on, Nina. We always end up doing what you want—'

'We don't.'

'We do.'

'How come we're here, then, not lying on the beach somewhere hot? That's what I wanted.'

For a moment Lou concedes surprise. 'You never said.'

'You never listened.'

'That's crap, I'm always listening to you.' Lou sticks out her arm, too late, as a minicab sails by, ignoring her. The flush sets deeper into her cheeks, and her chin, her fore-head and her neck burn furiously.

'Well done,' Nina snarls, daring herself to drop the shop-ping and walk away, to vanish forever in a puff of spite. It would be easy, she never need think of us again. Lou paces, scanning the traffic.

Later, when I understood better the universal shape of arguments and had developed a sensitivity to the lulls and pauses, thresholds and fracture-lines where insult-trading flashes into full-scale war, I knew that this was the point at which I should have taken sides. But threes are dangerous, and all of a sudden it feels as though I have been waiting five years for a moment like this, to show how evenly I love them both. Their voices crack. They have forgotten I exist. Any minute now, if I keep very still, someone will say something I can never forgive.

A taxi indicates and slows to a stop beside the Pay and Display. Lou lifts three of the bags, staggering to the kerb.

'Come on, Nina,' I mouth, but she shakes her head.

'I'll walk. I need a bit of space.' She shrugs.

Inside, the taxi is clammy and stale with human warmth. The window-wind slips in my hand and the leatherette seat pinches and sucks at my denim thighs. Lou slouches in the furthest corner, pressing her forehead against the glass and humphing as I ask the driver to go once round the block in case Nina has changed her mind. The car rocks sullenly over the pitted road, passes a cinema and a building site, boarded off and posted with flyers. Back on the High Street we hover behind a bus. Nina has gone only about ten steps. The weight of the shopping bags pull her shoulders, but her head is tipped defiantly. Perhaps we should stop.

'Drive on,' says Lou.

★

We wait on the deck of the *Otterburn* for hours, smoking and boiling cup after cup of milky tea. We let the steam curl up and lick our faces, making them shine. Lou's pale hair clusters at the roots. The afternoon has thickened into a sluggish dream of reconciliation, grey and warm and still with possibility.

'When you think what we were like when we first met, you know, we're not the same people at all.' Lou shuffles deeper into the bench, resting her head against my shoulder. Her eyes close, letting the words dissolve.

'Of course we are.' I look at her still hands, her thumbnail's smooth white rainbow, steady at the side of the mug.

'If I'd left at the end of Third and we never met again until today, I bet you wouldn't recognise me.'

'Lou,' I say in my mildest and most sympathetic voice, 'you are nearly six foot tall. Of course I'd bloody recognise you.'

'That's not fair.' She hesitates. 'You know what I mean. *I* might not recognise me.' A bluebottle zigzags through the muggy quietness and, far away, cars on the High Street roll to a stop as the lights go red. Deep in her ear she feels me speak: it tickles, she tickles all over and suddenly something slaps the back of her hand. She opens her eyes. There is a smear of blood below the knuckles and a knot of crumpled black gunk. 'Thanks –'

I pass her another cigarette. We sip our tea. 'Nina will come back, you know.'

'I know.' Lou wrinkles her forehead, shrugs as sunlight floods suddenly between the clouds, shadowing her face.

The narrowboats throb with colour and life. An old man creeps onto the foredeck of the *Kittiwake* to bathe his wrinkles. The invisible dogs in the boatyard bark. Children appear from nowhere, rollerskating up the towpath onto the pontoon. Their wheels clatter across the decking and their voices wobble. They sing and laugh as the vibrations jiggle their bones.

'How old are they, do you reckon? Nine or ten?'

I squint at them. 'Older than that.'

'I used to think eighteen was so grown up. On birthdays I used to look back at the year and cringe remembering all the stupid things I'd said or done or wanted.'

'Everyone does that.' I'm looking down. Our faces bulge in the canal.

'I suppose.' She flicks her fag ash over the side. 'I suppose I thought that when I was this old I wouldn't be so stupid any more.'

'You're not—'

She doesn't smile. 'It's just not good enough to go on turning over new leaves, excusing yourself from every accident or error of judgment – I was only thirteen, I was only fourteen, and so on – again and again, is it? After a while they aren't really mistakes or accidents any more – the pattern's too obvious. They're *what you do*. They're *you*.'

We look up as a footstep trembles the length of the boat.

Nina dumps her bags, swinging round the side-deck. 'You'll never guess what I've just seen – a kingfisher. I only realised afterwards that that was what it was, it flew so fast – it was like a tiny, electric-blue missile, straight down the middle of the canal.' The animation slips as she pauses for breath. 'Just thought you'd like to know.' She has waded through the remains of the flood in her basketball boots and stands in a pool, her ankle throbbing as though a sliver has been chiselled from the bone. She stares at us, blank and ready for anything. She has a cashpoint card, an up-to-date train timetable and a home to go to. She can do without us and the thought is liberating. She smiles because she knows she doesn't have to, apologises quietly as Lou squints back, considering the shape of Nina's chin and shoulders, black against the towpath and trees, considering how much she loves them after all.

'I'm sorry too – stressed about results, I suppose.'

That night we cook spaghetti bolognese with extra-lean mince and bay leaves and a mug of wine. Nina divides the pasta in three and I spoon over a lava-flow of sauce. Lou tops each with a storm of grated cheese. We eat by lamp-light, wrapped in blankets out on deck. Moths divebomb our hands. Mosquitoes plant themselves in the door-frame and wait for us to fall asleep. Somehow we drink three bottles of wine – two red, one white – and when we have reached that stage of drunkenness when even very recent events are hazed with a kind of Ready-Brek aura of warm goodwill, Nina agrees to compromise her strict no-smoking policy and we play a single valedictory game of confessions, even though we think we know each other's secrets inside out.

I wake up shining and cross. Grease covers my face like strips of bacon and when I get round to crawling to the shower room to pee and squint in the mirror, I know I will actually look the colour of uncooked bacon too: rindy with splashes of pink in each cheek and an overlay of green translucent shimmer. The sun has beaten down on us for hours. No one remembered to open a window before we went to sleep last night. My sleeping bag smells of chalk and glue and long-dead water birds. The feathers have bedded down, slipping off me drip by drip in the night, but I am still too hot, too lazy to open the zip.

Nina lies on the single bed, an outstretched arm away. For a moment I contemplate snatching her pillow, just to annoy her, just to see what she will do. She lies on her back with her knees up, poised. Her eyes are open. We stare at each other, silent, expressionless and frank – the way a wife might look at her husband the morning of their 24th wedding anniversary. She's been dreaming, her eyes are thirsty and I can see my bacony flush in her cheek. We don't even need to smile. She lifts her arm as though it were pushing

through mud, not air, and pulls her hand across her forehead like a heavy comb. The elbow flops back into place
with a hot, soft thud. Even the light is hot. The curtains
glow like amber coals. Time to speak.

'Sleep well?'

'Not really. Too much to drink last night.'

'Headache?'

'No.'

The top bunk creaks as Lou rolls over, kicking free of her
sleeping bag. I stare at the springs.

'Hangover?' she asks. We all speak slowly, like grand-
mothers with new false teeth. It sounds almost theatrical. I
fold myself in half, digging my heels into the mattress above
and, little by little, straightening my knees into the small of
Lou's back.

'Piss off. How old are you?' She leans over the safety rail,
peering into the gloom. Her hair flops down in a sad mohican.

'Watch it, or I'll tip you out.' We can't be bothered to get
up. We talk about power-showers and white linen shirts
and freshly squeezed orange juice and long, deep, turquoise
swimming pools. No one wants to be the first to move.

'Turn it back on!' Nina's voice bursts through the shower-
room walls, accompanied by the groan of the water tanks
guttering dry. The door sucks open and she scurries along
the passageway, dripping. Small white soap-suds burst in a
frenzy of perfect white circles across her collarbone.

Lou glances up from her mug of tea. 'What?'

'The water!'

I try the tap in the kitchen and the plumbing judders. Lou shrugs and looks at me. We make an effort not to smile. Goose pimples creep up Nina's arms and legs and the smell of sandalwood filters along the breeze. She says every woman should have a smell that's part of her personality and takes the same soap with her everywhere. It lives in a baby-pink, kidney-shaped box designed for travelling. She glares at us, shudders and flounces off to dry. I look away. The washing up will have to wait. 'What shall we do now?'

Lou leans back in her armchair, sipping her tea. 'Fill up at the boatyard, I suppose.'

'We'll have to get there first,' I mutter. 'I assume you've driven this thing before.'

'Not really.'

'What's that meant to mean?'

'I've watched.' She taps her fingernails against the side of the mug, staring at the ledge above the fire where the folded edge of Philip's poster rests against my Marlboro Lights. She stretches for them, luckily can't reach, her long arm flopping gracelessly, spilling the tea. 'Pass me that, will you,' she wheedles, twisting face to face with me in the next door chair. She flicks the liquid from the front of her shirt.

'My cigarettes? You must be joking.' I'm even further away and just as comfortable.

'The *poster* –' She points her foot at it, shuffling forwards until her toes nudge at its half-open fan. It flips to the lino. This is getting too silly to watch.

'Put it back,' she complains as I stand up, handing it to her.
I help myself to a fag. 'It's a test of my pediatric dexterity.'

'Your *what*?'

'Feet – Put it back!'

To annoy her I open it and read aloud, nice and slow.
Afterwards, I fold it again and drop it tantalisingly out of
reach.

'*Not fair.*' She thumps the lino with her heel.

'Will we be going through Shelton?' I wonder as she
pinches the unlit cigarette from between my lips. Before I
have a chance to snatch it back she's tossed it over her
shoulder like Henry VIII at a banquet throwing a bone.
Revenge.

'Why?'

'They're playing there tomorrow night.' I reach for a
replacement cigarette. Nothing that's touched that floor is
going anywhere near *my* mouth. Lou retracts her outstretched foot, looks long at me as though considering the
answer to some difficult, unspoken question.

'You want to go,' she says at last, simply. There's something abrupt about it, a sudden change of tone. 'I wonder
if he'll still be wearing that jacket..'

'Not to perform in.'

'God, it was disgusting. Do you remember?'

'I liked it.'

'It stank. It smelled of animals.'

'I liked that smell.'

'And the cuffs were black. If you looked under the collar you could see what colour it was meant to be.'

'Oh, well. I never got that close,' I smile, catching her out.

Lou blinks. 'That jacket was infested. It crawled. You could have seen the dirt a mile away.'

You told me you thought it was the sexiest thing in the school, I want to say.

'Ask him – I dare you.' Nina walked back to the base line, patting our last ball, one bounce every other step. She turned to face me. 'Ready?'

'Just serve it underarm this time,' I shouted, too late, as the ball slammed into the net. 'Ever thought of taking up football?'

'Piss off, bitch. *I dare you.*' We wandered around the court, collecting miss-hits. Wilson was taking us for Reproductive Education and this week she wanted everyone to bring something quintessentially masculine. *Sexy, in other words*, Nina had said. She'd been teasing me to get Philip to lend his jacket ever since. 'Shoelaces, quick!'

'Is he looking?' I bent in half, peeping at Philip's window between my knees. It was impossible to tell, but we always bagsied the end court, just in case. Bollard suspected we were up to something, but never guessed what. I straightened up. 'Ask him yourself.'

'I've got something already.'

'What?'

Nina tapped her nose. She loved secrets. With a shrug or

a wink she could transform straightforward, widely available facts into privileged information. She knew a hundred different tricks for irritating me, but *Did You Know* was by far the most effective.

Did you know – oh, I forgot, I mustn't say.

Mustn't say what?

Nothing.

What?

Nothing, I was just winding you up –

No you weren't!

I was –

It could go on for hours.

'Are you ready this time?' Nina swayed at the back of the court, staring at me ferociously. Bollard watched from the sidelines as I jiggled on my toes, spinning the racquet, a Wimbledon finalist, preparing to receive.

'Good, Porter, good,' she barked. 'It's refreshing to see you take some exercise for once.'

Nina's ball flew over the net, richocheted skywards from my flukily positioned racquet head and crashed through the branches of an apple tree just to the right of Philip's window. A confetti of leaves and blossom petals floated to the ground. The whistle went for the end of class and Nina grinned as I jogged off to fetch the ball, explaining to Bollard that we were going to stay on a bit longer, practising. We'd drop the racquets by her office door at the end of Tea.

'I'm knackered,' she sighed, throwing herself to the grass as the last of our classmates disappeared behind the Science

Block. A money spider picked its way up the side of her left shin. Cotton-wool clouds paraded silently across the sky. She closed her eyes, letting the world go red. 'Do you know what the first thing I'm going to do is when they take my braces off?' she murmured dreamily.

'Snog someone,' I guessed.

'Nope. Eat an apple. A Granny Smith.'

I pulled her to her feet and we mooched along the path to the Beech Trees, dragging our racquets through the gravel behind. Train-tracks are a kind of chrysalis, I thought, wishing I had needed orthodontic treatment too, that I could have some grand unveiling to look forward to, a moment of triumph when the real Beth would reveal herself, womanly and fully formed and beautiful, astonishing everyone.

Sophie leaned with her back to us on the far side of the gate, surrounded by Sixths, all smoking moodily, their silence the sort you get just seconds after the disclosure of some well-kept, long-kept secret, when the world as you know it lies at your feet in scattered shards. They crowded together as we drew near and for a long time no one spoke. Nina's eyes fidgeted from face to face as I lit up, inhaling awkwardly.

'I hear my little sister's taken up the evil weed,' Sophie said at last, changing the subject. Next to her, Heather Allen sighed, rested her head against the butt-trunk, staring up through a shifting green dazzle of leaves as the others looked on, their faces still puckered with silent, oversensitive concern.

Nina gave an apprehensive, hopefully reassuring smile. 'Only every now and then.'

'She shouldn't. She's got asthma, you know.' Sophie flicked away her butt and the other girls moved, as one, towards the gate. 'Mum and Dad would freak if they found out.'

'We're very careful,' I promised, ignoring Nina's glare. Heather Allen went pale.

We called at the Music School. Anna Birdwood had occupied Lou's usual cubicle. We gave her invisible V-signs and glowered through the cubbyhole, followed the passageway aimlessly as far as Philip's room and barged in, colliding on the spot as two pairs of eyes looked up. A music book lay open on the desk in front of them. Lou blushed. Philip smiled vaguely in my direction.

'Sorry—' Nina and I backed off, slamming the door and waited outside. Nina cupped her ear to the wood and wiggled her eyebrows as one of Lou's high, sing-song laughs came through the wall and Philip hummed a few bars, improvising an accompaniment on the baby grand. There was a silence, then the handle turned and we sprang back, jerked along the corridor with our fists in our mouths, all innocence. We lay in wait at the corner by Miss Wilson's room, ambushing her with tennis racquets.

'Hiya!' Lou brushed us off like flies, dodging through the glass door and out onto the path.

'Not so fast,' Nina said, grabbing her wrist. 'What was all that with Philip and you?'

Lou twisted free. 'All what?' she pretended.

'All that singing and laughing – yuk.'

'She's blushing!' I crowed as she skipped off, backwards, downhill. 'Come back. Answer the question.'

Lou turned her back on me. 'I can't, it's a secret.'

'What is?'

'Can't say.' She waved and raced away through the arch beneath the Science Block to Tea.

'Come on then. Let's start this boat.' Lou bangs her mug to the floor, standing up so fast that I think she's forgotten to bow her head. I have given up trying to understand why anyone over 5'8" would choose to live in a long thin tube like this. It must have driven Sophie mad and Lou's already broken two wine glasses and a desk-light, gangling from room to room like a daddy-long-legs in a jar. I follow her outside. The sky is cloudy, patched with blue, a labyrinth the sun knows off by heart. Two or three of our neighbours have already left and in their wake the *Otterburn* slips sideways like a loose tooth. Lou turns round, disorientated. Willow stubs, elder and giant hogweed whirl on the skyline. 'Where have we gone?' she wonders, staggering. Sophie's keyring jangles, glints in the sun.

The control buttons nestle neatly in a small rectangular panel with a rain-proof perspex lid. A row of green and red lights glitters along the top like mint- and cherry-flavoured sweets. There is a metal switch, a plastic switch called 'bilge', a line of mysterious black buttons, and a keyhole.

'What do I do, just turn it, do you think?' Lou squints doubtfully. 'Maybe Nina will know.'

'I doubt it. Shall I get the anchor?'

'What anchor?'

'You know – heavy, rusty, shaped like a hook . . .'

'*These* are the anchor, fuck-wit,' she laughs, pointing at a pair of murky ropes wound over the handrail. They double back from the pontoon, stopping at deck-level in a figure-of-eight, one each side of the boat. As Lou is guessing which key to try, I loosen them, pulling through and back, through and back, hand over hand. Water sprays my T-shirt as the last few metres snake through my dripping hands and the pontoon slips away. Drifting side-long into the *Singing Swan*, our fenders roll.

'Get ready to push us off,' Lou says, turning the key. The engine pauses, stutters into a low and smoky hum.

'Why aren't we moving?' I shout.

Lou shrugs. She reaches for the tiller, squinting along the boat at the trees on the far side of the winding hole. Nina pokes her head through the cabin door. 'What are you doing? Wait for me.' She ducks back in, to re-emerge in an old cotton jumper, on back-to-front, and what look distinctly like my favourite jeans. A cloud of exhaust hangs low and blue above the water at the back of the boat and a diesel rainbow ripples, gleaming on the surface like an inland waterways flag.

'Get us away from that boat,' Lou yells, and we swing obediently along the side-deck, heaving and pushing at the *Singing Swan* as the fenders drag. They squeak like birthday balloons about to pop. Our faces pink and a man out walking with his sunburned kids pauses to watch, unnerving us. Black cracks open at our feet. As Lou throws the engine into gear Nina takes her hand from the rail to wipe the shine from her forehead. The boat kicks. Someone bellows STOP and she flails for the handrail, finds it as we veer into open water, grabs hold, leaning now between the two boats like a felled tree. A bubble floats round from the engine, winks at us and disappears. The fenders bob. Nina's knuckles are white.

'Hang on!' I scream over the furore as she heaves herself away from the other boat. There is a splash and then a thud and then a dreadful silence as the engine cuts and slowly, almost deliberately, the *Otterburn* slips sideways back towards the pontoon. Nina's feet scrabble against the slimy hull. We are a *Blue Peter* generation and I should be able to find some way of wedging the boats apart using a billhook, a fender, and a worn-out pair of shoes. Instead the only thing I think of is grabbing her round the waist. I pull. She's small and boney – thin, and sort of jerky with fear. I hoist her sideways, jammed against my hip, and somehow, just before we crash into the side of the pontoon, she manages to kick free. The fenders squeal, then everything goes quiet. The family on the towpath wanders off. An aeroplane drones across the blue. Nina just breathes. We look down. Water drips from her shoes and jeans across the side-deck, splashing back into the canal.

'Are you OK?'

She stares right through me, nodding, and the colour

drains from her face. 'I think I'm going to faint,' she whispers as we shuffle round the side-deck, clutching the rail.

'What happened?' Lou hovers, keeps looking behind to see if anyone's come to bollock her yet.

'I'm going to lie down,' says Nina carefully. She doesn't want her voice to shake. I stare at the pontoon, at the back of the boat. They look OK. A trail of footprints slaps indoors.

'Nina fell in, sort of. What happened to you?'

Lou shrugs. 'Stupid fucking boat,' she mutters, kicking a pile of rope. 'There's something wrong with it.'

'Now we've crashed there probably is.'

'Oh fuck off.'

'Cigarette?'

'We should tie up.' She jumps ashore. I throw her the dripping rope and she wraps it round a post.

We light up, climbing onto the roof. It's radiator warm and suddenly I could fall asleep. We lie on our sides, watching the clouds, the swallows. When I stand up again, I think, I'm going to have the most magnificent, sickening head-rush.

'What have you been doing with these?' Lou stubs out the butt, pinching it disdainfully between index finger and thumb. Funny, the way you can suck a burning cigarette but once it's out you never want to touch the thing again.

'Oh, chuck it.'

'In the canal?'

I nod.

'We can't do that.'

'Why not? Everyone else does.'

'So?' She spits on her finger and rubs the ash-smudge, shaking her head.

'You don't mind leaving fag ends on the towpath, what's the difference?' I reason, blowing a perfect smoke ring. Lou doesn't see.

'On the towpath they get trampled into the mud and covered with leaves and grass grows over them,' she says. 'But in the canal they're visible. They float downstream with all the scum and shit and it's really disgusting.'

'In other words you couldn't give a toss about the pollution,' I interrupt triumphantly, not even bothering to stub out my cigarette, just throwing it into the canal in a defiant arc. 'You just want things to look pretty.'

'OK, OK,' she smiles. 'My motives are entirely superficial. But at least I'm not fucking up the canal.'

I squint across the basin. The water is changing colour before our eyes, burning from brown to mossy green. Sheets of light hang from the trees in layer on dappled layer of gauze. Lou's right, of course. Now we've done away with God it's what you do that counts, not why you do it.

Amnesty International came to school, like a circus, one night every year and set up a letter-writing station in Miss McKendrick's room after Sunday Assembly. We stood in line at the door. Reaching the front of the queue I focussed on the fluorescent ceiling, burning my eyes with floaty oranges and blues, looked anywhere rather than at the photographs pinned up on the opposite wall. The classroom windows gleamed and you could see right through your own reflection, deep into the first two feet of the world outside, the branches of some thorny ornamental shrub where shreds of Polo paper had faded for seasons, caught between the leaves. The tables would have been rearranged, making space for twenty-five at a time to sit and write, and the queue behind trailed down the passageway and out through the door. In front of me, sombre Fifths pushed back their chairs, shuffled to the canvas sack by the blackboard and dropped in their petitions one by one. I would sit at the desk and read the literature, copy out the paragraphs it recommended, sentence by sentence, right to the very last full stop.

Dear Sir, I am writing to express my concern about your government's disregard for human rights, specifically with regard to . . .

Lying here, lulled by the sigh of faraway jets, I wish I'd put it in my own words. Even then, the interventions had seemed too easy. They reminded me of the way some supermarkets in America celebrate the arrival of their millionth customer: champagne, a photograph in the local newspaper and five whole minutes to cram your trolley with whatever you want for free. Maybe that was how it worked with prisoners of conscience too. Perhaps it was simply a matter of numbers, and mine, the hundred thousandth letter, would trigger some brave new humanitarian response. Ten seconds after putting down my pen I would have forgotten how to spell her name, how many kids she had, how many times she had been raped. I would wait for Nina on the steps outside. We'd drift off, arm in arm, to get a can from the Common-Room Coke machine.

People don't realise how hard it is to reach eighteen and never have had to really work hard for anything. Nina and Lou and I were always clever enough and pretty enough and rich enough. The struggle in us didn't know what to do with itself. There was something awkward and foul about the way we said *third world*, *refugee camp*, *housing estate*, as though we knew they were places we had no right to name.

Lou slouches on her elbows. 'I had such a funny dream last night,' she says. 'I dreamed I had a goldfish. I'd been on holiday or something and no one had fed it for a year and it was incredibly hungry. Half its tail was missing. I sprinkled in some fish food and bits of crystallised fruit peel – for some bizarre reason – and it went crazy, eating everything.'

'Still feeling bad about Rossini?'

She looks at me. 'Rossini?'

'Your goldfish Sophie killed.'

'How the fuck do you know about that?' She frowns, sitting up.

'You told me – ages ago.'

'I told you *she* killed him?'

'Didn't she?'

'I can't remember now. She got the blame for it. She got the blame for everything.' Lou swings round, dangling her feet over the edge, making heel-prints on the saloon window below. She hesitates, trying to remember how the fish had looked as it lay there in the coffee-coloured earth. All she can see instead are Sophie's blistered hands. 'Anyway, someone said I should set it free, so I did. But the water in the pool was a sort of cloudy blue and I worried it might be full of sulphur—'

'That's yellow—'

'I know. Or sodium. The thing I hate about dreams,' she says, interrupting herself in a completely different tone of voice, 'is how you never know whether they mean what they seem to mean.'

'The only literal dreams are dreams about sex,' I tell her. 'And all the other dreams you have are basically about sex too, so on the whole it's safest never to tell them to anyone.'

'What's wrong with having people know you're dreaming about sex? Especially if they assume it anyway?' She beams at her own cleverness, then changes voice again. 'Maybe I am still feeling guilty about Rossini. Or maybe the goldfish has become a symbol of some other, more profound anxiety.'

'Such as?'

She shrugs. 'If I knew that I wouldn't be fucking dreaming about it, would I?'

'Maybe the goldfish is you! Here we are, surrounded by all this water, and there's not exactly a lot of space.'

We creep in to check on Nina. She has collapsed on her bed; my trousers lie in a soggy heap on the floor. It's dark in here and almost cool. She opens her eyes. She has a stunned, dumb look on her face, gives us a feeble smile and shifts as if to make room for someone to sit.

I touch her shoulder. 'How are you?'

'OK. I feel all floppy.'

'At least you got rid of some of that soap,' Lou says, grinning softly. 'We're going to see if we can get some help at the boatyard. Want to come?'

She looks from one of us to the other, shakes her head. 'I'll mind house.'

'OK. You sure you're all right?'

'I'm fine.'

We follow signs to the boatyard, doubling back along the towpath as far as the second fork, picking through brambles and ground-elder, slipping and skipping down the bank's soft sides. Faded tyre-tracks caterpillar through the mud between the puddles. In the distance, old man's beard and dog roses camouflage the rusty diamonds of a six-foot fence. The gate is open, propped back against itself with a breeze block that can't have been moved in years. Saplings struggle through the holes, between the snails. Ahead of us a bank of sheds and workshops steps away to the water's edge and a black-and-sand shadow lifts its head from the shady concrete, stares at us, yawns.

'Show no fear.' Lou squeezes my arm. Two more lion-sized Alsatians shake themselves into the sunlight, mill curiously backwards and forwards as we draw near. 'It's OK, they're wagging their tails.' A drill-bit shrieks through ply but the pigeons on the roof pay no attention and the dogs ignore us as we hover in the doorway, waiting for our pupils to grow. A stack of dusty, rough-edged 10x4 leans against the back wall and a varnish pot waits, open, on the bench in front. Apart from these the place seems empty. It smells of glue and wood-shavings.

'Go in,' I whisper, nudging Lou across the threshold. She tries a friendly-sounding hello and the drilling stops. Footsteps squeak across the concrete floor and suddenly there he is, right in front of us, tiny and shining in an apron of light.

'Hello?' He wipes an oil-smeared hand on the sleeve of his overalls, then combs it through his feathery hair. The dogs pad in, threading themselves around and between us, heads down, nudging our legs. As Lou explains, their thick tails bat our knees. You can tell he's friendly with Sophie from the way he listens, now, to Lou, as though he has expected her. As though he knows in advance what she's about to say. He has a sharp face, likeable, grimy and tanned. A quick, almost mysterious, sideways smile.

'I'm Gabriel. Sophie thought you might be down,' he says when Lou has reached the end of her speech. 'She asked me to keep an eye on you.'

'Typical!'

The dogs are calmer now, the grizzliest lies at his feet and watches us with a single, meticulous open eye. Gabriel stoops to rake his fingers through its shaggy fur. Somewhere out of sight a door slams shut in the breeze. 'You'll probably need pumping out too.'

'What's that?'

'Sewage.'

'Oh right.' Lou blushes.

'Do you build boats here?' I ask, to cover the silence.

'They used to. I'm just finishing a house.'

'A house?'

'A house on wheels – so we can go anywhere we like.'

He means a caravan, I think, distracted by Lou's face as the blood pumps steadily into her cheeks. Even her forehead bears the dark pink crush of cherry-stain. *Sewage.* Again and again her mind loops back to the thought of all that shit, her sister's shit. The thought of someone else smelling or even seeing it . . .

'Have any of you driven a narrowboat before?' he wonders, looking at me. Together we pretend Lou has wandered briefly into some other room, it's kindest. I shake my head. 'Would it help if I showed you how to work the boat?'

'If you're not too busy –'

He shrugs, acknowledging my effort to be polite. He walks us out of the workshop, looking back, once, as though to check something he might have left behind. He heaves the slide-door shut with an echoey slam.

'Are they guard dogs or pets?' I ask as we turn away, leaving the three Alsatians shoulder to shoulder in the middle of the yard.

He shrugs again and smiles. 'Depends.'

Nina is sunbathing on the roof when we return. She sits up, lifting her sunglasses, wriggles to the edge and lets her feet swing down.

'This is Gabriel,' says Lou, recovered. 'He's made a clip-together house which fits in the back of a van so he can drive it anywhere he likes. It takes a day to put together, and half a day to pack away again. He's sold the boatyard and now he's going to travel the world with his girlfriend, like gypsies.'

'Pleased to meet you,' Nina says, queenly.

'He also happens to know everything you could ever need to ask about boats.'

Gabriel steps aboard almost as though he owns the place, as once, before the Alsatians grew so big, he had. 'You know you shouldn't really sit up there,' he mutters. 'At least, not while the engine's running.'

'It isn't.' Nina slithers down anyway, flicking her hair. Seconds go by and no one speaks. He squints along the coach-roof. He doesn't seem to have noticed that we are all looking at him, ready for the next piece of advice. Any minute now, I think, one of us will reach for an exercise book.

'Have you found any tapes?' he says eventually, surprising himself. 'You know, just lying around?' His eyes flit systematically from place to place, as though checking off items in some mental inventory.

'Classical?'

'Bob Dylan.'

'No, sorry.'

He stares down into the cabin where Nina's sleeping bag lies, still unzipped and almost obscenely wrinkled, on the bed. 'I hear your parents are selling it,' he says, not looking at Lou.

'Well that's the current threat. One way of paying off my

sister's enormous overdraft.' She follows his gaze, shifting her weight self-consciously.

Nina is whispering something in my ear and it distracts them. 'A one-night stand, I bet you,' she breathes, indulging me with her most meaningful, flirtatious nudge, and suddenly the thought of Sophie and this wiry, uncomfortable-looking man entwined right there on Nina's bed seems irresistibly plausible.

Gabriel's instructions are clear and to the point. 'The main thing to remember about these boats,' he says, half shouting over the roar of the engine, 'is that they're very heavy and therefore very slow to react. The trick is to go at their pace. Take your time.' He pulls the tiller as far to the left as it will go and holds it there, nudging the small of his back. 'There's a pole on the roof. One of you go forward and push us off.' He points. Lou and Nina swap guilty looks.

Nina steps back. 'You go.'

'OK.' He gazes across the water. 'You can cast us off.'

'This?' She touches the rope with the tips of her fingers, distastefully. Lou has wound it round the handrail three or four times, fastened it in what looks uncannily like a slip-knot. A long loop dangles almost to the water below. Nina pulls at the swinging tail.

'Shall I push yet?' shouts Lou.

We've started to drift but Gabriel just stares into the distance. 'The biggest mistake you can make on a narrowboat is to hurry.'

We glide across the glassy basin at a stroll. Nosing along-side the yard quay, the bumpers barely squeeze. Everything is perfectly under control and Nina, Lou and I watch qui-etly, hardly even daring to look each other in the eye in case something makes us laugh and we break his concen-tration. He shows us how to tie up, then disappears into his workshop, returning with a map. 'Oh and another thing – you pass on the right.'

'What about when a boat is coming the other way?' Lou wonders brightly.

Gabriel seems to sigh, he nudges a dog out from under his feet and rubs his eyes. 'That's what I mean – you pass on the *right*; you overtake, if you have to overtake, which you shouldn't, on the *left*. It's the opposite of driving, in other words.' He checks the diesel and gas, and recom-mends a pub about five hours from here, halfway to Shelton, sketching for us on the back of an envelope how to walk there across the fields. He reckons we'll get to the concert tomorrow night in plenty of time. The tank sucks dry. As Gabriel disconnects the bilge-pipe we all look away squeamishly, kicking our heels in the sun-shine, watching the dogs. Drinking water wells at the neck of the hose and trickles free, writhing into the dark canal.

He comes as far as the first lock, watching us take the tiller one by one. 'We're on the river now,' he says as the engine battles upstream. 'Two days ago you wouldn't have made it as far as this. Current's too strong.' Flood-lines stain the meadows, the trunks of willows, on either side. A blue and white motor-cruiser slides out from behind a bramble heap, growing towards us as we iron the bend and Lou panics steadily bankwards.

'Oh my God, we're going to crash,' she jitters, gripping the tiller and yanking it the other way.

'Now straighten up,' Gabriel's calm voice eases us through the gap. 'There's always more space than you think.' At the lock he sends Nina and me ashore to open the gates while Lou holds the *Otterburn* in neutral. Waterweed drools from sodden ridges halfway down and a fountain spatters through the leaky sluice. A shadow falls across their faces as the boat inches in.

Nina follows me up the path. 'It's just like running a bath,' she mutters, peering down at them, waving the lock-key. 'Now?'

Gabriel nods. The gears wind notch by notch until the fountain spurts in a frothy, solid collapse and the bottom gates slam. Lou is shivering. She stares at the bulging blue rectangle of sky. Bright ferns tremble in the water-breeze. The silence down there is flat and dead and heavy with applause.

'You can let go of the tiller now,' Gabriel says kindly, but the words drown fast. Brick by brick the *Otterburn* floats up. The top of Lou's head inches over the parapet, climbs into a stripe of sunlight. There's something brave about her reappearing smile. We know they won't budge, but Nina and I shoulder the beams all the same, leaning into them, our bodies straight and slant, feet marching on the spot.

'Harder – push harder!' Lou shouts, cracking an imaginary whip as the water levels kiss, and slowly the doors ease open. Leaf-scatter swims in secret whirlpools.

'You're doing the next one single-handed,' I warn her, jumping on board as the engine kicks into gear. We wave at Nina, pretending to abandon her, though she refuses to take the bait and walks along the towpath, hands in her pockets, waiting for us to tire. Gabriel says he has to go. He prints his address across a corner of the map he's lent so Lou can post it back and recommends the *King's Arms* once again. Lou and I wave enthusiastically. Nina blows a kiss as we slip away.

'This is fun,' she says, adjusting her shades. She rests her hand on the tiller next to Lou's. The warm steel tickles her palm. 'Who can remember which of these knobs is the accelerator, then?'

Lou gazes sternly at the nose of the boat. The banks shift like scenery as we seem to motor on the spot. Sky shines steadily through the branches of underwater trees and upside-down willowherb as we plough ahead, wrinkling the silver foil.

This is it, I tell myself, looking back at the subsiding wake. Gabriel has disappeared below the lock's horizon. *We can go anywhere we like*. Nina scrambles onto the roof to sunbathe. Lou and I light cigarettes.

'God, it's hot,' says Nina suddenly. She rolls onto her belly. Her hair flops over the cabin door as she gazes down, squinting at a clutch of split-ends, snapping them one by one. She sighs. 'It's baking. Do you think anyone ever swims in this? Imagine that, Lou. You could swim all the way home – how disgusting.'

I think the water looks quite clean – at least there are fish in it. We duck beneath a sudden rain of branches as the *Otterburn* swerves. Lou's been day-dreaming, she hasn't heard a word we've said.

W e pushed up our sunglasses, like Alice bands, and crowded the booth. Fingerprints, scratches and smears of Brylcream misted the glass. One by one the ticket clerk placed three half day-returns to Farham on his side of the swivel, reading the price into a tea-stained microphone. We had the money, already counted out in coins, and Nina opened her fist, presenting it in a loud flat rush as the signal bell went. A 50p rolled across the metal seam and the ticket clerk clucked. He didn't like the way we blocked his window, and he probably didn't like our shades or our lipstick, or the way Nina snapped 'Hurry up, or we'll miss it' either. The half-moon span slowly and clicked. Tickets were exchanged for cash and as the train pulled in we charged across the platform, clattered down through the dusty tunnel and up again the far side. Carriage doors opened and slammed. It had been part of Nina's plan to arrive at the station late, but this was ridiculous. We had skipped lunch, jogging through orchards, across the pony field, and down along dogshit alley, rather than attract suspicion by taking a cab. Lou's face was pink as a raddish and my armpits were beginning to itch. The level crossing dinged and flashed as the barriers fell.

By train, the journey took about four minutes. A sherry-sipping, rose-garden commuter village, Farham had a church, a Post-Office shop and an off-licence well-known for its liberal approach to the purchase of alcohol by under 18s. Lou and I flopped into the nearest empty seats while Nina walked down the compartment, checking for mistresses.

'OK, Lou,' she said, returning satisfied. 'What year were you born?'

'Nineteen sixty-seven.' She closed her eyes while Nina stroked another layer of blue across the lids and fluffed her hair. 'Get off—'

'It'll make you look older.'

'What, messy hair?' She wound a strand round her index finger, tugged at it nervously.

'If only you had your ears pierced,' Nina sighed for the umteenth time.

'Mum won't let me.'

'So?' I twisted my new stud, the third. Already the train was beginning to slow. I hadn't even noticed the sun come out.

We walked down from the station, past the vicarage where Mrs Burton the Bursar lived with her husband and two grown-up stockbroking sons, and stopped by the off-licence.

'Make sure there's no one else in there before you ask,' said Nina.

'Nineteen sixty-seven,' Lou muttered, pushing in. She crossed the threshold and a buzzer trilled at the back of the shop. The door swung shut. Nina and I paced up and down outside, our eyes on the pavement. A Range Rover pulled in by the letter box on the opposite side of the road and a man in a Barbour struggled out from the driving seat with a large manilla envelope in his hand. Nina smiled at him, flashing her metal teeth.

'I'm starving,' I said. 'I didn't have breakfast. When's the next train?'

Nina checked her watch. 'Twenty minutes.'

'Do you think it's safe to smoke?'

She gave me a withering look. 'What's taking her so long?'

The Range Rover drove off and as the street fell silent again I tried to imagine living in one of those neat net-curtained houses, someone's wife, with a Hoover and nothing much more than the weekly coffee-morning to look forward to. The sort of person who would do the *Telegraph* crossword and practise thigh-toning exercises in the living room on a sweat-absorbant roll-out mat.

'What's going on? She's taking forever,' Nina said tersely. A front door slammed at the end of the street and a Royal Mail delivery van crawled by. By the time the offie door opened, at last, she was looking as though, had she possessed a gun, she would have marched right in and held the place to ransom. I stared at the rucksack, trying to work out if it looked heavier as Lou floated unsteadily away from the shop. Her mouth stretched up at the ends, lips thinning into an elated grin. She wanted to cheer and scream with triumph, to shake the cider to a frenzy, spraying it across the pavement, the precisely tended rosebushes, the letter box.

We stayed in the waiting room, a concrete bomb-shelter painted snot green and stinking of bleach with a one-bar heater that didn't work screwed into the wall alongside a paralysed clock. Nina put the rucksack on the floor, where the door would swing if anyone came in. Her eyes flicked over it, checking it was still full of booze, still safe. Lou stared at it too, bursting with pride. She beamed at us and Nina glared back superstitiously. She acted as though the place were bugged.

Lou smoothed her hair. 'Do I really look eighteen?'

'Nah, they just wanted your money. Did they ask?'

She nodded. 'There was a silence of resounding disbelief.'

The train came and we climbed in quickly, standing in the dim and sooty no-man's land between carriages as doors slammed and a whistle blew twice. The station backed off. Lou pushed the window down and stuck out her head as the train gathered speed. Sunlight flickered around her like a halo. Nina leaned against the Formica wall and studied the ends of her hair. She squeezed the rucksack between her feet. I took out a cigarette, happy. 'She's going to be insufferable.'

Nina rolled her eyes indulgently as Lou ducked in, pink-faced and giddy with rush. 'I think I've got about five-hundred flies up my nose,' she said. 'It's so weird, when you blink everything freezes and if you do it really fast it's like we're not moving at all.' She scissored her fingers and I passed her the fag. Behind her head a map of the South East Rail Network kinked out in red lines furry with the names of villages and towns I'd never heard of.

'We should get some food,' said Nina, looking up. 'Or we'll be totally wasted.'

'That's the plan.' I nicked my cigarette back off Lou, blew smoke in her face. The engine dropped a pitch, straining. Carriages jostled and the toilet door swung open, fanning light across the passageway.

'Do you think men and women's piss smells the same?' I wondered out loud, trying to remember the precise scent of the cubicles on House. They never seemed to smell of anything but disinfectant. Bright new terracotta roofs flashed by slowly outside, the poplars in front of them glittering in the sun. We passed the paper factory, pallets stacked up against the fire escape. The level crossing. There was a police car waiting at the gate and a tailback all the way to Menzies. A cluster of Fourths walked arm in arm along the pavement sucking ice-creams. We were slowing right down. Nina grabbed the rucksack, ticket ready in her hand.

Lou got off first, and went to find a taxi while we loitered inside. Our clerk had gone off duty. There was a woman, now, behind the glass. She had a golden ring with a coin in it, and a crucifix which sparkled with chips of diamond.

Lou waved and Nina and I climbed in, shuffling along the back seat. The rucksack glugged.

'Blue Pool, please,' said Lou to the taxi driver.

'What's that, then? Some new club is it?'

Nina leaned forward between the seats to give directions.

The Blue Pool was an old brick reservoir sunk in the crook of a clearing halfway up the beech woods, two miles from school. Early generations of Hawklies were said to have bathed there but its limpid days had silted into memory decades ago and, although the woods were zigzagged with footpaths, walkers seemed happily oblivious of its existence. Even in high summer the place was dark and chill. It smelled like autumn all year round, and the mud there never dried.

The taxi dropped us at the turn-off to a private drive. Life-sized sandstone eagles gazed from brick pedestals, one on each side of the gate, with calculating sandstone eyes as the rattle of the engine faded. Mare's-tails streaked across the sky, dissolving it into silvery wash. Hazel trees shivered inside their rough green leaves, and bluebells glinted through clumps of grass and ground ivy at the side of the road. Lou stamped mud from her boots as Nina shouldered the rucksack, looked around. A signpost pointed us away from the gates, uphill, along the edge of a green field, slippery with wheat and shaded white at the treeline where the soil was thin and the chalk beneath showed through. At the edge of the woods we came to a stile and, climbing over it, to a cavernous and earthy clearing. The ground was soft and bumpy where last year's beechmast had been trodden in but had not yet decomposed.

Nina turned left and we followed in single file. Patches of sunlight glimmered between the branches and the path was narrow and deep, grainy with sawdust and baked black mud. We were walking uphill now, around one final tangled shoulder and out along an open chalk scar, driven wide enough for a bulldozer and pitted with caterpillar tracks. Lou frowned at it. 'What's this doing here?'

I opened a new pack of fags. In the clearing far below us, felled trees lay in a row like thick cigars and, next to them, a chipped yellow matchbox JCB stood guard.

'They shouldn't be chopping down these trees.'

We lit up, smoked striding down the hill quickly. Bright streams glinted in silent diagonals across the track and the clearing swung in and out of sight. There were fewer beeches here. Self-seeded ash and elder crowded the gaps and if you looked for them you could see Coke cans, faded cigarette packets, crisp packets and cobweb-cottoned halfs of vodka silting up in the mulch beneath the brambles and ivy. Moths and mosquitoes blinked between the shadows.

The clearing smelled sweet, of freshly cut wood. Lou clambered onto the nearest trunk and pigeon-stepped along it, arms out like the wings of an aeroplane for balance. 'How much further?' she asked, jumping off.

'Not far.' Nina perched on the step of the JCB and tightened her basketball boots, looked up as a sudden burst of sniggering drifted from the bushes behind. We stepped on our cigarettes and swallowed our hearts. Froze like antelope, heads up, focussed and intent upon the hiss of savannah grass. Absolute quietness dropped from the trees.

'Who's there?' Nina called out at last. There was a flurry of whispering. Brittle twigs shattered like rain and Kate stood up, grinning uncomfortably.

'Oh, it's you,' she giggled, turning away. 'Sophie, guess who's here.'

Three more faces lifted from the gloom. 'Bloody hell, Lou. What the fuck are you doing?' Afterwards, Nina and I agreed it was the only time we'd ever seen Sophie look less than beautiful.

Lou tugged at her fringe, edged vaguely closer to me, as though for protection. 'Same as you by the looks of things,' she shrugged.

The sisters stared at each other but there wasn't anything to say. Sophie passed Kate a crumpled-looking roll-up. 'Off you go, then,' she waved dismissively. 'Have fun. And don't get caught.'

The faces disappeared. Laughter echoed across the clearing. 'Patronising old cow,' Lou muttered, hoisting the rucksack and reaching for a fag. Her fingers shook.

'Looks like you could do with a drink,' Nina said thoughtfully, squinting into the trees. 'The pool should be just along there,' she pointed. 'But we'd better not stay on the path any more.'

Garlic leaves squeaked beneath our feet as we kicked through the undergrowth, walking parallel with the path, then veering off once more as the earth gave way to squelching bog. Cobwebs smeared our arms and chests as we scrambled between the trees, climbing up and up until branches and foliage entirely screened the path.

'There'll be a clearing or something, just round the corner,' Nina promised. The knees of her jeans were caked with mud and she had twigs in her hair and a jaunty red welt on her cheek where a branch had flicked.

'I'm not going another bloody step without a drink,' Lou said mutinously. 'Talk about working up a thirst.'

We emptied the rucksack, laying out coats and plastic bags in a kind of jigsaw picnic-rug which slid to pieces the moment we sat down. One of the cider bottles rolled towards Lou's right foot.

'Open it then,' said Nina, and we watched as Lou unscrewed the cap, smiling at the crack-crack-crack of snapping aluminium. A rush of fizz spilled into her lap and dripped to the ground. 'Don't waste it!'

The sides of the bottle gave, bending in a voluptuous plastic clinch. Lou took a sip, blinked at the trees and swallowed. 'Fizzy. Sweet,' she pronounced, passing it on to Nina. 'So what's the story if we get caught?'

Nina gulped three times, flopped back against the leafy mud and closed her eyes. 'We won't get caught. Everyone in the whole bloody school's out drinking this afternoon. They won't be interested in catching us.'

'You saying we're not interesting?' I took a long swig, sucked in the hollows of my cheeks, glanced sideways at Nina, who nodded knowingly.

'I'm saying we're not naughty enough.'

'Speak for yourself.' I paused. 'We're gob-sisters now.' The bottle went round again, more quickly. Nina leaned up on an elbow, head in her hand. A mud stain spread slowly along the sleeve of her cardigan. Lou and I chain-smoked, competing to see who could flick the stubbed-out butts the furthest.

'Let's play confessions,' I said, remembering Lou's little secret.

'But Nina doesn't smoke.'

'She can pretend. Can't you?'

Nina shook her head and belched. 'Why don't all of us just tell a secret anyway? That's fair.'

'But then it's not a game—'

'And I haven't got one.' Lou blushed as we stared at her. Nina stood up, shook herself, and wandered off to pee. We wanted to finish the bottle before she returned but the bubbles meant we couldn't drink fast enough and Lou had a coughing fit. She looked closer, somehow. Bigger and more precious than she had before. The harder I stared at her face, the better it seemed I knew her so I kept on staring and staring and she didn't seem to mind, or even notice much. Her cheeks were white, and a funny red blotch burned in the middle of her upper lip.

'My bum's getting wet,' she murmured, flicking ash on her shoe. I couldn't even feel mine any more. 'We could do this every weekend – it's fun. I'm not at all drunk though.' Cider swished to the bottleneck. She gulped.

'We came to these woods in English, once, in my first year at Lockhurst, to talk to the trees. I left a chocolate digestive biscuit at the bottom of one, between the roots, and Hermione Lawrence went back the next day and only half the biscuit was left.'

'A squirrel ate it.'

I shrugged. 'I suppose there must have been some point to the exercise, we probably had to come back and write a poem or something about what we imagined they said – that or Mrs Hodgson thought she could win us over by pretending to be totally mad.'

'Maybe she really was mad. What did your tree say?'

'*I'm hungry.*'

Nina came back, stumbling, more twigs and a smudge of cobweb tangling her hair. She thrust out her hand for the bottle and put her eye against its yellow plastic sides. 'Nearly all gone. I'm pissed by the way. You only notice it standing up. Everything looks sort of bulgy.' She sat down on the wet patch, cursing as chilly cider seeped into her jeans. Lou tried not to laugh. Her mouth twitched.

'What's so funny?' said Nina.

'Nothing, I swear—'

'*What?*'

'It's just the look on your face.' She shuddered helplessly, exploded in a peal of whinnying snorts and Nina was laughing too, now, pausing only to gasp for air and take a swig. Her nostrils flared and she puffed out her cheeks, spraying Lou. It landed on her hair, at the back, and dribbled down her shoulder. Nina collapsed against me, shaking, her pink eyes screwed up, ready to weep. She cowered as Lou prepared to retaliate.

'If any of that goes on me, I'm warning you . . . It'll end in tears,' I promised, struggling to push Nina away.

Lou was standing over us now, taking a careful aim. She looked like a putto, or one of the winds.

'Mercy, mercy,' squeaked Nina, still laughing as the cider, warm from Lou's mouth, and flat too probably, rained down. They fell together, snorting and squealing, trying to remember how to breathe.

'Peace?' said Nina, opening the second bottle.

'Peace,' said Lou, and one by one they drank, turning their faces as they swallowed so I couldn't tell what was going to happen next, although I must have had an inkling since I was getting ready to run for it as they lunged at me, catching each other in the crossfire. I took a step, tripped on a root and half slipped half rolled back into them, landing my shoe in Nina's armpit, face down in the dirt. No one said anything. For a moment I examined the skeleton of a beech leaf, lying on the ground, three inches from my nose, like a consolation prize. I thought of the trees being hungry and the chocolate digestive and wondered whether to laugh or cry. The hillside went quiet. Birds rustled anonymously, fidgeting in the shadows, and bent twigs sprang into place. I drew in my knees and pushed up, giddy as a tobogganist eye to eye with the descent.

'You OK?' Lou peered at me, her face still shiny and wet – which was funny, since surely the cider fight had been hours ago. I raised myself slowly, found Nina sitting next to me, stroking her arm. She passed the bottle and I swallowed four long thirsty gulps.

'That's better,' said my voice.

There was a moment's silence, interrupted by Lou. 'I wonder if my sister came down here to keep an eye on us. She thinks I'm such an idiot.'

Nina frowned. 'She's the idiot,' she said heavily.

'What do you mean?'

'Nothing.' She shook herself. 'If we get caught, by the way, which we won't, we just had one bottle, OK? They'll gate us – nothing more. And obviously don't say anything about the others.'

Lou lit a cigarette. 'They'd still tell our parents, wouldn't they.'

Nina shrugged. According to Kate, the housemistresses kept an unofficial log of every time any girl went drinking. They knew the whos, whens, wheres, and whats of every single binge and took a purely strategic approach to punishment. 'It's only cider,' she said again. She read the label. 'Four point five per cent vol. If we're in the slightest bit drunk it's only because we didn't have lunch.'

'Or breakfast,' I muttered.

'You had six chocolate chip cookies at Break!'

'So? We should have brought crisps or something,'

Lou leaned back on her elbow, passing the bottle straight to Nina.

'Had enough?'

She nodded. 'Guess what,' she said, as though the thought had only just that moment popped into her head. 'I haven't practised today. Not once – *Poor violin*. Tomorrow my fingers will be all stiff.' Her face went pinched and rubbery. She had this way of looking suddenly luminous and on the verge of tears. 'That's the first time since hospital.'

Nina blinked at her shoelaces. 'Poor Lou.'

'What do you mean? I like my scar. It helps me concentrate.' She thought for a moment. 'Does that sound stupid?'

'No stupider than most of the things you say,' I teased.

She slid me the traditional withering look. 'Shall I tell you a secret?'

'I thought you didn't have any.'

'You've got to promise not to laugh?'

We nodded, shuffled up close, expectantly.

'Sometimes I think my scar is like a kind of sign — a charm or something. A bit like being haunted. I imagine it's Paganini's ghost or something, taken up residence, keeping an eye on how I play. I talk to it, in my head. Do you ever do that? Have imaginary conversations?' She paused. 'Am I mad?'

'Delightfully,' said Nina.

I shuddered. The hairs on my neck were standing up. 'Now tell us what Philip and you were plotting about the other day.'

Lou looked away, blinking soberly. 'I can't.'

'Go on.'

'No.'

'*Please.*'

'No.' She took a long, long drink.

'Oh go on,' I said at last, singeing a hole through the canvas tongue of my basketball boot.

'It's a secret, Beth. Forget it.' Nina was shredding leaves, absent-mindedly sprinkling the crumbs into Lou's hair. 'Jesus, you're obsessed.'

Lou looked at me side-on and nudged me in the ribs apologetically but I refused to speak. I closed my eyes, letting the hillside twist and spiral for a moment, sickeningly. When I opened them again the wood was the colour of disappointment.

The cider was nearly all finished now. Drinking it, we had to throw our heads right back. The liquid made a shallow, almost stony, rattling sound as it ran to our lips. Lou took the last fag from the packet and we agreed to share it when I came back from pissing. What Nina had said earlier about standing up was right. They laughed as I staggered into the fusty, leafless branches of an ash.

'Don't go up, go round,' called Nina and suddenly the thought of my cider-pee trickling away in a crumbly wash seemed almost sad. Looking back I could see Lou struggling to her feet. She came crashing after. Nina was packing up.

We decided to go the long way back, by road, since it was growing dark and Nina seemed to think we might get lost in the woods. We lurched downhill through garlic and twigs and leaf mulch, sinking giddily into softer and softer ground as the stream drew near and, on the other side of it, the path. Waterweeds shadowed the edges of the pools, their upper leaves bushy and furled like small shrubs, roots and stems submerged. I thought it might be cress but Nina said there wasn't time to stop.

'There must be a footbridge here somewhere,' she

muttered. Lou and I smoked our cigarette right down to the filter, trampling after Nina in single file as the stream shallowed and widened and the wood grew gloomy. Suddenly she stopped. She waved at us for quiet. Lou froze, one leg in the air mid-step, her face a caricature of surprise. We listened. The water trickled and gurgled, rushed and seethed in stereo.

Somebody say something, I thought, *before we get spooked*, but no one did and the water-hush took charge. We walked with our ears now, trapped between the two streams as they pinched us tighter and tighter. The ground gave way to a kind of peaty marsh, and umbrella-leaves clustered where the waters met. We stopped again, turned back. I thought I remembered a narrower place where a tree had come down a little way back but when we got there the water looked too deep for paddling and the branches precarious.

'We could make a bridge,' said Lou. 'Or throw in stones and step across.'

'What stones, you cretin?' said Nina, wandering off to look for a place to jump.

It must have been about a metre and a half wide, the sort of distance anyone could cover over sand, but the banks were high and precarious. Nina crossed her arms, anticipating trouble. 'You go first, Lou,' she said. 'You've got the longest legs.'

'Piss off, that's not fair. People are always picking on me. I've never been any good at long-jump and what if I land

funny on my wrist?' She stood beside me, staring into the
water. 'There's no way I can jump across this,' she muttered,
biting her lip. She took three long steps back from the
bank, shook off her coat, rubbing her hands and swallowing a few deep breaths, psyching herself like an Olympic
gymnast preparing for a double-back-somersault-and-twist.
She lowered her head, leaned forwards a moment on her
toes, ran at it and leaped, throwing out her right leg in a
clumsy sort of jeté and just about scratching the far bank
with her boot before she slipped back, jerky and screech-
ing, into the stream. We held our breath and waited as she
stumbled, splashed and somehow managed not to fall. The
quietness of the wood closed over us like ice. We wondered
if it would be OK to laugh.

Gathering her dignity, Lou turned round and looked at
us. The water came up to her knees. 'Fuck me it's cold,' she
whooped suddenly, stamping and smiling and wading back.
Mud-clouds swirled to the surface, one for every step.
Rotten leaves and snagged twigs floated downstream as
Nina and I looked on, amazed. 'What are you doing, spak-
head? You're meant to be on the other side.'

'I'm going to carry you across. Only hurry up, it's
bloody fucking freezing in here. Who's going first?' She
turned round, stooping, ready to piggy-back.

'Nina's lightest.' I dodged out of the way.

'Are you sure?' Nina put a hand on her shoulder tentatively. 'I bet you drop me in.'

'I won't.'

'You swear?'

'Well, now you've suggested it . . .'

Nina jumped on and they hooked together, shuffling awkwardly, Lou stumbling with Nina's weight. On the far side she staggered round, groaning as she deposited her load on the bank.

'I've got heavy bones,' I warned as she came back.

'I've got you,' she hoisted me a fraction higher and we lumbered across, slipping and sinking at the edges where the silt was deep. Nina pulled me up the crumbling bank and we both held out our arms for Lou.

'My feet are numb,' she stammered. 'And what's worse is I'm completely stone cold sober.'

We hauled her up the bank onto the footpath, and counted her through twenty star-jumps until she was warm again. She took off her boots, tipping out half a pint of water from each, and threw her socks in the bushes.

'That was an act of heroism,' Nina said. We hugged her and promised solemnly to be best friends for the rest of our lives. Then we set off again, along the path and down across the fields towards the road, marching faster and faster until all you could hear was the sound of breath and footsteps.

'Warm enough?' asked Nina, as we swang out into Mill Lane.

Lou nodded. 'So long as we keep moving.' After the woods it suddenly felt bright again, open and exposed. Lights were on in the windows of the Old Mill, throwing out faint lines across the lawn and glimmering into the road more faintly still. Almost-shadows leaned in, kissing our feet. From somewhere behind the house came the ceaseless crash of a waterfall. We linked arms, Lou in the middle, huddling close.

'Will we be back in time for supper?'

'I've got a couple of Pot Noodles on House.'

The clouds were grey like steel and the fields on the crest of the hill ahead dusky and almost indistinguishable. Something in Nina's pocket clicked with every second step and as we tramped along the tarmac our long coats swung in unison, brushing together at the back. Dried leaves trilled in the hedgerow. The headlights of a car on the top road, far away, turned slowly in our direction.

'Keep walking,' said Nina as Lou squeezed both our arms. 'Don't act guilty, we've just been for a walk, remember. Nothing wrong with that. We got a bit lost, that's why we're out so late.' The headlights dipped and flickered, vanished where the lane curled back on itself, then reached out once more in two long dusty beams.

We didn't let go until the very last moment, when it was already close enough to see us and brake. We leaned back into the siding, single-file, and watched the grass turn green and then no-colour again as it slid past slowly, drew to a stop. Reversed. It was an old white Metro. An only too familiar Musicians' Union sticker peeled at the bottom left corner of the rear windscreen.

A window wound down and Philip leaned out, smiling at us evenly. 'Nice time of day for a walk,' he observed, staring at Lou's wet jeans. 'What happened to you?'

'She fell in a stream,' said Nina, trying to sound sensible. 'We're rushing back to get her to bed.'

He nodded, turned again to Lou. 'You must be freezing. Hop in, I'll give you a lift.'

'Oh no, we're fine.' Lou smiled. 'It's not on your way or anything.'

'That doesn't matter. You'll catch cold otherwise. Come on, jump in all of you. The door's not locked. It won't take a minute.'

Maybe he hasn't realised, I thought, as I shuffled across to make room for Nina in the back, depositing a streak of mud on the seat between us. A dog-eared road map frayed on the floor at my feet. My kneecaps brushed the back of Philip's seat. Lou walked round in front of the headlights and folded herself in next to him. Slammed the door too hard. Nina opened her window and elbowed me to do the same as the car whined uphill backwards, looking for a place to turn.

'We've been walking,' Lou said tentatively.

'Where did you go?'

'The woods.'

We sat in silence for the rest of the journey, not trusting ourselves to speak. We must have reeked, of cigarettes at least. Philip stared hard at the road ahead. When I caught his eye in the rear-view mirror he looked away. He stopped just short of the gates. 'I'll let you out here,' he muttered.

Nina and I mumbled thank yous and climbed out, waiting for Lou. He must have been lecturing her. At last the

passenger door clicked open and the engine revved. Lou
stood like a statue by the side of the road as the car's wheels
twisted at her feet. She didn't even notice. Just for a glimpse
of a second her face glowed red in the tail-lights as Philip
drove away.

We moor along a meadow as the afternoon sky begins to grain with dusk. Nina nudges us slowly through the shallows, tiller hard left, and Lou leaps ashore, standing clear as I throw mallet and pins. The mallet thuds into soggy earth and the iron pins ring. I jump after them with a second rope. We fasten the *Otterburn* parallel against the bank and Nina cuts the engine.

Our ears have grown accustomed to its chugging growl and the hours have floated by like a film with the sound turned off. Birds chirruped noiselessly behind the whir of the projector and now, as the sound of the engine fades, nature presses in. I have a heartbeat. It pounds in my thumb as I lift the mallet, drive the pin. Lou hums – maybe she's been humming all afternoon – and I can almost hear Nina's festering discontent. Somewhere, out of sight, a lane runs parallel to the canal. Mud-clouds sink into mirrory darkness at the back of the boat.

Nina shuffles along the gangplank, pigeon-stepping into the field barefoot. She picks between the nettle-stands and thistles, grinning stupidly. I look at Lou. We're all grinning stupidly, it seems, beaming at nothing in particular. Our sunburned faces ache and the meadow is dizzy. We drift across nibbled grass to a break in the hedgerow, slide over a stile, floating out to where a bridleway leads up to the bridge, to the top of the world. The bricks are warm and worn. We lean on them, lizard-like, soaking our guts with heat and staring down at the silver ribbon of canal. Just for a moment we've been rendered speechless. Behind us the bridleway kinks through potato fields, sinking below the treeline where bright cars interrupt the tarmac, whistling like wind. Footpaths fan out cross-country. We can see everything now. It is delicious, floating up from the water-level into this uninhabited oxygen. Lou hawks a gob-stopper of phlegm, dangles it over our three reflections and spits. 'We could play pooh-sticks,' she muses idly.

Nina flicks her hair. 'I wonder where the nearest phone box is.'

'Who do you want to ring?' I wonder, and they shake their heads at me as though I've gone stark raving mad.

'Remember at the end of term we did those tests – you know, what were they called? *A Levels!*' Nina looks almost exasperated. Lou tips back her head, turns slowly on the spot. They're bored. They're waiting for me. They have been waiting for me all along.

Cows have gathered on the meadow's horizon like a change of weather, a crowd of curious black and white clouds. The gangplank sags beneath my weight. The water below is clear now, glassy shrimps fidget over stones and mud, burying themselves, then changing their minds in a swirl of panic and sand.

'See anything interesting?' Nina opens a bottle of wine. She stands on the coach-roof, looking down at me, waving her glass. 'Better watch out, the beef is coming to get you.' Gazing across the fields, she is delighted by the thought of her own conspicuousness. Up there she is a landmark – the tallest thing for miles. Midges drift across her face like smoke. Flicking her hair, she nets them. Her head is a battlefield of torn wings, severed legs. 'Steak!' she shouts, clapping her hands. Behind me the creeping thunder hesitates, momentarily bemused. Lou puts Bob Marley on the ghettoblaster.

'Hamburger!' Nina stamps at the cows but the music drowns it out and she's dancing now, swinging and dipping to the reggae beat, her hands and empty glass held coyly, politely, behind her back. She sways and wiggles and croons at the animals as they tiptoe to the edge of the water, heads low, eyes raised, nudging each other out of the way. They snort as she rocks and shuffles, staring back at her but Nina can outstare anything, she loves to be looked at long and hard. Lou passes me a glass, turns up the volume, singing along.

'Come up here – it's brilliant, you can see for miles,' Nina spins a pirouette and then another, twisting round and round until the thick August hedgerows seem about to take off, whirling of their own accord. She staggers, reaching out, as though to haul us onto her level one by one. Half a glass, and I am dancing too. Lou waves her arms,

Egyptian-style, as Nina and I shimmy and bop, wailing the chorus into make-believe microphones. We empty our glasses twice and the cattle gaze crazily, almost captivated, almost petrified.

It's Lou who turns away first. The bottle is empty and she wants a cigarette. Her mood has changed. She stands below us, leaning against the deck-rail, staring at her reflection as the last notes die and the play button clicks up. Nina vanishes into the loo to paint her face. The spell is broken. The devoted attention of the cows begins to cloy. Their saucer-eyes moon at me, lecherous. I curse, give up on them and hide inside, banging on the shower-room door, 'Hurry up will you, I need to piss.'

'Piss in the field with the rest of the cows,' Nina shouts back. 'You've made me smudge my eye-liner.'

Lou stands in the doorway, rubbing her arms. 'I've been bitten,' she says sadly. 'They always bite *me*.' Suddenly everything seems personal. She picks up one of my jumpers from the table, ties it round her shoulders. 'It's cooling down a bit out there. All these fish keep jumping for flies. I wish we had a rod, then I could catch us supper.'

Releasing her face from the mirror, Nina saunters in, drunk. A new woman. 'I'm not eating anything that's grown up in that disgusting water. It's green.'

'It's only algae. Good for you, probably.' Lou lights the fire.

Nina ruffles her hair. 'You can't be cold!' she frowns, as Lou opens her hands before the element, staring at their silhouette. Her eyes are burning, watery reflections. I want to say her name but that seems almost dangerous, like calling to a sleepwalker, or an acrobat mid-air. With some people you never really know for sure when they are happy, when they are sad. Blue gas streams up the flue, twisting out into the twilight.

'If I still played violin,' says Lou eventually, more to herself than either or both of us, 'tomorrow would be just another day. A levels wouldn't matter. I probably wouldn't even have taken them. Apart from Music I suppose.'

Nina backcombs her hair. Dust and midge wings scatter invisibly across the floor. 'If you still played the violin you wouldn't be here to enjoy *tomorrow being just another day*,' she says. 'Your parents would have taken you away from Hawkley long ago. You would probably never have been allowed to see us again, all your friends would be other musicians. And the only person in the world you would feel you could trust would be your shrink.'

'That bad?' Lou wonders.

I'm inclined to agree. Nina's black hair crackles and the strands at the back fly out from her shoulders in a static, glittering tent.

We lock the boat and hide the gangplank, swish through the meadow again and up to the bridge, turning left down the bridleway, following Gabriel's map. Swallows dip from the violet sky, looping and swerving over the canal, killing flies. A bat zigzags in front of us, flutters like a quick, gigantic moth. For a moment, Nina and Lou walk hand in hand in front of me, the way they used to, headed for the village

shop for fags. What did we talk about, back then? Philip.
Clothes. Nina walks lopsided, half on grass, half on the
mud, almost childishly petite in comparison with Lou.
From the back, I guess, she could pass for an 11-year-old.
Lou leans Nina deeper into the verge while Nina tries to
hold her ground, stepping neatly round the matted entrails
of a pigeon casualty. Darkness washes the colour from their
clothes.

'Bethy, Bethy,' they croon, reaching back for me. 'Stop
lingering.' They hold me one on each side like policemen
and we quick-step through the midges, keeping our
mouths shut tight and blinking them from our eyelashes.
We communicate by nod and squeeze. Half a mile on, the
bridleway forks and we follow the wider track, parallel now
with the canal. There are houses in the distance, a village.
Headlights beam up from the sunken lane ahead. A mare
and foal stand by a paddock gate, listening. The birds have
stopped. It is a beautiful, dreamy night.

No one notices as we come in. The bar is heaving.
Waitresses hurry past with plates of steak and chips, taking
orders for coffee or desserts. A man with ketchup-spots on
his blue and white checked shirt asks if the chocolate
gateau comes with cream. His girlfriend folds her paper
napkin and sighs. Nina scurries off to find somewhere to
sit while Lou and I queue for drinks. A hook-nosed
woman in a raspberry-pink cardigan and gold hooped earrings squirms past clutching three full glasses of white
wine.

'That'll be you in twenty years,' I mutter, pushing Lou into the empty space.

She grins. 'I never wear pink.' 50ps clatter from the fruit machine behind us and a cheer goes up as heavy money spatters free into the lip. A circle of men in rugby shirts eye the gambler as he stuffs his pockets with fistfuls of coin and shoulders to the bar, pushing in front of me. He has a purple spider's web tattooed across his forehead. At the sight of it Lou panics. 'I'll just go and see what Nina wanted,' she mumbles, ducking away.

Spider-man plants his elbows on the counter and nods to the bartender.

'What can I get you?' She's looking straight at me. It takes me by surprise. I hadn't decided yet.

'A pint of cider – Three pints of cider, please.'

Spider-man presents me with an unpleasant look. 'Are you eighteen?' he sneers.

'What's that?' Nina frowns at the triangle of pint glasses as I lower them away from my chest. Lou reaches out to help.

'Sorry, I didn't know what anyone wanted.' I wipe my hands on my jeans, then take a sip. You have to be in the right sort of mood for cider. I can't think why I've bought it now. Nostalgia, perhaps. Nina gulps, grimaces and leans back in her window seat. Fingerprints mist the rims of the empty and half-empty beer glasses she's shunted out of the way and we roll our sleeves, avoiding the soggy mats and crisp crumbs left scattered across the table like ancient schoolboy code. A three-quarters smoked cigarette, filter up and still alight, balances against the ashtray. Framed reproduction sporting prints have been screwed into the nicotine-stained walls. Faded blue and green hardbacks lean against an old-fashioned stoneware lemonade jar on the shelf above the door to the toilets.

The rugby shirts stagger back from the lounge bar, loaded with pints. To save on drinking time, they've bought in two or three rounds at once.

'Oyoy, what's this? Invaders!' the fattest one hollers, elbowing the empties back to the middle of the table and slopping the full. A lager-lake drips to the carpet, spattering Lou's jeans and Nina looks up, annoyed.

'We didn't think anyone was sitting here,' she says in her most reasonable voice, but the words sound prim and plummy and you can tell this won't be the end of it. Lou and I pick up our glasses, ready to move.

'Don't go,' says the fat one, clapping his neighbour across the shoulder, spilling more beer. 'There's room for everyone. Here, sit on my knee –' He belches, whipping up hurricanes of laughter from his friends as they shuffle along the window-seat, pushing Nina further and further into a cul-de-sac. She slides her drink along after her defiantly, refusing to be intimidated, nods at Lou and me to do the same.

'I'm Harry,' leers the shrew-faced giant next to me. He sits with his legs spread. Huge white hands bulge palm-down dimpling his fleshy thighs. 'So, ladies, do you come here often – as they say – and, if so, how come we haven't done this sooner?' He looks at me. Oh God, he seems to

have singled me out for himself. As he speaks he jiggles his
knee against my leg. I flush and stammer, struggling to
think of a snappy reply.

'We're on holiday,' says Lou. Nina's neighbour is whispering something in her ear, an intimacy she doesn't much
seem to enjoy. Symmetrical muscles bulge in her cheeks as
she grinds her teeth.

'On holiday,' nods one of the other rugby shirts. 'That's
nice. Where are you staying?'

'On a boat. My sister used to live there.'

I send Lou an urgent kick under the table, but I think
I've made a mistake because she just carries on talking, on
and on, about Sophie, her mum and dad's decision to sell
the boat, tomorrow's A level results – anything and everything that pops into her head.

The whisperer flinches and stares at Harry, then leans
across, flicks beer in his eye. Harry grins. 'What's that for,
dickhead? Wasn't me.' He turns to us, self-righteous now
and slurred. 'Don't worry, we don't give a shit where you're
staying. Honestly, some girls think just because a man is
friendly to them in a pub that all he wants is sex.' He shifts
his leg away from mine and turns to his friends, discussing
the afternoon's game. At our end of the table the silence
drags. Our ciders look as though they're going to last forever.

'I wonder if Gabriel's here,' says Lou at last. 'Sophie
didn't mention they were friends.'

'There's a lot she doesn't mention,' Nina winks, relieved
that we have found a topic of conversation at last.

'What's that supposed to mean?'

'Nothing.'

'Nothing *what*?'

'They had a fling.'

'How do you know?'

'I can tell.' She tips her head back, swallowing the yellowy fizz as though it were medicine.

Lou's face colours with slow surprise. 'My sister wouldn't shag Gabriel. He's too small.' She laughs, imagining them together – dancing perhaps – his forehead resting on the boxy silhouette of Sophie's straight and gorgeous shoulder.

'Fascist!' Nina looks pissed off. She pushes her empty glass away and squeezes through the crack between table and wall. 'No one wants the same again, I assume?'

We hold our breath until she's out of sight and then, as one, stand up, relinquishing our stools in search of somewhere less exposed to sit. The rugby shirts whistle and jeer and everybody turns to stare. A couple of young-looking, safe-looking men at a table by the fireplace gesture at empty chairs. 'Thank you,' we mutter as they budge up.

'God, Nina's touchy tonight,' says Lou.

'PMT.'

'Is it now? I forgot.' Lou sighs, happy to think that some things – even in the unregulated adult world – are still predictable and therefore precious. Then her contentment slips once more into mild and curious disbelief. 'She's wrong about Sophie, you know. I know my sister – Gabriel's not her type.'

'Whatever you say,' I shrug, remembering the way he'd gazed at Nina's bed, as though it had never occurred to him until just then that someone else might lie there, sleep and dream there. That some other body might eventually press Sophie's print from the mattress. He wasn't handsome, exactly, but I could see what she might have found attractive. He had an open smile and eyes like chocolate.

Nina comes back, drinkless. We wave at her and the rugby shirts wave too, mimicking. 'Over here, darling,' the one called Harry coos, falsetto.

Nina gives him the V. 'I can't believe it. Fucking barman wanted ID.'

'I'll go.'

'No, hang on a mo,' she mutters, sorting through her purse. 'My rail card's in here somewhere. I'm sure it is –' A photobooth snap of the three of us, taken just after exams, at the end of term, flips to the floor and Lou's new neighbour stoops gallantly, returning it.

'I'm about to go up for a round. Would you like anything?' he wonders.

Nina tucks the photo between two £5 notes where, in theory, it won't get crumpled and opens her mouth to say no. She looks up, holds her breath as she sees him for the first time, changes her mind. 'Three rum and pineapples. Thank you,' she murmurs, fluffing her hair. 'You'll need a hand . . .'

He follows her back to the bar while Lou and I sit awkwardly and smoke and make desultory conversation, trying to act as though strange men bought us drinks every night

of the week. I pretend not to understand the hand gestures
the rugby shirts are throwing across the room in our direction. Lou blushes and the stranger sat opposite looks round.
'Take no notice of them,' he smiles. He spins his beermat.
'Students?'

'Us? Sort of – just left school.'

'A wonderful time.' He nods wistfully to indicate that
this would be a suitable moment for someone else to take
a turn questioning, but neither of us can think of an appro-
priate place to start. He's in his twenties, middle-class,
employed; his probably mediterranean tan has faded; his
jacket and shirt veer just to the fashionable side of conser-
vative – nothing in his appearance sparks our curiosity.
Nina has comandeered the only eligible man in the room,
as usual, and we slump with relief as they return. She's
laughing prettily, little by little dripping precious juice from
the glasses with every step. She gestures for me to shove
along so they can sit together and all five of us swap names.
Nina's catch is a Robert; the thuggish name diminishes his
appeal. Eyes down, we sip our drinks in unison. I've never
had rum and pineapple before, it tastes of holidays – lazy
and romantic – the sort of holiday I haven't been on yet,
the sort of holiday you'd never want to end. Lou pinches
me under the table. The fattest rugby shirt is staggering in
our direction, swinging from chair to chair like an ape, a
cigarette hanging from his bottom lip. He points himself at
Nina, standing so close his crotch is barely a hand-span
from the tip of her nose, and gazes down. 'Got a light?'

Nina makes an effort not to breathe. She shakes her head

and he turns reluctantly to Lou, then, even more reluctantly, to me. Inhaling, he touches my Zippo hand, as though I trembled. Robert is telling cadaver anecdotes, preparing Nina for the year ahead. He qualifies next summer.

'Are you a medical student too?' I ask his friend, Nigel, who blinks in the negative as half a pint vanishes down his throat in a single gulp.

'A lawyer, actually.'

'How interesting.' Lou gives a vacant smile, staring through her fringe as Robert and Nina lean together for the very first time and kiss. It's Nina's fastest seduction yet.

The rugby shirts thump the table, suck their teeth. One of them murmurs, 'Fucking slag,' loud enough for everyone to hear, and Lou and I sink our foreheads to our hands. Nigel glares across the room on Nina's behalf but the snoggers kiss on defiantly, flushed necks twisting from side to side like the necks of dancing birds. Robert's hand slides along Nina's shoulder blades, his fingers circle her vertibrae one by one.

'Well this is embarrassing,' Nigel says at last. 'Ignoring them obviously isn't going to work.'

It isn't quite clear which 'them' he means, but Lou and I nod all the same. We finish our drinks. 'I think we'd better go.'

'Will you be OK?'

'Sure. Come on, Nina.' I tap her arm and she breaks off, looking at me with the glazed confusion of one who has suddenly woken from a long, deep sleep. 'We're going.'

Robert leans back in his chair. His mouth is shiny with drink and spit. 'I'll walk you home.'

A purple van pulls up as the pub door swings shut after us, washing our faces with light. The brakes groan. Gabriel jumps out. 'Not going are you?' He hurries across the tarmac, a single Alsatian trotting after him. It sniffs at Lou.

'We're making a speedy getaway,' says Nina, squeezing Robert's hand.

Gabriel trawls our faces for clues and stares at Robert suspiciously. 'Boat all right?' he asks Lou at last.

'Yeah.' She fidgets like a sulky child, kicks at a clump of grass, decapitates a dandelion that's sprouted through a crack in the paving stones, won't look him in the eye.

'Do you really have to go? I wanted to talk to you — about your sister.'

Lou glances at Nina bitterly. 'I already know.'

Gabriel frowns. 'Please. Come inside. I'll buy you all a drink.'

'We can't. We're going back,' she mutters, crossing the road into darkness.

Gabriel regards her disappearing back, then turns to Nina and me. 'Tell her we were sorry not to say goodbye.'

Nina nods, too chuffed to wonder what he means. She loves a good public vindication, almost as much as she loves a public seduction. As if to remind us of his presence, Robert clears his throat. 'We should go after her,' Nina says to Gabriel. 'She'll only get lost.' The night has grown warm. Retreating, we wave once, turn and walk away. In

spite of ourselves, we're reassured by Robert's heavy tread.
If I really stare hard I can just see Nina's white neck curv-
ing back as she looks up into the moonless, starless sky.
'Fuck, it's dark,' she mutters, bumping into Lou. 'Why
were you such a cunt to Gabriel?'

'I wasn't. We were going. We couldn't go back in there.'
Her basketball boots scuff the lane impatiently. 'Come on,
let's go.'

'Admit it then – that I was right about your sister,' Nina
calls.

'Maybe we should hold hands.' I strike a match and
everything goes black and bright as our pupils shrink back.
The world turns green and shadowy, then gutters out. We
straggle down the lane. Lou runs her fingers along a garden
wall, touches air and stops. As she draws them back a wire
twangs. She screams and suddenly I am screaming too, at a
different pitch. It sounds almost musical. Nina and Robert
rush up. I strike another match and Lou examines herself in
the light. Three little domes of blood leak up from a scratch
above her knuckle.

'Oh,' she sounds disappointed. 'What happened to you?'

'Just keeping you company.'

For a moment Lou looks balefully at the barbed-wire
fence behind us, then the match goes out. 'Will I have to
have a tetanus jab?'

'I don't bloody know,' says Nina, dropping behind.
Robert clears his throat and now we can hear whispering.
Their murmured, shy one-liners grow fainter and fainter as
Lou and I walk ahead. She puts her arm through mine. At

Hawkley, in Third, we used to hum the Bach Double Violin Concerto if we ever got scared walking back from the Beech Trees after dark. Lou would take first violin and I'd be second and we'd see how far we could go without laughing or breaking off for breath. I had to adapt my part to a two-octave range but Lou could do most of the notes for real. She had a sweet voice.

'Shh!' Lou stops dead in her tracks. 'What's that?' We've come as far as the bridleway, leaving the lovers to mouth their own duet. All I can hear is the irregular sigh of distant cars. Close beside me, Lou shifts weight.

'What is it?'

For half a minute she makes no reply. She probably hasn't even heard the question. 'I don't know,' she says at last. 'Nothing. Forget it.' She sighs and I feel myself relax.

'What did you think you heard?' We move off.

'Something on the other side of the hedge, I think.'

'Footsteps?'

'You heard them too?'

'No. Maybe. I don't know – Where are the others?'

There is a pause. 'I'm glad I brought that air-pistol,' Lou says out loud. She stops again and this time I can hear the definite swish and thud of a footfall, not twenty feet behind. For an instant we freeze, then run for it, pelting down the bridleway, not daring to stop until we reach the bridge. The canal flows silently below. A lonely bellow rings through the warm night air and Lou looks back. 'Oh shit, it's following us,' she wails.

'*It?*'

She points. Splodges of blurred white glimmer behind us in the water-light, plodding steadily in our direction. The cow lets out a second moan and we shriek. Lou's fingernails pinch my arm, dragging me after her as she runs for the safety of the stile. Panicking, we scramble over, uncover the gangplank and run aboard. The fire goes on, and then the paraffin lamp. We stare at each other, trembling. Begin to laugh.

Lou carries the lamp outside. She sets it on deck. Thick shadow slants up from the benches and our bare throats glow. The scent of grass and mud and water floats in through the saloon as we fetch blankets. Outside again we lean together. Her hair tickles my neck, it smells of beer and smoke and the camomile tangle-free conditioner we found in the shower-room together with so many other tubes and ointments, moisturisers, creams and gels – a sort of cosmetic biography, a confession of admitted imperfections, abandoned, open, on the shelves for any-one to read. Quickwash shampoo with extract of rosemary for bounce and shine. Clearasil. Aapri face mask. Anti-ageing wheatgerm oil. Sophie thinks she's growing old.

The gangplank creaks as Nina steps on board, catching her breath.

'Got rid of Romeo?'

'He's gone back for wine. I heard you screaming – everything OK?'

'Yeah.' Three feels safer than two, but even so we pull in

our drawbridge, check the location of the boat-hook just in case.

'Let's stay out until dawn,' says Nina, gazing through the fuzzy light. Her eyes flit up to the bridge and back again as she lies across from us, languid and poised and ready for anything. She wets her lips. Her flawless teeth gleam delicately as she smiles. Unseen, a goods train drags itself across the horizon. Far-away flashes of lightning spark and crackle from the rails. The air fizzes with insect wings, the fluttering of restless birds. Nothing sleeps tonight. Everything is busy and curious and close.

Lou sighs. She lies on her back, arms folded across her chest. Hidden beneath the sleeve of her sweatshirt, her fingertips trace a slow forgetful loop across her collarbone. The tip of her cigarette glows bright, then faint again, then bright. 'Is it tomorrow yet?' she wonders. Giant moths beat up a storm in my ribcage. It's funny to think that one phone call in the morning sets them free, to think that a decade from now exams and school will have become so unimportant we might not even remember this moment, this holiday. Knowing that its significance will fade makes the night seem precious, suddenly. If only time would stop just here, exactly now, before we sober up, while Nina and Lou and I are equals.

'What's body temperature?'

'Thirty-seven degrees.' The air is warm like a human touch. Lou stretches. Nina combs her hand through her hair. She glances up at the bridge once more, its arch a slight black shadow in the purply canal. Gravel spatters the water, an elbow-nudge. Yes, there is definitely someone up there, leaning against the rail, watching her. She shudders hot and cold. An army of insects creeps across her scalp.

Drying mud crumbles along the bridleway, cows in the field stand back as footsteps swish through meadow-grass and Lou jumps up, swinging the lantern. 'It's Robert,' Nina says softly. 'Give us a hand with the gangplank.'

'Are you sure?'

She looks at me as though the question is almost too simple to bother answering, but I know she knows what I mean. 'Of course I'm sure.'

He waits at the water's edge, the edge of darkness, as Lou and Nina struggle with the plank. 'I've brought the wine,' he mumbles, waving it like a password and jumping back as the wooden end lands splat in the mud at his feet. Nina stretches out a hand to him and it's as though the furrows of their fingerprints have interlocked. She pulls him aboard, reckoning the weight of his bashful enthusiasm in a single touch. They climb to the roof and she turns him slowly, showing the view, as Lou and I search the saloon for something clean to drink from. Over our heads, the ceiling creaks.

'Do you believe in love at first sight?' Lou whispers, rinsing the coffee ring from one of yesterday morning's mugs.

'What's love got to do with it?' I'm halfway through before I hear what I'm saying.

'*What's lo-ve but a second-hand emo-tion . . .*' We sing it, standing astride with one fist by our pelvic bone and one,

for the mike, at our mouth. Our eyes close and our noses
crease at the top like only the noses of blue-blood rock-
divas can. We stamp and strut and hum the instrumentals,
fall about laughing as the verse comes in again and neither
of us can remember the words. The roof has gone suspiciously quiet. Oh God, please don't let them be going to
do it right here.

Lou coughs heavily and carries the mugs and glasses
through, clattering them against the bench as loud as
she dares. Nina and Robert separate. He passes the bottle. 'We're going for a walk, so only pour two glasses,'
says Nina, heading for the loo. 'We'll take the rest with
us.'

Robert looks down at us self-consciously.

'Do people call you Robert or Rob?' I ask.

'Robert.' He tries a smile. He doesn't have anything to
say to us.

Lou and I chatter defensively, ignoring him and showing
off, allowing ourselves the occasional surreptitious sideways glance to check he's listening. 'The important thing
with booze,' says Lou, 'is knowing your limit. If I drink
more than two-thirds of a bottle of wine you can be certain
I'll puke.'

'Depends if you've eaten or not.'

'No. Even if I've had a three-course meal I still can't take
a bottle of wine.'

'That's cos you're so skinny. You should line your stomach with yoghurt or milk.'

'Would low-fat yoghurt work?'

I shrug. 'Ask Nina. Bloody Marys work, for hangovers, I know that. We had them the morning after Dad's Fiftieth.'

'What's in a Virgin Mary?'

'Tomato juice.'

'You mean the blood's the *vodka*?'

'I suppose—'

'That doesn't make much sense.' The words go woody and her tongue seizes up like an arthritic joint. We pause and sip, blush simultaneously as our brains interpret what our mouths have been saying. It's like *don't mention the war* in *Fawlty Towers*, but Robert stares through our embarrassment unperturbed. He doesn't know. Lou pinches a cigarette, lights up as though it were a matter of life and death which, in a way, I suppose, it is.

'Give us a drag,' I say, to break the silence. Where the fuck is Nina anyway? Has she changed her mind? What does she think she's playing at, leaving us here like ancient aunts wheeled out to admire the boyfriend? Who does she think we are, her mum and dad? Lou examines a mozzie bite on her wrist, rubbing a drop of wine on the skin as though she genuinely believes it's going to help. She scratches it luxuriously, looking up cat-like, as the water-pump sings. There is a loud splash close to the boat. Huge black butterflies flicker and swoop beneath the bridge.

When she comes out Nina has one of Sophie's blankets draped around her shoulders, poncho-style. She's brushed her hair. Sandalwood loses itself in the scent of wine and cigarettes. She twists the cork from the corkscrew, stoppering it into the bottle with the heel of her palm. Robert jumps down from the coach-roof. 'Ready?'

She nods. 'Let's go.' She blows us kisses, runs down the gangplank after him, doesn't look back. Shoe-prints settle in the mud. Their footsteps fade. And now a different kind of quietness descends, intense and unexpected and completely exhausting. It's a kind of relief. Lou yawns.

We watch for them crossing the bridge – imagine step by step the bristle of cropped grass, cold dew soaking their trousers like the ghost of a doubt – but no one passes and I feel lonely, suddenly, and left behind. They must have gone the other way. In silence we swallow our wine, smoke a few cigarettes. Moths and daddy-long-legs flicker around the lamp. It's so quiet now you can almost hear the flow of the canal.

'Eighteen is old to be losing your virginity,' Lou says at last.

'Maybe she's not.' She claimed to be on the Pill for her complexion, but I never could tell exactly what Nina got up to away from school and, when I asked, she'd only look at me with a kind of secretive, teasing smile. One autumn term she covered her bedside wall with holiday snaps, lovingly Blu-Tacked edge to edge in a glossy montage. Rupert Everett look-alikes with floppy hair chuckling confidentially or pouting in shades or sunbathing, asleep on some permanently sun-drenched English beach. *Who's that?* I'd asked, pointing at each square jaw in turn. They had the names of heart-throbs: Charlie, Josh, Oliver – the syllables had dropped from her lips like precious stones. At least she'd had the decency to blush. Day by day, the Blu-Tack hardened, corners popped free. She'd pressed them in again, wrapping her thumb in loo paper so as not to mark the pictures with fingerprints. The heart-throbs grinned. I couldn't really imagine her with any of them. '*Mind your own business*,' she would have said if I'd asked, and that's the thing about virginity.

'She might have lost it ages ago.'

Lou pretends to look hurt. 'She would have said.'

'Not necessarily. What's it got to do with us?'

'Nothing, I suppose,' Lou yawns again. 'But it would have been nice to know.' We heave in the gangplank and hug ourselves with blankets, flopping on deck together, drunk and drowsy, fighting off sleep. We lie on our backs staring up at where there should have been stars. We listen to each other breathe. Lou sighs quietly. 'I believe in love at first sight,' she murmurs, closing her eyes.

Asleep, cocooned in the rough blue wool, drizzled with dew and giddy with the speed of time, Lou's cheeks burn with two bright cherries and her eyelids ripple and pulse. Her fingers twitch. The planet tilts towards the sun again and birdsong circles the gloom. Someone is whispering at me to *Wake up, Beth. Wake up!* Twigs and gravel scatter the deck. Nina waves, points at the gangplank, shivering.

She smells of moss and washing-up gloves, runs her fingers through her hair. Fragments of broken-up, dead leaf drop out. She brushes the mud from her shins and waits. I could have asked her anything I liked. The moment passes.

'Thanks Beth. You're a star,' she says, as if somehow we aren't quite friends any more.

'Not having lunch?' Pablo nodded at our empty trays as we drifted the length of the food counter, Nina's nose wrinkling with exaggerated disgust. She shrugged.

'Too hot to eat.' She took a banana, shook her head as he offered two. Lou and I helped ourselves to Granny Smiths, clasped them behind our backs like prayer-books as we slipped past Miss McKendrick at the Dining-Hall door. A swarm of giddy Fifths huddled and fizzed across the Quad from the Science Block, buzzing with near-hysterical chatter. This was their last day of lessons before exams in June. Now they had two whole weeks of Library to look forward to. *Only a month*, worried the swots. Divided up subject by subject, in accordance with their individually approved revision schedules, it seemed like no time at all. We waved at Kate.

'Be my partner in tennis this afternoon?' asked Nina, collapsing on the grass outside. I flopped down next to her.

'Can't — it's Orchestra.' With Parents' Day only four weeks away we were rehearsing, now, twice a week.

Nina sighed, hoiked up her skirt, exposing maximum thigh to the sunlight, and scowled as I bit a chunk from my apple's lurid green cheek, crunching noisily. 'Go on, then, abandon me – I don't care!' she proclaimed, peeling her lunch. 'Maybe the lovely Wormwood will be my friend.'

'No she won't, you sad prat. She's in Orchestra too.' I swallowed and grinned. Lou closed her eyes, listening to her freckles pop in the heat of the sun. Everyone had had the same idea, it seemed. The Orchard Lawn murmured, striped with Hawklies sunbathing in colonies of two or three. Somebody screamed as a wasp dive-bombed their forehead and we all looked round.

'Must be her birthday,' Nina said, nodding at Heather Allen as she hovered by the Library door, clutching a bunch of lilies wrapped in polythene. 'God, I wish I was eighteen.'

'So *old*!' Lou sprinkled lawn-mowings in a pyramid over her discarded, browning apple-core. She pulled me up.

Nina was pretending to be asleep. 'See you at Tea,' she called as we stumbled away.

It was hot in the Music School. The air felt sticky with rosin and wax. Someone had been eating salt 'n' vinegar crisps in the Rehearsal Room – Philip perhaps, though it seemed funny to think of any grown-up eating crisps. He leaned against the concert grand, sorting out parts. 'Lend a hand setting up, will you,' he summoned, looking at me.

I widened my eyes. 'What about Lou?'

'Lou's got other things to be getting on with.'

'So have I.'

But he wasn't listening any more. 'We'll see you at three,'

he said to her. She nodded. Skipped from the room before I had time to interrogate.

Philip looked pleased with himself. 'How's your sight-reading this afternoon?' he wondered cheerily as I dismantled the nearest stack of chairs and slid them to the centre of the room. They skidded well, colliding in a crush of tipped backs, a tangle of legs. As the last chair clattered sideways into a music stand, he cleared his throat and stared at me a moment, puzzling. Then shook his head, lifted a finger to his lips. 'There are people practising next door.'

'Oops, sorry.'

Outside, a queue of doleful musicians reached right down the corridor as far as the instrument store. Everyone, it seemed, could think of something they'd have preferred to do that afternoon – tennis, swimming or athletics. More sunbathing. Even an hour of French translation work was deemed the more attractive choice.

'Hurry up you lot. Sit down. Be quiet,' Philip bawled, pretending to be the kind of teacher kids instinctively obey. 'There's a lot to get through today.'

'You say that every week,' muttered one of the flutes anonymously.

Philip gave us his twinkliest smile. 'And this week it's true.'

Not quite in unison the front desk cellos raced through Bach's first prelude. Heather Allen quickly grew bored of practising harmonics, twisted her bass on its spike, slapping the sides like a bass player in a jazz club. Anna Birdwood wormed to her seat importantly. She fished a

freshly sharpened pencil from her pencil box and placed it
on the lip of the stand. To avoid the possibility of any
loose tendril brushing her cheek or forehead or neck and
distracting her from her important role as Leader of the
Seconds, she had her hair pushed back behind a squashy
blue velvet Alice band.

There was a moment's hush as Philip passed the music
round, then gradually the mutterings and twitterings grew
louder again. I slipped through to the front and sat by
Anna, balancing my violin and bow across my knees
uncomfortably. I shuffled, stared at the triangle of space on
the far side of her chair, but she wouldn't budge. She pen-
cilled our names across the top of the music, hers first of
course, and settled back. Squashed against my left elbow at
the front of the violas, Hermione Lawrence laboured
through the first few lines, nodding and whispering to herself as she counted, trying to get the tune.

Philip stepped into the throng and clapped his hands for
silence. He flashed a mocking, patient smile at Ella Barker
as she scurried into place, last, and everyone tittered. Then
desk by desk the room fell quiet again. 'Only four weeks to
the concert, now,' he said, as if we didn't know. 'And to
show how well you've been playing and how confident I
am, today I thought we'd start on something new.'

Hermione waved her bow to ask a question. 'Can I open
the doors? It's really stuffy in here.'

He nodded. 'Quiet everyone. Shh. It's not a difficult
piece, technically. But – as the most sharp-sighted of you
will have noticed – it's an arrangement for solo violin

which means that most of the time the orchestra is *accompanying*. You're going to have to follow the dynamics marked, and *watch me* all the time.' He paused for effect. 'And just in case some of you were wondering why Lou's not here, she's next door, working on the solo part. She'll be joining us later, once we have a feel for the piece. She's been dreading this afternoon for weeks, so let's be kind to her and give a round of applause like they do in professional orchestras when she comes in.

'We'll take it all the way through so you can get a feel for the piece.' He rerolled his sleeves. 'Quite slowly, since we're sight-reading. Solo violin starts with the melody, so I'll hum it for you.' He waved the compass points gently, then paused, a mariner summoning winds, and gripped the baton, fingers motionless. Anna Birdwood raised her violin and puffed out her chest, blocking my view with her left hand. She held still, showing off as Philip broke his pose.

'It's a wonderful piece, by the way. Incredibly romantic, as the name suggests. I think you're going to love it.' He swallowed, looked round at us once more with all-encompassing confidence as he lifted his stick. Slouched backs straightened of their own accord.

'Any more little secrets?' I wondered, slouching against the piano lid, watching Lou pack away.

'No.' She wiped the fingerboard, dusted the belly of the violin. 'He wasn't sure we'd have the rehearsal time,' she said. 'That's why I couldn't tell.'

'So?' I gave her my mortally wounded look, but she

never did know when I was serious. Philip came over,
threw himself down on the piano stool and spread his hands
above the keys like Ashkenazy steeled for the performance
of his life. He hesitated, winked at us, launched into Scott
Joplin three or four times too fast. It was his party piece.

'She played well, don't you think?' he said, lifting his eyes
from the keyboard and grimacing at a scatter of wrong
notes. Lou looked simultaneously pleased and mortified.
She knows how brilliant she is, I thought. She doesn't need
me to say it. Hawklies hardly ever paid each other compliments. It was a kind of unwritten rule. Protection against
anyone getting too big-headed. Lou's cheeks glowed with
success and she looked away from us modestly. The
Rehearsal Room had emptied fast. Stands and chairs lay
crooked and teetering in the thunder of some great stampede. The floor was slippery with pencils. Sheet music
flopped at the foot of the piano like flat, exhausted birds.
The Rag Time came to an abrupt, chaotic end. Philip ran
a hand through his hair and smiled. 'I think it's going to
sound really good. We've got some excellent string players
you know.'

'Especially in the Seconds.' Lou slotted her violin neatly
into its velvet-lined compartment, fastened the velcro
choker and closed the lid.

I recommended she take a running jump and Philip pretended to be shocked. He followed us out. 'See you later,
then,' he called as we linked arms, skipping away from him
under the Science Block arch, past Sophie's study-unit, to
Tea.

The Dining Hall was humming. 'Have you heard? Caroline Price's mum's been killed in a car crash.' Nina patted the empty seat beside her. Lou and I took a corner each.

'When?'

'This morning. In a car crash – that's all I know.'

I opened my sandwich, stared at the triangles, one in each hand: yellow butter, purple jam. You wouldn't have known they'd ever touched. I flipped them face-down on the table and pressed. It wouldn't have been right to eat just then. We trailed outside. The sun was still shining. Shadows leaned across the Orchard Lawn. Why is it bad things always happen to the people you have treated wrong? I wondered, remembering the fluff from Mrs Price's tissue, fraying as she unwrapped our pilfered Parents' Meeting treat, the goey collapse of thick sliced white that stuck between Caroline's front teeth and the mustard tang and chew of gristle. She'd kept a comb in her make-up bag and used to slither it absent-mindedly through Caroline's hair at every opportunity, smoothing and settling the centre parting as her daughter's right hand twitched to bat her off. I tried not to imagine in any more detail my own mum crushed against the steering wheel of her navy blue Volvo Estate. 'Lou's playing a solo in the Parents' Day Concert,' I told Nina, changing the subject.

She brightened instantly. 'Hey, that's marvellous. Congratulations.'

We went for a fag at the Beech Trees after supper. It was a hazy evening, warm and thick with flies. Nina swatted at

them ineffectually with the end of a dockleaf. Sophie and
Heather crept round from the far side of a holly bush, nodded at Lou, crept back again. Other voices, some we
recognised, muffled between the trees. Somebody laughed
quietly. A pigeon broke through the canopy and everyone
caught their breath. A branch shook, new leaves fluttered
and sighed as an empty fag-packet dropped through the
undergrowth. There must have been twenty of us hiding
there. Those who spoke spoke in a mournful tone, though
Caroline had been taken home at lunch.

'It's just everyone's nightmare,' Natasha's voice murmured. Everyone kept saying this, over and over. I couldn't
help wondering if the death of a father would have seemed
as bad.

'Shall we do face-packs tonight?' said Nina.

Lou offered to bags the bathroom.

We said goodbye to Nina at the Music School. Philip's car
glowed golden with sunset by the side of the tarmac path.
'Do you think she ever feels left out?' Lou wondered softly.

'What Nina? No.' She had plenty of friends: older
Hawklies, pen pals, cousins, a pair of fifteen- and seven-
teen-year old brothers who lived in the house next door.
Crammed into holidays and weekends, a whole other life
that we were never allowed to know about.

We flicked on the lights in the Rehearsal Room. Lou
had to practise in there because of the acoustic, Philip said.

Kate wandered past the windows on her way for a fag.
Alone, I thought, *that's funny*. Her hair hung down her back

in a thick half-black, half-purple plait. Wrinkling between
the tops of her DMs and her paint-splattered dungarees, a
couple of lime-green socks glinted luminously with every
step. She smiled at us and winked.

Philip came in rubbing his hands. Pound coins rattled in
his jacket pocket as he shook it off and slid it across the
piano lid. He ran a hand through his hair and stared at
Lou, his knotted face easing into a trance. He hadn't
noticed I was there.

'Fetch me before you go,' said Lou and I watched as he
seized up again, his lips went blotchy in the harsh fluorescent light.

He'd gone when I picked her up nearly an hour later.
She packed her violin, zipped the case and stowed it in the
cupboard on the shelf above mine. 'Philip's got a crush on
you,' I whispered, slotting my arm through hers. We side-
stepped through the frosted glass doors and out into the
evening. 'He fancies you,' I said again, but she had turned
her face away and wouldn't respond. We stopped walking
and she pulled free.

'I forgot to lock my violin. I'd better go back,' she muttered, stepping off through curtains of dusk. 'You go on. I'll
see you in the bath.'

'Quick!' Nina burst in, pink from the stairs and fizzing
with news. I pulled my hair free, shaking the T-shirt inside-
out. She stood in the doorway shifting from foot to foot
and wouldn't step across the threshold, as though afraid
that coming too close might damage her excitement in

some way. 'Put your clothes back on. Something's happened to Kate. There's cops everywhere. Come and see.'

I must have sat down quite suddenly, or fallen perhaps.
The mattress squeaked. 'What do you mean? Is she OK?'

'Dunno. She's in with Dr Goodman. See you downstairs,' she said vanishing. I struggled back into my
dungarees and ran out. A self-important hush whispered
along the corridor's grubby magnolia walls. News had trav-
elled fast. Staring doors opened onto empty or half-empty
rooms. In O Dorm a 45 crackled round at the hub. The
Beach Boys in P had been turned down as a mark of
respect. A bath ran unattended in the single bathroom on
the landing, the taps almost completely buried in a mountain of fat white bubbles. Emily Waterhouse thundered
after me into the buzzing hall.

Thirds and Fourths swarmed in front of the noticeboard
where Matron stood with two policewomen. Snippets of
information passed from girl to girl in a furious kind of
three-dimensional Chinese whispers. Somehow Nina had
managed to elbow her way through the crowd, she leaned
against the radiator outside the Study door, listening so
hard she didn't see me wave. Natasha stared through the
window as a third uniformed outline paced up and down
the drive. Squeezed in at the edge of the windowsill,
Harriet watched carefully for signs of an announcement.
'What happened?' I asked her.

'Skinheads,' she spat, as though that were all anyone
needed to know. 'Five of them, on school grounds. Friends
of Kate, apparently.' An elbow knocked my shoulder and

the throng heaved open, letting the policewomen through. Their walkie-talkies muttered and fuzzed acknowledgement.

'Have you caught them yet?' someone shouted as the front door slammed. Everybody craned for a sight through the window as the officers regrouped and hurried off to find their car.

'Calm down,' called Matron. 'There's nothing to worry about. Go to your dorms.' A few of the last arrivals, nearest the stairs, turned round again nonplussed and did as they were told.

'That's the last time I smoke at the Beech Trees,' Ella was muttering as she squeezed past.

'What did they do?'

'They followed her back.' Harriet scrambled to the floor. 'Tried to force her, twisted her arm and shit, really nasty.'

'And they could still be here? Up by the Music School?'

'I guess so. Lucky for Kate Dr Goodman was out walking Winks.'

A gang had collected round Matron. I shouldered through it, searching for Nina.

'Have you seen Lou?' I whispered, dragging her into the Study.

'No.'

'I think she's still off House.' I closed the door. 'She went back to lock her violin. She's probably on her way now.' The table had been pushed against the wall and wooden stools stood in a circle in the middle of the room ready for tomorrow's drama class.

'And now it's twenty past nine.' Nina frowned. She flicked off the light, knocked into stools and chairs as she crossed to the window.

'What are you doing?' Splinters of lamplight from the path outside slanted across the window-seat, catching the edges of the mantelpiece, the cracks between floorboards. The room settled into stripey, dusky focus: shelves piled high with dictionaries, text books, and lever-arch files over-flowing with diagrams and essays. There were photocopies scattered across the tables, doodled-on scraps of paper and silly notes littering the floor, pen lids and biros lost forever behind the cushions of the window seat.

The window opened easily. Nina stepped up. She crouched and shuffled out, letting herself down in short jolts, hands shifting grip from the edge of the sill to the thin iron frame itself. Her basketball boots scrabbled against the outside wall as she released herself and fell, with a fluttering thud, against the roses. She cursed and looked back in at me. 'Coming?'

'To look for Lou?' I stood on the ledge and wiggled my socks in her face. 'I'm not wearing any shoes.'

'Wimp.'

'Out of my way then.' I sat down, dangled my legs and launched myself, landing with a loud crack.

'What the fuck was that?'

'A snail,' I muttered, reaching in to pull the window shut. The flowerbed was stony and damp. I scurried after Nina across the lawn to the gloom of a cherry tree and we crouched there, thrilled by the open emptiness of the grass horizon. The classrooms ahead of us glittered glassy and dark. Desklights shone warm lozenges of concentration through nearby study-unit windows where Sixths scrawled timed A level essays, or frantically copied out notes. Someone sang along to a Cat Stevens tape.

We sidled from tree to tree and shade to shade, crept up on the Library unobserved and darted into the Orchard. Faint clouds of apple-leaf glowered through the dusk.

'Do you really think the skinheads are still around?' I murmured. Behind us, floodlit sycamore shadows lurched across the walls of the Admin Block in sharp black zigzags. '*Do you?*'

Nina pointed. 'Shh—' The Library door had opened. Three girls stood in the porch-light, staring into the trees.

'Who is it?' They were too far away to tell.

'They can't be looking at us,' said Nina. The girl in the middle stretched up, scraping the red-brick arch with her fingertips. She groaned, then wrapped her arms around the shoulders of the other two and flopped between them, as though about to crash and stumble all the way down the Library steps.

'It's Heather,' Nina said.

We edged a little closer to the Gym, preparing to make a dash for it beneath the Science Block arch the moment they looked away.

'Keep to the shadows,' Nina muttered under her breath. 'They must have seen us by now.'

The girl on the right sat down, resting her elbows on her knees. She leaned against the cold brick balustrade and

Heather squeezed in close, one step up. She was playing with her hair, pulling her fingers through the curled ends over and over, dreamily. They seemed to be waiting for us to make a move. Then from behind the Changing-Room wall came the sharp, shrill heart-attack of a wolf-whistle and Heather looked up. She combed her hand one last time through her hair and rose to her feet. We heard her say goodbye, or goodnight, and then her face dipped out from the porch-light and she was on the tarmac path, half strolling, half sauntering into the dark. She passed by close enough to hear our scalps peel, close enough for us to smell the smile on her face. A man's hand and a leather cuff reached out, settled around her waist and pulled her in behind the shadow of the wall.

Nina was squeezing my arm. 'Guess who that was,' she whispered.

I had no idea.

'Pablo.'

'Pablo from the kitchens Pablo? No way—'

'I bet you a tenner.'

'How do you know?'

She touched her nose. Heather's friends stared wistfully into the darkness after her, then slipped back into the Library. A light went on in one of the upstairs bays. A silhouette leaned forwards, pulling the window to. Suddenly it seemed very quiet and very late. Nina tucked her hair behind her ears. Somewhere, far away, a door banged shut. We stepped from our hiding place, walked to the edge of the light, linked arms and ran together through the gleaming arch, panicking into the darkness on the other side. We stopped on the threshold of the Chemistry Lab, waiting for our hearts to slow and our eyes to re-adjust. The Music School stretched out, brooding on the crest of the hill like a fortress. Lights were still on in a few of the rooms. Rectangles gleamed in the double glass doors.

Nina saw first. She didn't speak, or make a sound of any kind, she just stopped breathing. Heather and Pablo wandered into view.

At first I thought they must have had a lover's tiff. He had unwrapped his arm from round her waist and they weren't even holding hands. Then the Rehearsal-Room light licked over them and I stopped breathing too. The woman I had thought was Heather was Lou, and Philip was the man.

They walked slowly, even through the light, so slowly that Lou looked as though, at any moment, transferring her weight from one foot to the other, she might lose her balance completely and fall. As though walking were no longer a natural physical act but rather one which required her full attention. They veered left and right with every step, swinging sometimes together, sometimes apart as they approached the path. Lou's arms were folded across her chest. Philip gripped his hands behind his back. They stared at the ground ahead and as they wound closer we could hear the swish of the grass beneath their feet. His jacket creaked. Her black skirt caught against itself and brushed between her legs.

For a long time neither of them spoke. Then, as they reached the path, Philip asked if she'd be in trouble for staying out late. He sounded softly matter-of-fact. Lou looked up, blinking into the light ahead. She felt her feet on the tarmac and stopped, disorientated. 'What time is it?'

'Nearly ten.'

'I'll be OK.' They were moving faster now, towards us, side by side along the narrow path. Philip let his hand swing loose, relaxing in the safety of the light and glancing at her, just quickly, just once. They turned the corner, disappeared from sight.

Nina and I held still, following them in our imagination. Slowly my feet came back to life. Nina's teeth chattered.

'Did you know about this?' she said at last.

I shook my head. We moved away from the doorstep numbly and headed back along the main path, reckless with surprise, too stunned to notice or care who saw us. We were thinking fast. We shuffled possibilities and reassembled facts. Rewrote recent history. Sometimes I'd blink and everything would slip into real time for a second or two. Then, just as suddenly, I was with Lou again in the Music School and we'd be laughing, scoffing or scowling at Philip behind his back.

Nina rapped at the Study window. The brass latch had been twisted shut, the curtains drawn. Faded roses glowed like bruises through the sun-tattered lining. She rapped again, harder, but no one came and after a while we wandered round to the front door, ready for a bollocking.

Mrs Wilson looked up as we walked in, narrowed her

eyes as though she found it hard to credit our audacity, and glanced at the clock. She was in the middle of Pocket Money. A cashbox and register sat open on the table in front of her and Isobel and Anna Birdwood lounged beside her in a two-person queue.

'We just went to fetch a file,' Nina said quickly, walking by empty-handed. 'For Chemistry tomorrow morning – there's a test.' We carried on, brazenly, towards the stairs. So long as we made it to the landing we would be all right.

'And where do you think you're going to now?'

Nina's left foot had hardly touched the bottom step. She pinched me. We turned on the spot.

'I don't remember either of you asking my permission,' Wilson mused. 'And I've been sitting here the last half-hour.'

Anna's mouth twitched at the thought of what we all knew would be coming next. Isobel grinned openly.

'We didn't think we'd be so long,' Nina began but Mrs Wilson broke her with a look.

'I don't want to hear your explanation, Nina, though I'm sure it's quite convincing. Instead you can both report for extra-work on Wednesday after lunch. One hour each.'

Nina opened her mouth in protest.

'Save it. I've just had Louisa Greene in late with the very same excuse, or maybe you knew. No, you girls have been taking a few too many liberties with the school rules lately and I want it to stop.'

'She knows about the cider.'

'How could she?' I had followed Nina up to her dorm.

I didn't want to have to look at Lou just then. I felt like hiding. 'Want a bath?'

'It's too late now,' she said, kicking off her boots and slumping moodily in front of the mirror. She peeled back her lips, inspecting the pewter-coloured tracks inside.

'*When you're stra-ange*,' Ella and Natasha sang, swaying and twisting along to the music on their beds. Natasha pretended her deodorant bottle was a microphone. She crooned at us through her eyelashes.

'Oh grow up,' Nina snapped.

'Who's in a little bait then?' Ella thudded to the floor and the record skipped. 'What's wrong with *her*?' she mouthed.

I shook my head, curled at the toe-end of Nina's bed. 'Heard anything more about Kate?'

'She's fine,' Natasha said. 'She's going home for a couple of days.'

Nina rolled over and groaned. A hand reached out from under the duvet, fumbling for its watch. I threaded carefully between the lockers and chairs, sat on the edge of the mattress and shook her shoulder.

'I am awake you know,' she yawned. 'I've even had a shower. But it was so bloody cold afterwards and I couldn't think what to wear.' She leaned up on her elbows, blinked at me through a mess of damp-smelling hair, her face already smooth and wide awake, fresh-looking where mine was puffy and stupid with sleep. 'I wanted to nab Lou's skirt.'

'She's gone already,' I whispered. Ella was still asleep. 'Just put on your jeans.'

'They're in the wash.' She sat up, flicked her hair. The knot at the front of her towel had loosened, slipping down her chest.

'So take the skirt.'

'I don't think I could. Not now.' She shuddered. 'Did you talk to her last night?'

'No, everyone was asleep.' I parted the curtains. The sky

was blue, chimneys leaned across the lawn below in crisp black shadows. Nina's mattress creaked as she hauled herself out. She straightened, smiled at her face in the mirror and bared her teeth. Only six months to go, according to the orthodontist. She dreamed of running her tongue along the smooth enamel, like an actor in a Colgate ad.

Outside a slow procession straggled along the path towards the Dining Hall. Harriet and Natasha mooched in front. Natasha was wearing a stretchy white mini-skirt and her knickers showed through. You could see the VPL from here. I turned back to Nina. She'd helped herself to a pair of grey-checked trousers from the cotton heap on Ella's chair.

'Are you ready now?' We were going to miss the poachies. Everyone went to breakfast on poachie days. The trick was to be passing the counter just as Pablo slithered a new batch under the lamp – that way they'd still be runny inside.

'Almost,' she stuck her hand in her mouth, pinched off the exhausted rubber-bands and flicked them at the bin, hooked powdery new ones into place and yawned. The elastic stretched in neat symmetrical parallelograms.

'Maybe we just imagined the whole thing,' I hoped, but Nina shook her head. She shrugged.

'Come on.' We stumbled down to the hall where Valerie sat, in Mrs Wilson's chair, reading the TV page at the back of *The Times*. Walked out into the high bright morning.

Lou spent Tuesday mornings in the Music School so we

only caught up with her at Break. We sat in the Dining Hall, by the fireplace, watching the canteen door. Nina tipped back in her chair, sucking at the rim of her plastic cup. She nudged me as Lou came through the main door, skipping the queue for biscuits, and poured herself an orange squash. She stood alone, scanning the tables. We had decided not to wave, we wanted to observe her, hoped for some kind of confirmation, I suppose. Others were watching, idly, now too. She turned away as Anna Birdwood walked by, laughing. Flicked her hair self-consciously, sipped her squash once, then abandoned it on the corner of the nearest table and turned away, ready to go, as I relented, jumping to my feet and calling out to her, half frantic with sudden, sharp regret.

'Where were you last night?' she said, shuffling between the chairs as though nothing had changed. She crouched on the floor between us, looking up, relieved. 'I thought we were going to do face-packs.'

'We were, but *someone* came back late and then there wasn't time.'

'I wasn't back late,' she blushed. 'Not very.'

'At least you had a responsible adult to see you to the door,' said Nina. 'Much safer, with all those skinheads around.'

'What do you mean?' She looked from Nina's face to mine and back again, screwing her mouth into a kind of breathing question-mark. She tried to look astonished, then outraged.

'You weren't going to tell us, were you?' Nina pounced.

'There's nothing to tell, and how do you know any-way?'

Nina tapped her nose. One by one she dropped her jammy dodgers into her cup, watching the coffee level rise and then fall again slightly as the biscuit dissolved.

'Are you having an affair with him?' I asked.

'Don't be an idiot!' If she had trusted herself to look us in the eye she would have known then we didn't believe a word of it. 'He walked me back because it was late and we'd been in the Music School, *practising*—'

'Yeah, right.' Nina stood up to go. Ella was pissed off about the trousers, she had to change. 'Coming?'

Lou trailed after us into the Quad. 'There's nothing going on, I swear,' she insisted as Nina marched ahead, leaving me stranded between them at the top of the Changing-Room steps. 'Why does everyone assume that every time a man and a woman have a conversation they must be having sex as well?' she complained. 'It's so *adolescent*.'

On House we slipped into the single bathroom for a fag. I rolled my cardigan under the door and Lou opened the window. We shared one, looked in the mir-ror, blew Marilyn Monroe air-kisses. Afterwards we cleaned our teeth and squirted on more perfume. Lou flapped my cardigan, wafting smoke into the oxygenless morning air.

'You smell like a tart's window-box,' Nina sniffed when I dropped in to fetch her for Chemistry. Matron tutted past us on her way to P Dorm where Catherine Scott was

ill in bed with a septic ear. The corridor reeked of cigarettes.

'I hope you've been practising the Romance?' Philip
smiled, tuning my violin for Orchestra.

'Not like you have,' I mumbled, shrugging.

'What?'

'Never mind.' I stared at him, fluttered my eyelashes. 'I
didn't say anything important.' The D string slipped,
twanging like flat elastic and he looked away. The bridge
creaked as he tightened it again. Hermione had opened the
windows. Birds sang in the apple trees, hidden behind a
swirl of leaf. The Rehearsal Room hummed with girls.
Rossini today: the timps were out. Philip and Lou pretended not to be watching each other's every move. They
milled between the music stands in an elaborate, halting
dance.

The kettle screams. Lou is breathing a sirocco in my ear. Fragments of mud and grit stick to the side of her face where it lay pressed against the sweaty deck. Her blanket lies rumpled and ticklish between us, and her hair smells diesely. She whimpers as I lift myself to my feet, then mutters 'Fuck' in a normal voice, opens her eyes and sits up, wide awake. Behind us Nina pours boiling water into three mugs of Nescafé and bites the last peach. She's slicked back her hair in shiny black furrows, water-spots dapple her linen shirt, and her forearms bristle in the shade of the saloon. She must have washed very quietly. 'Afternoon,' she murmurs cheerily as I stagger through to the shower-room. My dehydrated brain seems to have glued itself to the inner left wall of my skull. It lolls like a jelly-cube stuck to the side of a mixing jug, sagging and wobbling with every step.

Water on the bathroom floor soaks my socks and the mirror is fogged. Nina has left her watch by the soapdish at the edge of the basin. It's quarter past twelve. I wonder suddenly if Caroline Price has got her A's. She'd always wanted to be a vet but something about her laugh, her hair and the size of her tits meant no one thought she could be serious. She'd had blue eyes, and eyelashes that clung together after Swimming in lazy curling triangles and for a moment I missed her with a kind of physical regret, the way you always end up missing what you used to ignore. Lou sips at her steaming coffee. She's feeling sick, she says. We all are.

Locking the boat, we troupe past chewing cows and up to the bridge. Coins tap in the pocket of Nina's cut-off jeans, their rhythm building up in our heads like a marching song as we head towards the village, towards the phone box, hurrying reluctantly. No one links arms.

'What if it's out of order?' says Lou as the bridleway filters into tarmac. We huddle in the dusty verge and a Land Rover whooshes by. Whispers of straw flutter loose from bails on the back seat, landing in a golden trail. Lou veers into the middle of the road, balancing along the dotted white line, arms out, like a tightrope walker. The road grows wider, neat grass smoothes suburban banks. Ahead of us, the telephone box appears to glow.

'Who's going first?' says Nina, knowing full well it will have to be her. Lou and I wait outside. We sit on the lawn with our backs to the glass, picking daisies, slitting our thumbnails down their hairy stems to make a chain. When Nina comes out again it's more than a handspan long. The door creaks, we can hear her crossing the grass. 'Next please,' she announces in the voice of one who hasn't been marked as low as 'B' since she was thirteen years old. We let ourselves steal a glance at her wide delighted grin.

'You go.' Lou stretches luxuriously, lies back with her

eyes shut, sunbathing. These days she's good at pretending not to care. The daisy chain sprawls in kinks across her bumpy midriff. Nina chucks some coins.

'It eats up money,' she beams.

Amazing, I think, dialling home: a phone box with no graffiti. Someone's even left telephone directories, unchained, for general public convenience. No cobwebs either. Through the glass Nina and Lou look clean and clear. They are ignoring each other, their eyes are closed but Nina can't stop smiling. 'Mum?' The envelope flicks and tears and I wonder if Dad's paper-knife has sliced through Nina's careful smiley face. The print-out trembles in my mother's hands. She holds her breath as she reads. Then: 'Well done, darling.' Her sigh into the receiver tickles my ears. I dance across the grass to Lou, who opens a single, questioning eye.

'Your turn. Fingers crossed.'

'Congratulations,' Nina says when Lou has gone.

'Congratulations yourself.' I topple beside her, lie on my back stamping the ground. Nina wraps the daisy chain twice round her wrist, tucking the loose ends under and round. She shakes it in the sunlight.

'Don't you know how to finish it?' I hold out a trembling hand.

'Of course I do.' We banter happily, trade cheerful slights, concentrating only on the genuinely trivial. I stare at the sun and the sky turns giddy. Splodges of colour – insubstantial reds and greens evaporating into patches of white, a shade of bliss – float across its blue.

Lou sticks her head out from the door of the telephone box. 'They're engaged,' she wails.

'So try again.'

'I have. I need a fag.' She comes back, lights up, pacing. I've never seen a cigarette turn to ash so fast. She stubs it out on the yellow of a daisy, rolls her shirt-sleeves, marches back in. This time Nina and I allow ourselves to watch as she lifts the receiver, slots in her 50p and waits for the tone. Her lips are still and after half a minute she slams the phone down again and pushes out, kicking the slow door shut behind her, white with sudden rage.

'You know, this is so fucking typical of Mum,' she mutters savagely, pinching a second cigarette from the packet and striking a match. It snaps. She's scraped off half the gunpowder. I flick my Zippo. 'She knows I'll be trying to phone.' She tries again, flings the receiver down and shouts through a crack in the door, 'And now it's bloody eaten my money!'

'Press the reject button,' Nina says helpfully.

'Fuck off – I'm not a total fuck-wit, you know.'

Bollard handed us dustbin-liners for extra-work. 'Start with the flowerbeds outside the English Block, work round to Science, the Music School, Art and Design and the car park. I'll be checking up on you from time to time,' she said, 'so no dawdling.'

The black bags fluttered behind us, snickered like devil-wings, uncreasing, fresh from the chrysalis. 'There was a man Maths teacher once,' said Nina, 'who shagged the Head Girl.'

'Really? Here? When?'

'I don't know. They got married, I think.'

'But Lou's only fourteen.' Sometimes, even to each other, we seemed very young.

'Same age as Juliet.'

'Juliet?'

'As in *Romeo and*.'

'He's taking advantage of her. She's just a kid. She doesn't know what she's doing.'

'You just wish he was taking advantage of you.' Nina

pinched a Mars bar wrapper from beneath the leaves of a curry plant outside the English Block, released it with a gesture of grand indifference into her billowing bag.

When no one was looking we distributed the contents of the Admin Block bin between our two black sacks and trailed across the Orchard to the Science Block, stepping fag ends into the mud rather than having to pick them up. Two laps of the Music School, one outside, one in, yielded a clutch of ring-pulls, a crushed Coke can, the gold foil from a bar of Dairy Milk, a Rolo wrapper and a box of matches, which I kept for later. Lou was practising, alone, in Philip's room. She stood with her back to us. Beethoven muffled through the glass.

'That's the piece,' I said to Nina. 'Isn't it beautiful?'

'Hollywood music,' Nina sneered.

One Friday morning Philip drew up the piano stool for me to sit on. 'No, don't open your case just yet,' he said, adopting his favourite position, one leg draped against the radiator, even though the heating had been switched off months ago. He looked seriously into my eyes, folded his arms across his chest and wondered where to begin. 'Is everything all right?' he tried.

Too general. He'd have to come up with something more inspired than that. I answered with a vaguely mocking nod.

'You seem upset.'

'I'm fine,' I smiled.

'Be straight with me, Beth.'

My eyes were shiny like mirrors, throwing back at him his sympathetic look. 'I am. I'm fine.'

'So you're not angry about anything?'

'Like what?'

'I don't know,' he sighed. 'You tell me.'

'No. I'm not angry.'

'Good.' For a moment I thought the heart-to-heart must be over. Then he refolded his arms, right over left this time, as though there was some other matter he wanted to discuss. He tipped his head on one side. Looked even more serious, even more quizzical than before. The trick with caring-sharing teachers is to let them take their time. The more you rush, the more they think you're trying to hide. You have to give them their say, appear to be listening with an open mind, that way they imagine it's gone in.

'I need to ask you a favour,' he said at last. 'It's about Lou.'

What a surprise, I nearly said out loud. Nowadays everything revolved around Lou. I wondered if Anna Birdwood had noticed too, or was it just me he'd lost interest in? He'd abandoned the staccato technique and put me back on Kreutzer and Bach. His enthusiasm had been replaced with mild despair. He'd given up telling me I could be as good as Lou. He didn't yell, '*Bounce the bow!*' or shout when I forgot to bring a pencil. He didn't wince at my intonation or chuckle with delight as he worked out clever new fingerings. He didn't tell me my vibrato jerked. He didn't flinch when my bow scuffed crossing the strings or exclaim, when nothing had gone too badly wrong for several minutes, '*Now you're playing! At last!*' He didn't check I was practising, or want to know what I had worked on over the previous week. Instead he asked if I was 'well', and from the tone of his voice I knew he wasn't really interested in the reply. Nothing I did could disappoint him any more. I'd lost him. It was as simple, as severe as that.

Three or four times a day I determined to win him back, then changed my mind and vowed to boycott our lessons for the rest of term. I'd walk right past his window, go to the Beech Trees and sunbathe instead. Take shelter and smoke if it rained. My hair would rat-tail down my back and plaster my forehead. My face would be pale yet flushed, almost tuberculoid, and when he came crashing through the undergrowth, stumbling and sliding on the wet grass, drenched to the skin, he'd be delirious with joy at having found me safe at last. In spite of himself he would admire my reckless disregard for school rules and I'd accept his jacket, shivering as he placed it across my shoulders, momentarily overpowered by the musky, animal smell of the suede. I'd walk with a haughty self-composure rare in one so young. He'd hold me with a passionate, protective arm and pull me close . . . I hung about in the Music School. I stood in his mirror, practising scales, shuffled my fingertips along the stick until they felt all wrong. Rehearsed a hurt and faintly disapproving smile. For weeks I'd had the feeling tears lurked somewhere at the back of my face. It felt hollow and watery, as though I were about to catch cold. I practised the Kreutzer and the Bach phrase by phrase and bar by bar, hoping he might walk in and be impressed.

For a moment I wondered if he was going to ask me to play go-between.

'She's practising so hard,' he said, 'she's going to kill it. Try and distract her, can't you? And *make her eat.*'

'And you honestly don't fancy him in the slightest?' Nina repeated, shaking her head at Lou, who shrugged uncomfortably. It was hard to be so categorical. There were bits she liked. She liked his hands, the crop of rough, bluish fuzz that spread across his chin in the afternoon. The fact that he was older, she supposed, that a grown man might really be interested in her. She took it as a compliment.

'He's nuts about you, Lou,' I promised. 'He practically told me so.'

'What did he say?' Nina stepped aside to let Miss McKendrick pass on her way to the English Block. 'What did he say?' she asked again as soon as the teacher was out of range.

I looked at the ground, at the cracks in the tarmac path and the trodden-down patches at the sides where grass should have been. I thought of telling a substantial lie. *He wants you to meet him at the Beech Trees, midnight tonight* — something like that. After all, if they loved each other, who was I to stand in their way? No one must ever know the extent of my true emotions. I looked at Lou, linked arms confidingly. 'He said you're killing him.'

'Bollocks.' In spite of herself, she blushed.

Nina performed a half-pirouette and flicked her hair. 'She fancies him, she fancies him,' she sang, skipping away from us towards the Quad. A gaggle of passing Fifths turned to stare, shaking their heads with mock indulgence as Lou's flush deepened.

'Who's the lucky man?' drawled Kate. Since the night of the attack she wouldn't even walk to breakfast in groups of less than three.

'No one,' Lou shook herself free. 'This is getting particularly tedious,' she muttered, running away.

He often stayed late at the Music School, coaching her. They worked on style and interpretation while I listened at the door. His muffled words were heavy with innuendo and for every silence I deduced a kiss. I wondered whether he had found her scar, if he had been allowed to touch it, tried to imagine what music they would play across each other with their quick expressive hands. I knew there was something between them, and I knew I was being ridiculous. She didn't even think he played the violin that brilliantly. He had no feeling for Beethoven's complexity, she said.

To be a great musician, she said, you must also be an intellectual. It's no good hoping the emotion will carry you through, or smothering the piece with sentimentality. At The Covelli Music Academy they had been given reading lists for each of the great composers – to add a philosophical and historical dimension. Now she started reading *Thayer's Life of Beethoven*. Mr Wilkes, the Librarian,

had permitted himself a quick smile, just on the left side of
his mouth, directing her to the relevant bay. Nina bet me a
Mars bar she wouldn't get further than paragraph five, but
week by week the bookmark plodded on. The ends of the
pages crinkled in the bath. Frazzle crumbs thickened the
spine. I left my Mars bar and a coral pink rose nicked from
the bushes at the back of House on Philip's windscreen, like
an out-of-date Valentine.

Everyone seemed to be dieting just then. At half-term
builders had come to put private cubicles in the shower-
room on House. Zoe Ross had been sent home to fatten
up. And it was true, even Lou, the skinniest of us all,
avoided the Dining Hall. I mentioned it to Sophie, who
summoned her up to her study unit for a talk. 'All this crap
about needing to be thin – it's a conspiracy,' she said. 'If you
don't eat, your brain won't work. Your fingers won't work.'
But Lou insisted it had nothing to do with dieting, she just
didn't have time for food when, on top of everything else,
there were end-of-year exams to revise for. Sometimes she
crept through to snatch an apple, or a Marmite sandwich at
Tea. Each week her mum posted a fresh supply of chicken-
flavoured Doll Noodles, Pot Noodles and Cup-a-Soup.
Otherwise it was crisps and chocolate from Tuck.

Her face changed shape and under her eyes the shadows
turned a deeper, darker grey. She looked more nearly beautiful than before – she was a lovelorn heroine, suffering for
her art – and rumours spread from class to class. Anna
Birdwood took particular delight in fleshing out the mass of
circumstantial evidence. She kept her speculations plausible,

that way the make-believe soon hardened into fact. Lou
was horrified.

'Never deny,' said Nina. 'Never deny. Much cleverer to
agree with everything they say and make them feel ridiculous than fuel the controversy by trying to stamp it out.'

Lou scowled through the lecture. She tightened the cord
on her dressing-gown, clutching shampoo, soap and chocolate to her chest. If she didn't go now the bath would
overflow. 'I can't do that – just think what trouble Philip
would be in.'

Nina smoothed her face, let out a patient, saintly sigh.
'Only if it's true,' she said, pronouncing every syllable.

'You can't patronise me, I'm reading *Thayer*,' Lou
snapped. We followed her down the corridor to the bathroom. 'I just don't want to get him in shit.' She shut the
door in our astonished faces. Anna Birdwood swaggered
past on her way to the Study. 'Must be love, love, love,' she
sang.

Lou extinguishes her seventh cigarette. Butts lie scattered in the grass by her feet like spilled chips. She fidgets, picks her fingernails and stares at us resentfully. Only part of this, I guess, is an act. Nina lies propped on a single elbow, snapping off blades of grass into strips of sharp, identical green. When she has collected a handful she'll inch slowly into range and I am waiting for the inevitable lunge.

Lou stands, ready to try again, muttering, 'This is the absolute last bloody time.'

'You said that before,' Nina reminds her. Below us, a green and yellow bus decelerates noisily, pulls in at a shelter almost completely camouflaged with ivy and bindweed. Three old ladies help each other down. One of them carries a walking stick and a dirty-white dog. The other two pull trolleys full, it seems, of scrunched up newspaper. As they shuffle away from us, downhill towards the village, Lou's Mum, Evelyn, gets off the phone to the police. Nina sprinkles my hair with grass, then nudges me in the ribs. 'She's through,' she mouths.

Lou stands neat and still inside the telephone box. After a while her money runs out and her mum rings back. Our stomachs churn. Now I'm the one left chain-smoking. The daisies have wilted in the sun.

'She's getting bollocked, I bet. Mummy's threatening to stop the allowance.'

'Blaming it all on us more like.' I squint at the cornflower-coloured sky as an aeroplane charges silently through billions of billions of particles of gas.

'I can't see why you need A levels to go to Art college anyway.'

'Snob.'

'Do you think she'll do retakes?'

'Might not be that bad—'

'Come on, what else are they talking about?' Nina flicks at a greenfly, leaving a tart yellow smear on her wrist.

'The weather. How much Daddy will get for the boat.' Suddenly a brilliant idea suggests itself. '*You* should buy the boat.'

'You must think I'm insane.'

'Come on – you'd get a discount. It'd be much cheaper than renting rooms. Then we could have sentimental reunions – one a summer till we graduate.'

'Just think how cold it would be in winter, though. And it's much too far away from town. I'd get lonely.'

'There's always Gabriel. You two should be well suited.'

She glares at me, side-on. 'Is that, by any chance, a reference to my height?'

'Actually, I was remembering how good you used to be

at woodwork—' I cower as she throws a second fistful of grass.

'I *was* you know!'

'Bollocks. I was about a million times better than you.'

'That's such a lie. Remember when we had to make dovetail joints and yours wouldn't fasten together and whatshisname held it up in front of the class to demonstrate and all the sawdust sprinkled out.'

Nina looks at me, thinking hard. She blinks and laughs. 'That wasn't *my* dovetail joint, you idiot. It was yours.'

'No it wasn't.'

'Yes it was.' She watches a sequence of pinks with gathering momentum streak across my face: candyfloss, raw salmon, raspberry – the colours of confusion, doubt and, finally, defeat. She's right. I've misremembered. Here I am, about to dedicate my final teenage years to the study of History, and I can't even think back to 1985. 'Anyway, it proves my point about you and Gabriel,' I stammer, looking away.

We moved to the Quad for Orchestra practice. Tomorrow the seating would go up: 25 rows of clip-together, flip-down plastic, stepping up to meet the clock. Underneath, at the back, you could monkey-walk between the bolted props. Everyone looked ill in the concrete light. Finger-joints cracked in the perpetual cold. Kate and a huddle of other Fifths, aimless in the lull between exams, clapped enthusiastically as Lou crossed the floor, the smatter of applause fading fast to hushed embarrassment. Philip tapped his baton, fishing for eyeballs. Then he turned to Lou. 'Are you ready?'

I am a femme fatale. I am reading Thayer. She wrinkled her brow. 'Can I have an A?' She stared at the oboes, then at the viola section in front, at Philip's DMs. Her cheeks were burning but her hands were like icicles and this just a rehearsal – what would her nerves be like the night of the performance? Anna Birdwood pretended to whisper in my ear, distracting her as Philip ran through the tempo, and she had to get him to say it again. A Fourth at the back of the cello section sniggered. *I'm reading Thayer and I can play it twice as fast as that if you want to know. I am the best musician in this room so no one laugh at me.* She looked up, different somehow. At first I thought she was staring at me. Philip stood motionless on the podium, gripping his baton. Lou shouldered her violin. Silver strings bit into the finger-board.

Nina hurled into my dorm. 'Where's Lou?' she demanded.

'In the bath as usual, where else?' Still warm, a heap of clothes and underwear lay on the floor by her chest of drawers. I scraped the mascara from my eyelids with a fold of bogpaper dipped in Ponds and threw it at the bin, trailing after her. A sea of Fourths parted reluctantly, stepping aside to let me through.

'Tell Nina to look where the fuck she's going next time,' said Millie, stuffing biros and cartridges back into her pencil case. I crossed the landing, knocked on the bathroom door.

'Lou, is Nina in there?' The tap went quiet, followed by a whispering pause. Someone drew back the bolt and a peach-scented wall of steam spilled into the stairway, choking me. 'What's up?'

'Lock the door.' Nina shuffled back to the loo-cover. She crossed her legs like a buddha, leaning against the water-pipe's fibreglass padded spine, crunching Hula Hoops. Lou lay stretched in an oval of smooth green water, hiding her face with her hands. Scalding forearms covered her lurid chest. A Twix and a Bounty bar melted into their wrappings, layer by layer, between the taps. The tiles were shiny with a million beads of condensation and the window had steamed up. Outside, a slow blue twilight welled and deepened against the glass.

'What's up?' I said again, when neither of them bothered to reply.

'Something *happened*,' Nina said deliciously.

Lou breathed. Tidal-waves rolled down from her heart towards the overflow. Her back and shoulders seemed to glow where Philip had touched her, yes, actually touched her, through her clothes, kneading the soreness away and smothering her muscles with gentle pinches where she'd said it hurt. She didn't dare lean forwards, but how could she wash without us catching sight of the finger marks? Peeling off her T-shirt ready to bathe she'd half expected to find scorch marks patterning the plain blue cloth, for it to tatter and crumble into dust in her hands. If only it had. That way at least she'd know she hadn't been dreaming.

Turn round, he'd told her, placing one hand either side of her neck. Loose strands of hair had caught in the sweat of his fingertips, looping their sharp ends up to tickle her face. She melted and swayed in front of him, swallowing hard as though afraid her ears might pop. A catapulting heart led riots through her chest as she held her breath, silent and terrified by the thought of what might happen next. For a moment she thought she might fart and clenched her buttocks secretly. Then, after a couple of minutes he broke off. *Better?* She turned so they were face to face, standing so close there was nowhere to look but the

hollow just above his collarbone where the skin was tanned
and ruddy, waiting. *I hope I haven't made it worse*, he'd said at
last, stepping back with a quick, self-conscious laugh. She
took a deep breath.

'You should have kissed him,' Nina said, shuddering.

Lou lowered her hands, slowly dipping them in the
water. She wasn't sure. Her old music teachers had touched
her, after all. It was a kind of language to them. And all
term Philip had prodded and brushed and nudged, like a
couturier pinning velvet to a mannequin. *You must remember, Lou, that making music is, first and foremost, physical – like
throwing the discus or riding a horse. Your fingers must be strong
and energetic. Your right arm needs the stamina of a triathlete.
Why do you think the great Kremer, preparing to perform to
thousands in the Festival Hall, stands the same way every Susuki
four-year-old learns to stand in lesson one? It's scientific. This –*
minutely repositioning her foot with the side of his mud-
creased boot – *is the only way to do it. Posture is the origin of
sound.*

It wasn't, of course. She lifted a knee, stretching her leg
like a lady in some shaving commercial. Bath water trickled back into the tub.

'Well?' said Nina.

'I never used to fancy him at all, but now with the solo
and everything—' Lou sighed. 'It's so *intense.*'

I stared at the mouldy, peppermint-coloured pipes below
the washstand, hating them. Nina crunched another Hula
Hoop and shrugged, tipping her head to listen as a pair of
leather shoes marched upstairs, drew briskly to a stop out-

side. Knuckles rapped at the door above my head. Invisible fingers twisted the handle impatiently.

'Won't be long,' called Lou, switching voice.

'It's Mrs Wilson. Let me in now.'

I drew the bolt, stepping aside as she pushed in quickly and looked round, shocked to see the three of us crammed into so small a space. She sniffed. She rummaged beneath the folds of Lou's bath towel with her eyes, inspected our pockets and sleeves for the tell-tale outline of a roonie pack. No one went to the Beech Trees much any more. It was safer, in a way, to smoke indoors.

'Honestly, you've got perfectly good dormitories to chatter in,' she said at last, crossly. 'What *are* you all doing in here?'

It didn't need answering and she was embarrassed now. We waited politely for her to go. Her footsteps faded into the hubbub.

'Better be careful. She's out to get you,' Nina warned then. Looking down, Lou soaped her scar. The water must have been very hot. Her face was throbbing.

Twenty minutes after lights out, House was ours. Goodman and Wilson made one final circuit, admonishing late showerers and threatening the rowdy with extra-work. They sat at the pocket-money table in the hall, skim-reading whatever remained of the morning's newspaper or discussing girls. Gradually the crashes and thuds from the dorms upstairs would dwindle and fade to a fragile, restless quiet. In spite of themselves, Fourths and Fifths would fall

asleep. The housemistresses would check the ground-floor
windows one last time, say goodnight and disappear into
their respective flats, locking the door and snapping out the
lights. This was the moment I waited for. 'Come for a cigarette?' I whispered.

Lou rolled over. 'Haven't got any.'

'I have.' I rattled the matchbox.

'Are you sure they've gone?' She sat up in bed. The buttons on her nightie gleamed. She folded back the covers,
nudged into her slip-ons and shuffled quietly across the
bare boards as I shrugged my coat on over my pyjamas.
Valerie turned on her side with a heavy insomniac sigh as
we closed the door. Shadows slithered up the bannisters
from the blacked-out hall below and timid, jerky footsteps
creaked across the ceiling. It was funny to think of the girls
upstairs creeping from dorm to dorm the same way Lou
and I crept. Whispering to each other identical baseless
reassurances.

We locked ourselves in the loo at the end of the corridor. There was a windowsill – high up but wide enough to
sit on so long as you hugged your legs for balance. Lou
struck a match. The orange walls glowed. Cigarette smoke
drifted in vanishing puffs towards the dim silhouette of an
old iron fire escape. Outside the trees were silent.

'I still can't believe it,' Lou said, speaking at my reflection
in the mirror. 'I mean, teachers don't usually give massages
do they?'

I shrugged, looked down. 'Was it sexy?'

'What do you mean?'

'Did he do it in a sexy sort of way?'

She didn't answer. Maybe she couldn't tell. Instead she blew a smoke ring. It collapsed upon itself in a vaguely circular, exhausted cloud.

'Did he say anything afterwards?'

Lou paused. 'Not much. It was just a bit embarrassing. He's got a girlfriend, you know. An oboe player. Once he told me her name but I've forgotten now. Gwynneth or something—'

'Men always talk about their girlfriends when they want to have sex with someone else,' I muttered glumly. Lou just shrugged. She pushed her foot against the sink, hoisting herself up onto the window ledge. The panes groaned as she leaned against their ancient leading. She didn't bother with *Cosmopolitan* or *Just Seventeen*. It would never occur to her to begin a sentence with the words *Men always*. Fag ash fizzed in a dark grey smudge at the rim of the plug-hole.

Unbolting the loo door, swinging it wide in the face of a ghost that looked like Mrs Wilson only without the make-up, two-dimensional somehow, the first thing I thought was *How much has she heard?* Only then did I remember why she must be standing there. Compared with what Philip may or may not have intended massaging Lou, the possession and smoking of cigarettes seemed like a trivial offence, but suddenly the air in the corridor was too hot to breathe. The smoke we had so carefully exhaled through the open cubicle window seemed to waft back in, like dry ice in the disco sequences on *Top of the Pops*, betraying us.

Wilson said, 'Come out here where I can see you.' She

wore a long plaid dressing-gown. Her face was pale and shiny with night cream, her quiet voice flat with disappointment. I had imagined the corners of her mouth would curl up, witchy and cruel and satisfied, but nothing in her face could be described as even remotely triumphant as she turned away from us – more like sad, or tired, or bored. Lou's hand reached for mine in the darkness, grabbing it and squeezing hard. Colgate spread its sticky, minty mess across the tips of her fingers. She looked at me for half a second, less than that, questioning. I blinked and it was done. Our fingers separated, mine to hide the toothpaste tube, forcing it through the hole in my coat-pocket lining, hers to her mouth.

At the stop of the stairs, by K Dorm, our silent procession stopped. Wilson peered into our faces, one by one. The landing light gave her yellow skin. She might have been dead for centuries. I clenched my shaking hands behind my back and took a breath. The passageway tasted of stale tobacco. Lou's mum and dad were going to freak.

'You know the punishment for smoking, don't you?' Wilson seemed to chant.

'Lou wasn't smoking. She doesn't smoke,' I said out loud, looking her straight in the eye for honesty. Wilson sighed. How many times had she been through this performance?

'I couldn't sleep,' Lou explained. 'I've been worrying about the concert. Smell my breath if you don't believe me.'

'Thank you, I already can. Go to bed. You can expect to have to account for yourself to Dr Goodman in the morning.'

'Yes Mrs Wilson. Sorry. Goodnight.'

The housemistress refocussed her attention on me. 'Empty your pockets.' Into her receiving hands I piled a biro lid, a tissue, an old cotton-wool bud, a box of matches and three spare Tampax. I turned the linings inside out. 'Where are your cigarettes?' she asked.

'That was my last. I was going to give up. I know how bad it is for you—'

'I'm sure your mother and father will be pleased to hear it.'

A small voice, scratchy with hope and desperation, trembled through my heart attack. 'Do you really have to tell them?'

'How else should I account for the fact that I'm suspending you?'

As a matter of fact, Lou's A levels aren't that bad. They certainly don't seem to justify the expression on her face as she drags towards us over the daisy-scattered grass. It's as though her mum has sucked the energy from every cell, it flashes back along the wires, a kind of mouth-to-ear anti-ageing treatment, leaving us the 99% fat-free, freeze-dried shell of an 18-year-old. The phone-box door grinds back on its hinge.

'We have to hurry home,' she says flatly, leaning over us, blocking out the sun. 'Sophie's gone missing and Mum and Dad need to search the boat for clues.'

'What do you mean, *gone missing*?' I squint at her. The sky shines bright and blue behind her, blotting her face. A pigeon swoops in through her ear, then out again the other side, flapping lazily for height.

'She never went to London, apparently. And when Mum and Dad rang the TV place no one there had ever heard of her. They've called her friends but they're as mystified. The last time anyone heard from her was Tuesday afternoon when she rang the college telling them not to forward her post. And guess what – Mum spoke to her Moral Tutor and apparently she didn't even sit Finals, let alone get a First. Turns out they've been worrying what could be going on all last term. Some man, Mum seems to think.' She stuffs her fingers into her pockets, then pulls them out again, examining her nails.

'Is there anything we can do?' Nina holds out a comforting hand, which Lou affects not to notice. She stares at the flattened grass at her feet. This was the moment, looking back on it, when everything changed.

'No. Let's go back to the boat,' she says eventually, calm as ice.

Nina and I trot after her, winded, reaching out with sympathetic little nudges and grasps. We want to cover her with touches. Squeeze and pinch her out of herself until she cries. We want her to speculate horribly, or rage, or laugh it off. *Sophie? Gone?* Instead she gazes into the middle distance, face expressionless. We need to reason with her: whatever she's imagining it can't be that bad and Nina and I have results to celebrate. It's not that we're impatient or anything, but why did this have to happen now? We grab her arms, walk three abreast along the middle of the lane. '*What exactly did your mum say?*'

'*Have they been to the police?*'

'*Oh Lou, she'll be OK. I'm sure there's just been some misunderstanding –*'

'*Maybe she's gone off on holiday –*'

Lou blinks. We won't let go. When cars come we lean into the prickly verge like runaway prisoners, manacled all for one.

They banned me from the premises for 48 hours. *Next time*, the Head blinked, *it would be 72*. Then 96 and so on until my fourth offence, at which point I would be asked to leave for ever. 'We believe in giving our girls a chance,' she said, nodding me out. 'I hope you will have something more constructive to offer the school when you return.'

I closed the door quietly. Lou still leaned against the waiting-room wall, her forehead to the window, fingering the calloused leaves of a yucca plant. 'Well?'

I shrugged. The taxi would be here any minute and I still hadn't packed. We took a detour through the English Block. At least I could spend the time revising for exams. 'What did Dr Goodman say?'

Lou grinned. 'Just a whole load of crap about choosing my friends more carefully – where do they get it from?' She slotted her arm through mine. 'By the way, Nina says to say she told you so.'

'So much for martyrdom!'

Lou's face twisted into an awkward smile. She hadn't

expected me to rush to her defence – by daylight it seemed almost embarrassing, as though I'd made some formal declaration of loyalty which both of us knew she'd never reciprocate. 'What will your parents say?'

I shrugged. What would anyone's parents say?

'Mine would have taken me away.'

'I know.'

She stayed with me through Break and waved me off as the taxi rolled over the ramps, the indicator blinking left for town. I sat in the front without my seatbelt fastened, wishing we could crash. Not even Dad would be mean enough to bollock me in hospital.

Suspension, I discovered, was like being ill, when you feel bad but not too bad to lie on the sofa watching *Sesame Street*. I was aware of it all the time, the way you are aware of a swallowed paracetamol, stuck halfway down your throat. The chalky edges of my disgrace jammed solid and wouldn't go down.

I sat in the kitchen, staring across a rainy patio and through the trellis into an equally rainy patio next door. Meg and Steve, my guardians, left for work at eight o'clock and, in theory, I had the house to myself all day. In practice, neighbours kept dropping round, and the phone rang every other hour. Steve had managed to persuade Meg that it would have been inhumane not to give me a set of keys – *what if she needs to pop round to the corner shop for a pint of milk, a KitKat, or twenty B&H?* – and this was the penalty. She seemed to think I was about to bunk off, jump on a bus and spend the afternoon wandering up and down Oxford

Street enjoying myself. The fact that I had come away from Hawkley with precisely £1.76 didn't appear to change her mind. She was pissed off, I suppose. She'd read about teenage rebellions in the Sunday supplements – celebrity columnists wingeing on and on about their kids, their sisters' kids, the kids from the estate across the road – but if I had to smoke the very least I could do was make a reasonable effort not to inconvenience them by getting caught. Four years ago, when Mum and Dad first asked them to be my guardians – *it's just a formality, really* – no one had mentioned anything like this.

'You've done it now,' Dad blustered on the phone. Long-distance, he sounded so close. 'Consider your copy-book permanently blotted. We are never going to live this down. I hope you're proud of yourself because people will remember for years, you mark my words. It'll crop up on every school report, and you might as well forget about Cambridge—' The connection hissed as Mum picked up in the bedroom. Her breathing sounded light and calm, the way it sounded last year when she rang to tell me Bendico had been put down.

'That's enough, Hugh, let me speak to her.' Dad's end clicked. The paracetamol bobbed again at the back of my throat. 'Beth, are you there?' I swallowed. 'Don't pay too much attention to your dad, he's just upset. We both are, you silly girl. You know why you mustn't smoke, don't you!'

'I'm sorry.'

'Every day doctors are discovering more bad things it

does to you.' In spite of myself I sniffed. 'I want you to promise me you'll stop at once.'

'I have.'

She hesitated. 'Go on, tell me you promise.'

I crossed my fingers, twice on each hand.

The world is divided into cowards and braves and there's no telling which you'll be until the instant everything falls apart and instinct takes over. Everyone knows this. Growing up we wait and wait for the moment. Sometimes it never comes. Hour after hour I sat in Meg and Steve's kitchen, running through those three or four seconds at the top of the stairs, by K Dorm, over and over again. Committing them to memory I thought how everyone deserves a friend like me.

I bought a packet of ten at Waterloo and arranged my knees, ladylike, in the smoking compartment, watching as the Thames slipped by. Getting back to Hawkley felt like a homecoming. I squinted through the trees at Farham for a glimpse of the off-licence. The sun must have been shining while I was away. In two days the wheatfields had turned from blue to golden green. Dusty-leaved poplars shivered as the train swept past and in the yard outside the paper factory the stacked pallets hardened and bleached into kindling. Nina and Lou would be in Library right now. I hoped they'd missed me.

The platform was bare, so blindingly bright I dropped my ticket and had to fumble for it on the hot concrete, while the guard watched from his little booth, clicking his cutter to the tune of *Three Blind Mice*.

'You're not one of these drug-takers, then?' The taxi
driver examined my pupils while we waited for the barriers
to lift. He pointed at the newspaper rolled on his dashboard.
'Five sixth-formers, expelled for using marijuana,' he
summarised. 'Page three.' It was the *Gazette*. A shot of
the Head, cut out from last year's whole school
photograph and enlarged to 3 × 4, stared kind but stern
from the headline. The journalist didn't give names. A car
behind us honked as the gates went up. 'It was in the *Daily
Mail* this morning too.' He peered at me for a reaction.
'Hadn't you heard?'

Away from town the lane wound sickeningly. I stared
straight ahead. The village shop flickered by, then Miss
Dudley's house, the turn-off to the woods and the Blue
Pool. We passed the war memorial. Someone had scrubbed
the birdshit off the Hawkley sign, ready for Parents' Day,
and there was a notice I had never seen before – School:
Please Drive Carefully, it said, in bright red capitals –
knocked into the verge. Morning lessons weren't quite over
yet, the place looked deserted. A tractor hummed up and
down House Lawn, striping the grass, and Matron stood by
the front door waving to Dr Slime. His car door slammed.

'Sorry to be back?' she smiled, as though I'd gone to
Paris, or been lying in the shade of a palm tree on some
tropical island sipping rum.

I waited for the taxi to drive away. 'Is it true – about the
drugs?'

She nodded, folding her hands. 'I hope *you* never try
anything as dumb as that!'

I dragged upstairs to dump my bags. If I was quick I might catch Nina in Break. She'd know what had been going on. She'd talk.

Lou sat cross-legged on my bed. 'I borrowed your sweat-shirt – hope you don't mind.' She held out a handful of coconut rings, nicked from Break.

'No thanks,' I rubbed my gums with toothpaste, flopping across the mattress next to her. My duvet felt cold and it didn't smell right. It smelled as though a stranger had been sleeping there.

Lou looked down at me, munching urgently. 'Have you heard?'

'A bit.' I arched back, stretching. Upside down the dorm looked cold and white. Beds and locker-tops darkened a floorboard ceiling.

'The cleaners found it in Heather Allen's drawer in her study-unit the day you left. Goodman managed to talk her into ratting up the others. The only one they didn't catch was Guess Who.'

'Who?'

Lou leaned over, whispering. 'My sister. Nina says she knows for a fact that she was involved.'

'You're joking—'

'On my life, I swear. Can you believe it! God, she's lucky – the police were here and everything. It's been a nightmare – everyone going round blotchy with tears. They've had a crack-down on fags as well and yesterday Harriet threw an egg at the Head.'

'*You're joking!*'

'Don't worry, she missed. But Philip's devastated. Half the orchestra's gone, just like that. And be warned – he's not best pleased with you either.'

I sat up. 'What have I done wrong now?'

Lou shrugged. 'Missed a rehearsal. Come on, or we'll be late for Geography.' A shoulder-bone clicked as she heaved me up from the bed.

'Sounds like you need another massage,' I teased.

'Oh God,' she glared at me, half laughing, half stern. 'Don't you start!'

'Start what?' I batted my eyelashes.

'Nina told Natasha who told Wormwood. Everyone knows now.'

Somehow Nina managed to avoid me until just before Games. I found her in the Changing Room. 'We're doing the eight hundred this afternoon. *Fun!*' She clipped her gleaming hair into a ponytail. Double-bows lolled above the grass stains on her nearly new Green Flash. One pink and one blue pompom peeped round her ankles at the back of each shoe. Below her pleated grey skirt her legs were smooth and shiny and beginning to tan.

'Did you miss me?' I asked, ignoring the scowl Bollard directed at my late arrival, my state of dress.

'Not particularly. Too much going on.' She smiled again at her reflection in the mirror. 'You better get changed.'

'Lou says you told Natasha about the massage.'

Nina shrugged. 'She didn't really mind. And anyway, I found out something juicy in return.' She glanced over her shoulder. Bollard's glower darkened the lockers behind. 'Apparently Pablo didn't sell the drugs.'

'I never thought he had.'

'Where have you *been* the last few days?' Nina rolled her eyes.

'London, where do you bloody well think?'

She blinked. 'Better go back there, then, and fetch your sense of humour.'

'Piss off. So who did sell them?'

'I don't know. It could be anyone. The kind of person you'd least expect.'

'Like?' I suspected she knew better than she was letting on. She flicked her ponytail and tapped her nose. Bollard breathed into her whistle.

Once around the hockey pitches is bad enough. Twice kills. Sweat runs into the eyes and you begin to glow and each breath rasps through the chest like a rusty saw. The running track bulges, black and red hallucinations dot the view. I didn't know it then, but the 800 metres would come back to challenge me every summer for the next four years. And every time, remembering that afternoon, I wondered again who Nina could have meant. In Fourth I volunteered to work the stopwatch while Bollard recorded times in her attendance register, but Caroline stepped in at the end and I had to go round alone with everyone watching and shouting and Bollard's voice ringing out loud and clear above the others, 'Run, girl! That'll shake the tar from your lungs!' She knew how much I hated it and if I managed to produce an Off-Games note for the appointed day she'd blow her whistle, gathering the class, and announce a change of plan. 'Beth can't run with us this afternoon. Get into pairs.' And everyone would cheer because that meant tennis for an hour instead.

We warmed up in the shady corner of the hockey pitch, not far from the Music School. Philip and Mrs Wilson were arguing in the Rehearsal Room. The sound of their voices drifted across the long jump, through the apple trees.

We set off immediately. Lou takes the tiller. Reeds slip under in our wake, resurfacing shiny with canal-lick as ducks and moorhens bob in the shallows. Water bubbles tick and pop behind the engine. The canal is glassy and monotonous with heat. Electric blue. Algae glows green and fish leap under the bank. Nina arranges herself on a blanket across the coach-roof, sunbathing. She closes her eyes, imagines she's in another country, far away. The painted iron panels are a warm, almost deserted sandy beach. Gentle waves laze and spill in the distance. Robert is there. A breeze ruffles the coconut palms and the hairs along her forearms curl and bleach. She feels her collarbone burning.

Lou still stares ahead. I want to be there for her, ready to listen the moment she decides to speak, but tire of waiting. Flopped in the shade, on Nina's bed, I day-dream as the sky backs off through the cabin door and passing branches loom then disappear. Philip, whose face I can picture only by accident now – it's been so long – recognises us and winks as he takes his bow. I gaze at Lou's hand, resting on the tiller, her anxious silhouette, and suddenly it's obvious. Gabriel and Sophie. That's what he was trying to say last night. *She's fine. She's coming with me. We'll send you a postcard from across the world.*

I wake up dizzy. The afternoon is so hot Nina thinks seriously of jumping in. She crouches on the side-deck, cooling one set of toes at a time, kicking at twigs and waterlilies as we motor by. Footprints pepper the decks with leaf-mulch as she steps the canal's dank gently rotting perfume into every room. She ties an old handkerchief round her too-heavy hair, rubs suntan lotion into her shoulders. Uncorking the last of the wine, she empties it into three tall glasses, scrapes in ice from the bottom of the freezer, but celebration seems unthinkable now. Lou doesn't even notice hers. Her eyes are fastened on the waterway ahead. The ice melts quickly, leaving a heap of scale at the bottom of the glass. Fruitflies paddle up the curve of the meniscus. Silently we work the locks.

'She's going to get sunstroke. She should take a rest,' Nina says, inching her sun-blanket further from the engine's growl. 'I'd actually quite like another go at driving.'

'Aren't you bored, Lou? Want to swap for a bit?' we suggest every half-hour. I hover beside her, imagining it a companionable silence. Sunlight glitters on the water, silvers our arms and feet with scars of flickering white. Suzanne Vega tinkles intermittently from the ghettoblaster by Nina's side. Her glass lies empty, rolled against the handrail.

'Lou, do you want your wine?' she calls.

I pass it on: 'Did you hear? She says do you want your wine.'

Lou blinks and shakes her head.

'You sure?'

'Yes.' The syllable sounds cold in her mouth, like a pebble.

'Is there anything I can do?'

'About what?' She looks at me, pleading dumbly. 'I'm OK. I just need space. To think, you know.'

'I'll go then.'

She nods, interrupting herself with a single word. 'Gabriel?'

'I think so. Will you tell your mum and dad?'

She shrugs. The deck is hot beneath my feet, the handrail hotter. Suzanne Vega sings louder now. Nina and I share Lou's wine, picking out the flies, wiping them on the hem of our shorts. 'Do you think Sophie's all right?' she wonders quietly in the gap between songs. 'Maybe she's been kidnapped.'

'Come off it, the Greenes aren't that rich.'

'What then?'

'I think she fell in love.'

'I can't believe she didn't sit Finals.'

Of course you can't, I think, remembering how Anna Birdwood had crowed all term, once, for getting a Distinction to my Merit in Grade Six violin. 'I'd rather fail than get a mediocre pass,' she'd gloated. 'That way at least no one can think you've tried.' A tanker crosses the road-bridge ahead of us, its aluminium sides flash suddenly in the sun. I wipe the sweat from my forehead.

'She had everything,' says Nina.

'So do you.'

'And so do you.' Our voices echo through the tunnel. Goose pimples creep up our arms in the concrete chill.

Arriving by dusk, we moor alongside a redeveloped wharf. One of the warehouses has been converted into flats. Geraniums and pansies cluster in pots on the show-home balcony one floor up. Below them coach doors open to reveal a craft shop selling enamelled water-jugs and knotted rope. A toddler stands sandwiched between his parents on the quay, dazzled by the boats, a stream of melted vanilla ice-cream running down his chin and T-shirt. Dusty rainbows glitter at the back of the boat and the sun hangs low and crimson in an almost colourless sky. I prop myself against the deck-rail, smoking. In front of me the water, sky and sun all wait their turn to disappear. Cloud-wisps burn with apprehension. The air is warm like a bath, and every move kicks up a swirling, feathery aftermath of dust. Traces of perfume, faint and unexpected, stir a thousand insignificant thoughts as Nina wanders out. My lungs are aching with vague, pre-emptive regret.

She's showered and changed her clothes. Her last clean T-shirt, creased and gritty from the bottom of the bag, flatters the afternoon's tan. She glows. Her squeaky hair lies in dark, neat parallels. Slowly, as the evening closes in, their edges will crisp and crumble, loose strands fly away. She crosses the deck and leans beside me, so close our shoulders brush. Before she speaks she weighs, quite carefully, which words to use.

'Could you and Lou drive the boat on your own, d'you reckon?' Her quiet voice is minty with toothpaste. 'I was thinking I might go home. There's a station here. I can get a connecting train to Oxford.'

'What about Lou? You can't leave her, not now.'

'You know, Lou and I were never that good friends.' She moves away from me, turns round, staring back into the saloon so there's no chance, not even a remote possibility, that our eyes might meet. 'Sometimes I think I only bothered with her because she was so brilliant.'

'I had no idea you were that cynical that young.'

'Come off it, Beth, everyone gets turned on by talent. Don't tell me you never hoped a bit of what she had might rub off. You loved going round with her — bathing in her reflected glory or whatever you say. We were only kids, it doesn't matter, but you did, of course you did.'

I drop my fag butt. It floats, is motionless, slowly absorbing the canal. A seagull flaps low above the water — creaking, heavy and grey. The water-pump groans as Nina wanders into the saloon, tired and embarrassed by her little speech. Long ago, whole seconds ago, she must have realised there could be no reply. Leaving tomorrow is an act of betrayal no matter what she says and trying to make me hate her for it just won't work.

'Got any moisturiser?' Lou stands shadowy in the

doorway, fresh from the shower and blushing to have spoken after so many hours of silence.

I smile at her. 'Look in my bag – have you burned?'

'That's one way of putting it!'

'I've got some after-sun if you like – jojoba something. I'll get it for you.' Nina's feet slap the lino. Her voice rings with its usual affectionate, half-secretive, half-mocking catch.

'Thanks.' Lou runs herself a drink. She watches me pass through to the bunks, undressing. 'You weren't going to have a shower, were you? Only the hot water's all gone.'

Giddy with the forgotten steadiness of dry land, we swerve across the pavements, following brown tourist signs to the Shelton Civic Hall. We're early for night-life, but the shops are shut. The scent of barbeques drifts from dry back gardens into the empty street and a rusty white Metro stops at the traffic lights by W H Smith.

Each year Parents' Day began with the arrival of the School Photographer. Notices appeared at strategic points across the grounds demanding the presence of every girl on House Lawn at 11.10 sharp. Trousers and hats would not be tolerated. Nina shouldered my reflection from the mirror, pulling at her skirt to straighten the hem.

'Très chic.'

'Are you sure it's not a bit short?' She twisted, craning for a view from behind.

'I thought you wanted us to see your pants.'

'You're such a fucking prude.' Wallpaper poppies faded as the sun went in and bright screams drifted across the lawn as early arrivals milled between the gym-benches, tables and chairs. A stream of Fifths trailed from the Geography Block with yet more furniture. I checked my watch. Nina was changing again. Now we both wore Laura Ashley dresses, long and flowery and smelling of shop. She sneered in the mirror, back-combed her hair. 'Satisfied?' She bobbed a curtsy, breaking her pout with a quick sarcastic smile. We threw on overcoats, fancying ourselves as French Resistance heroines, and swooshed downstairs.

The lawn was crowded now, dizzy with chatter. Someone had fetched a whistle for Bollard and she strutted along the tables like a lion-tamer, cracking an imaginary whip as Wilson bustled, directing us into years. 'Thirds over there by Miss McKendrick.' She pointed at a faraway figure waving from the shade of the oak. Slowly our year arranged itself in order of height. Isobel King, the tallest, crowed and waved at Caroline, five heads back. Best friends separated, moaning bitterly.

'Jesus, it's only a photograph.' Nina and I unlinked and mooched in opposite directions.

'Back to your places NOW,' McKendrick yelled as the middle of the line broke into a rebellious conga. She picked up again, checking names off the register. 'Where's Lou?' A conspiracy of muffled snorts followed the silence and she frowned at me.

I shrugged. 'I'll fetch her, shall I?' But McKendrick shook her head. She walked along the line numbering us, one-two, one-two, all the way down. Almost suddenly the lawn fell quiet. Fifths were already filing tentatively along the tables at the back of the stand. The Fourths stepped up onto chairs in front of them and Ella got extra-work for pushing Valerie. Someone wolf-whistled as Philip and Lou appeared from the path behind the Library. They separated. Miss McKendrick waved and glowered at Lou.

'Where have you been?' she snapped.

'I didn't know—' Lou gesticulated wildly. She stepped into place ahead of Isobel, caught my eye and grinned.

'Why do *we* have to sit on the grass?' moaned Nina as the number two's trailed off in straggling crocodile. Philip hovered at the edge of the lawn. Next time I looked he was gone. The mistresses had taken all the chairs. Bollard sat on the far right, legs spread in a glowing, shadowy V beneath her pleated skirt. She'd loosened her hair from its usual scraped-back ponytail. Dudley and McKendrick had applied identical lipstick. Mrs Allen sat with her arms crossed high on her chest and a low hiss washed from the back as the Head walked forwards to take her place between Goodman and Wilson, stepping on the hem of Lou's dress as she went.

The photographer held up his hands for quiet. 'Hello again,' he shouted. 'Haven't you all grown since last year!' Nobody laughed. 'OK, let's get this over with, then we can go and have a cup of tea.' He ducked beneath the camera-felt, jostled the tripod, re-emerged looking distinctly ruffled. 'Just to remind you – no sunglasses, please, except for medical reasons. No hats. I want you to look straight ahead and when I hold out my arm like this –' he demonstrated '– I want you all to smile.' As he disappeared again behind the camera 50 or 60 girls reached into their pockets for shades. The arm went out. The camera chugged steadily from right to left and a hush of giggles rippled from the back as Harriet and Kate jumped down, racing to get their mugs in twice.

Parents were due to arrive after Break. Nina, Lou and I

sat on a wall outside the Art Block shivering. Mercedes and BMW Estates bumped into the buttercup field. Millie and Natasha were ushering at the gate. Already the furthest corner of the field was a shining metallic grid. Car bonnets ticked.

'If Mum's wearing her green culottes I think I'm going to die,' said Lou. She wiped a strand of hair from her mouth.

'Are you sure it's OK for me to have lunch with you?' I said again.

'Come to mine if Lou's picnic runs out,' suggested Nina. 'Mum said she was bringing strawberries.'

'Everyone brings strawberries. Oh fuck, here they are.' Lou climbed up on the wall to get a better view of the car. She waved, jumped to the ground and wandered off.

Rainclouds with brilliant white puffy edges chased overhead from House to the Dining Hall. Summer dresses flapped and wound themselves around our legs like salty towels and thrilled titters rippled across the lawn as picnic blankets and tablecloths buckled in the wind. Half-empty paper cups flipped abruptly, scattering wine. Golfing brollies flowered at the first suggestion of rain, snapped back into neatly accordioned buds as the sun came out again. Corkscrews, knives and extra plates were passed from group to group as stressed mums realised what they'd forgotten to pack. Nearly everyone seemed to be eating smoked salmon. Isobel tossed a squeezed-out lemon half over her shoulder at Anna Birdwood. In the flickering shadow of the cherry tree, next to Lou, Emily Waterhouse's family huddled round an earthenware mixing bowl of wholewheat pasta salad.

Lou's mum, Evelyn, helped us to fizzy grape juice while her dad uncorked a bottle of champagne. Sophie tasted it, pulled a face, then swallowed the rest in one when Evelyn wasn't looking. Her father shrugged as she refilled her glass.

'Oh Dad, the concert's not for hours and hours. Please can Beth and I have some wine,' said Lou.

'You just have. *Whine — get it*,' joked Piers.

Lou scowled at the sickly-smelling yellow liquid. 'It's not fair. Everyone else is drinking.'

Evelyn refocussed her attention. 'I'm not having you perform in front of the whole school drunk,' she said.

'So where are these strawberries?' Sophie had pushed her breadcrumbs into a pyramid at the centre of her plate. She couldn't stop fidgeting.

'You'll have to fetch them,' Evelyn threw her the keys. 'Your idiot father left them in the car. Beth, why don't you go and help her, dear.'

We zigzagged between the picnic rugs. Turning the corner out of sight, she smiled at me. 'Got any fags?'

I nodded, blushed as though the question were in fact a compliment. I wondered where Nina was sitting, hoping she would see. 'Outside or in?'

'Out.'

We wandered up to the Beech Trees, leaning in their shadow, out of the wind. 'Whoever invented the concept of Parents' Day ought to be hung, drawn and quartered,' Sophie said.

'Hanged,' I corrected automatically, kicking myself for having butted in with such a prim irrelevance.

She inhaled. 'Where are your mum and dad?'

'Brussels.'

'God, you don't know how lucky you are.'

'At least it's your last.'

'That's true.' She squinted through the hedge, across the hockey pitch, the orchards, the tennis courts and round to the Music School where a tiny, far-away Philip leaned from his window, staring back. He couldn't see what he was looking at. 'Will Lou be brilliant tonight?'

'Isn't she always?'

Sophie allowed herself a bitter-sweet smile. 'Stupid question, huh?' She tapped a flutter of ash from the end of her cigarette and far away a window slammed suddenly: cause and effect. 'What did she tell you about her scar?'

I shrugged. 'I can't remember. We don't talk about it.'

'Does she still blame me?'

'She said it was an accident.' I shrugged again.

'Of course.'

Philip gave us an absent-minded nod as we passed him on the path, he seemed to shamble and jerk simultaneously, crippled by nerves.

'Come in with me a second,' said Sophie, forking off for the Music School. 'Just need to pick something up.'

I followed her to the instrument store, watching from the passage way as she scrabbled in her cardigan pocket, feeling for the key. Lou's case was easy to unlock. The silver zips peeled and she reached inside, closing her fist so I wouldn't be able to see what she had taken, though anyone with half an imagination could guess.

'How come you didn't get caught?' I asked on the way to the car park when no one else could have been listening.

'They didn't want to catch me,' Sophie smiled.

Nina stole a bottle of wine. When the clouds opened and everyone scrambled for cover and chaos took control, she pinched it from a cool-box left unguarded by the Study window. She bundled it in her overcoat and smuggled it on House unseen, hiding it beneath her pillow then hurrying back down to the hall where about two hundred squeezed-together parents cheerfully chattered the shower away. The leaded windows fogged. Steam rose from the shoulders and neck of Mr Greene's elegantly tailored cream wool blazer. Tea was served in the Gym. A gang of Fourths had been bribed to help the kitchen staff carry in twelve trestle tables loaded with damp sandwiches and shining chocolate eclairs. Afterwards, the mothers and fathers of unmusical girls were encouraged to leave. For the rest there would be a few hours' lull. Hotels and restaurants in town filled steadily as exhausted parents forced themselves to fit in yet another meal. Lou's family had booked a room in a nearby B&B so Evelyn could change. Nina hopped from foot to foot waiting for them to hurry up and go, then dragged us to her dorm, closing the door mysteriously, and pulled out the wine with a flourish.

She tore the foil and pushed at the cork with the end of her toothbrush, denting the palm of her hand. 'I'll hold, you stamp,' she ordered, kneeling beside the bottle, looking up at me. I pushed down slowly, wobbling and tentative at first, then harder and harder until the cork gave, all at once, in a rush and a geyser vomited white wine down the front of the Laura Ashleys, spattering us to the skin. Lou sprang back. We cursed and laughed and sucked the cotton. Nina rinsed the peppermint smears from her tooth-mug, filled it to the brim. 'Here's to the end of term.'

'Dutch Courage!' said Lou. She only meant to take a sip or two, a glass at most, though it would be hard to measure and Nina kept reaching for the bottle, topping us up. The wine was warm and sour, you had to gulp or retch, and every time they swallowed Nina and Lou made pickled walnut mouths. We had arranged ourselves crosslegged on the floor by Nina's bed and passed the mug like eight-year-olds at a birthday party, waiting for the music to stop. Greedy eyes followed it from hand to hand. When her turn came round, Lou would hesitate. So long as she only sipped in turn she couldn't possibly take more than her fair share and a third of a bottle of wine wasn't much. Two glasses' worth. When her father let her drink at home she had that much easily, or more. It barely affected her. She reached for the empty bottle, studied the label. Maybe this was stronger than the stuff they had at home. Her stomach ached from laughing so much at something Nina had said but now she tried she couldn't seem to remember what. She pinched herself. *Sit up straight.*

Her mind went fuzzy. For a second she thought she might throw up. Someone leaned over her, reeking of alcohol. There was a hand clamped to her forehead and the rim of the enamel mug, heavy with water this time, pushed itself between her lips.

'Drink it!' barked Nina, rummaging through Ella's tuck-box for a jar of Nescafé. 'This'll sober her up.' She sprinkled a tablespoon of granules onto her palm and dropped a pinch onto the tip of Lou's obediently shuddering tongue.

'How about a cold shower?' I suggested.

'Isn't that for men with erections?' sniggered Lou. Nina offered more Nescafé.

We changed into our concert clothes: skirts, as serious and dark as possible, no jewellery, brushed hair. Lou wore a burgundy-coloured velvet dress. Nina walked between us to the Music School. A plastic knife lay white and greasy-looking in the wet grass at the edge of the footpath.

'I can't remember the notes,' said Lou. 'I can't remember how it goes.' Our smart shoes jittered on the tarmac. I hummed the opening bar to calm her down as Anna Birdwood swayed past, overtaking us. 'Good luck, Lou,' she smiled. 'Break a leg.'

'Break your own,' Lou muttered, clenching my arm. The burglar lights outside the Admin Block snapped on.

'How are you feeling?'

'Stop asking me that.' She swung her case from the shelf in the store-cupboard, bashing the wall, and we followed her into Philip's room. It was cold, he'd left the window open. Under it, raindrops beaded the ledge and stained the floor. Polish clashed with the scent of cut grass, summer leaves. The light outside was poignant and exaggerated. Apple trees gleamed in the dusk, then sprang back, vanishing, as Nina flicked the switch. Lou opened the case, stared almost malevolently at her violin.

'What if I can't do it?' She held it away from her, the way you'd hold a muddy cat, as Nina and I flopped to the floor, leaned back against the radiator, looking up at her.

'Start with a scale,' I suggested after a long silence. 'Something easy.'

From the way she lifted her bow, shook back her hair and cradled the chin-rest, collecting herself, you could tell she was expecting it to be easy but the first note crunched and she sprang away from it, as though the heel of the violin had bitten her throat.

'Are you always like this before a concert?' asked Nina.

'No.' She took a deep breath. 'I need a cigarette.'

'Are you still feeling drunk?'

She blinked at us. 'Just sick.'

'Nerves. You'll be fine. Just concentrate.' Nina was beginning to sound unhelpfully anxious. Lou's face threatened tears.

'Come on, Lou,' I joked. 'Or Anna will stand up and have a go.'

'OK, you've convinced me,' she said blankly, lifting her bow, closing her eyes.

We said goodbye to Nina at the door to the Dining Hall. Pablo was wiping down the last few tables after supper. He winked and crossed his fingers, grinning at Lou. A tray of salt and pepper pots rested precariously on the canteen ledge between the tea and coffee urns. Philip came over, self-conscious in his navy-blue suit. He wore a creased white shirt. His tie was striped with slips and welts, as though the grey silk had been shredded and then glued together again. He kept his hands jammed in his pockets. 'Everything OK?' he smiled.

In the background a pair of flutes accelerated through the 'Flight of the Bumblebee' while Susie Hargreaves thundered low accompaniment on the timps. Anna Birdwood stood with her back to the room, rehearsing the fast bits from the Rossini. Behind us Ella cracked jokes for the cello section.

We dumped our cases on an empty table, as far from the others as we could go. It stank of dishcloth. An ooze of ketchup dried in the plastic-cracks. Lou examined her fingers, peeling back a hangnail until the skin beneath blossomed with tiny red cells that slowly welled into a single gleaming sphere of blood. I took out my violin, wiped away the rosin-dust with my thumb, squeaking the sticky wood. Then Philip called everyone round. 'I just want to say three things: look at me; don't play in the rests; and, most of all, enjoy it!'

Lou took her finger from her mouth.

The Civic Hall's peppermint-green walls are garlanded with plaster vines. A plaster grape-and-pomegranate cluster hangs above the clock. White plaster putti, one on each side, kiss the shining fire-escape sign. To the left of the door a wooden plaque gives thanks for the restoration to donors and craftsmen alike. Nina points out a spelling mistake and smirks. We follow her through to the back of the hall where a girl with a tablecloth folded round her waist is lounging shyly behind a makeshift bar and help ourselves to complimentary wine. Already the front two rows are littered with programmes, jackets and bags, but the room feels empty. Apart from the waitress and a baby sleeping in its mother's arms we are the youngest people there. We sit near the back and wait. Nina rests her head on my shoulder.

'Wake me up when it's time to clap,' she yawns. Three drops of white wine slop over the rim of her glass. 'When my grandchildren ask how I celebrated my A level results I think I'm going to have to lie.' Her eyes are closed. She sucks her thumb.

'You can say you went to a gig.'

'Maybe classical music will be trendy by then,' says Lou.

Nina shrugs. 'Maybe pop music will be classical.'

The room fills slowly. Floorboards echo and scrape and laughter ripples from the bar. A steel-haired woman sits by Lou, huffing and sighing, her forehead glistening as she struggles from the grip of a hand-knitted cardigan. Her fingers shake with the strain of every button. She looks at us sideways, unfolds a score and a glasses-case from her handbag, resting them one above the other on her knee. Lou stares straight ahead. She blinks and shuffles forwards an inch as Philip walks on stage and this is the first thing I can't quite believe: he's wearing the same blue suit. Four years on, his hair is the same, his face is the same, he walks with the same good-humoured, vaguely ridiculous bouncing swagger. For a millisecond, as he squints into the smattering of applause, I'm ready to fall in love again. The baby grunts, threatens to cry.

'My daughter,' he confides tenderly. 'Upstaging me again!'

The audience laughs. Heads turn and the mother blushes. I haven't noticed her before. She seems very young. Nina pinches me, leaning up to my ear. 'It's whatshername – that Sixth expelled for drugs,' she whispers.

Lou's eyes flicker from the stage, hesitate, sliding back as Nina inspects her memory. 'Heather Allen! Shit, I *knew* I recognised her.'

Philip's introduction comes to an end and the rest of the players slip into their seats. They shuffle their music stands, fold over the corners of the scores, performing a dozen minute ritual adjustments. Nina closes her eyes again, sinks to my shoulder. She smiles the way a boa constrictor might smile, digesting a new-born lamb.

No one expected to see a fourteen-year-old soloist walk on stage. The parents shifted in their seats and wished they could have gone home in the interval. They folded their hands and knees and rearranged their faces, kindly, hoping the embarrassment, when it came, might not show through. Lou's faint smile did not inspire confidence. The dress made her look stringy and gauche. The violin scroll jutted uncomfortably beneath her arm as she bowed, hair flopping forwards in a fluffy mess, and the chin-rest creaked. She flushed, acknowledging the tentative applause and Philip lifted his hands for calm. Lou smoothed her hair behind her ears and squinted once into the audience. She cradled the violin, squared it against her shoulder with the grace of a marksman taking aim.

I never heard her play so well. The notes unravelled, twisting and looping themselves into a new kind of Beethoven that lingered, flew at the tips of her fingers, fresh and candid and impossible as brilliance itself. The phrases stretched then hesitated. Languid and passionate by turns, the melody paced out its halting, sinewy seduction.

Almost as soon as it began, it seemed to end. The Quad resounded with ecstatic quietness. In front of us, Philip glowed. Sometimes I like to think that was his last moment of happiness.

Lou tucked her violin under her arm and bowed. She turned to him, stepping up onto the podium to shake his hand as the applause crescendoed. An old man at the front stood up, and then a family three rows behind, and suddenly half the Quad was on its feet. Nina put her fingers in her mouth and whistled furiously as I crept off stage and Philip spread his arms, lifting them in a collective hug, signalling the orchestra to take a bow. Only now were we allowed to stare at the audience. I beamed at Lou's mum from the wings. *What's she done to her face?* I thought. I'd never seen her smile before. Her eyes were shining. Mr Greene clapped like a loud emphatic machine and Sophie thundered her heels, a jerky staccato that growled from row to row and rumbled across the aisle to every corner of the auditorium until, when I was sure the seating must collapse, Philip released his hands and the orchestra sat down. I walked back slowly across the stage, half hidden behind a huge bouquet, and the audience roared as I handed it to Philip and Philip handed it to Lou. Hawkley girls cheered from the balcony and I remember noticing how badly the florist's ribbon clashed with Lou's red dress as she leaned forwards, tilting her cheek for a congratulatory kiss. I remember the whites of Philip's eyelids fluttering shut as she shifted weight. His lips went rigid, his shoulders seized, he shied and, falling, the violin wrenched and splintered and snapped beneath Lou's weight. The wolf-whistles faded at the backs of our throats.

Lou lay very still on the concrete floor, listening to the audience reel. Crushed white lilies cushioned her head. The polythene wrinkled and sighed accompaniment as she breathed and she could feel the springy outline of a petal rub her eyelashes when she blinked. She blinked again. She didn't want to think about what else she felt. The shards, the silvery ridges of unsprung strings, the knotted scroll. The chill of the concrete seeping up through velvet into her shiny, melted chest.

A man's voice brushed through her vagueness, whispering urgently in her ear. His fingers pinched her arm. 'Are you OK?' he said. His breath was like a warm wind. 'Can you stand?' Polythene rustled again as someone pulled the bouquet free and they lifted her head, returning it very gently to the floor as murmurs floated from the audience. She thought she'd like to stay there, listening, a little while longer but the hands were gripping and pulling her up, right up to her feet for yet another bow. She'd never heard a sound like that before. The buzzing dimmed. She looked at her feet, so far away it gave her vertigo, and folded the shattered violin under her arm. Philip and Beth will carry her away. Her mum and dad push through to the gangway. Sophie stands frozen to the spot.

Sitting here, side by side, I have the feeling that this is the way our friendship was always meant to end: accompanied by Philip's string quartet.

'We've been invited to do some recording — it's an amazing opportunity. It's been a while in the pipeline, maybe I should have mentioned it earlier,' he told the Head, explaining his decision to leave. But there were other reasons. Everyone remembered, everyone knew.

Lou is in another world. She never played again after the fall. Smashed beyond repair, the £3,000 violin lies in its velvet-lined coffin somewhere cobwebby at the back of Mr Greene's garage store. Hawkley withdrew the scholarship and last year, when her turn came round, Anna Birdwood led the orchestra. Lou's fingers grew weak and shaky. Music to them had only ever been a sequence of more or less repetitive strains. She has forgotten how to play — that's gone for ever — but listening is something she can never unlearn. Her scar aches, longing for Paganini's ghost, for the days before irony when it was possible to think of something that fanciful.

Nina leans against my shoulder, dreaming or daydream-
ing of Robert, her A's, of catching tomorrow's first train
out of here and never writing back.

We'll meet up, of course, in the holidays. A café in
London. We'll be wearing different clothes, and make-up –
ethnic jewellery. We'll take folded £5 notes from new,
nearly identical, Guatemalan purses and each insist on paying for the other's drinks, which will all be cappuccino.
Nina will scrounge a cigarette and I will watch amazed
and disappointed as she lights up, drawing heavily on the
low-tar filter for maximum punch.

At first we'll make an effort not to talk about school, but
the gaps and pauses will be too uncomfortable. Someone
flicks the occasional throwaway nugget of information into
the heap of ash between our coffee-cups. Reaching in for
it, the tips of our fingers powder grey and stink for the rest
of the afternoon but suddenly all that matters is that
Caroline Price is pregnant, Anna Birdwood has had a nervous breakdown in New York and Isobel King's dad got
taken to court by the Inland Revenue the week her
mother's breast cancer was diagnosed. For thirty minutes
we'll be best friends again as rumours are analysed with
almost cloying enthusiasm for we have new lives and new
allegiances too, and anything is better than having to mention these.

We'll kiss goodbye – we never used to kiss before – and
slide home riddled with unpronouncable discontent. Send
postcards saying how lovely it had been. Wait for the memory to fade. We will be grown up about it, which means

philosophical. It's healthy and natural for old school friends to drift apart.

We'll change, but not as much as might have been expected. In spite of our careers, our husbands and our children we will wake up cold at dawn. A kind of unremitting homesickness will follow us for days, for weeks at a time and as we grow older we will look back on this evening and remember it as the very last night, not just of Beth and Nina and Lou, but of youth itself. We were only eighteen, we'll think, leaving our Volvos in the supermarket car park, remembering how young our daughters had seemed when they were that age. How much they still had to learn. How careless they had been.

Nina lifts her head as the last notes fade, looks round disorientated, then remembers where we are. She runs her fingers through her hair and sighs. My collarbone tingles and aches. I blink at Lou. Her eyes are glistening. Her hands unknot and her shoulders ease. The muscles of her heart push blood along arteries she doesn't even know she has and her scar contracts. One knee hollows itself against the other. The mosquito bites on her forearms sting. 'OK?' I smile at her. Glowing, she nods. The palms of her hands beat like a metronome as the musicians take their bow. The baby cries. Men and women in the front rows fidget with jackets and bags. Keyrings clatter. Polished shoes shuffle and squeak across the gleaming floor.

Nina stands, ready to go. She smooths her T-shirt, nudges between us, squeezing into the aisle where Heather

Allen paces, jiggling the child. She hadn't meant to get so close. She stares at them, wondering if she'd been wrong, all those years ago, about Pablo, whether the older woman – we are all women now, no matter what our fathers prefer to think – will recognise her without the brace. 'What a beautiful baby,' she says uncomfortably. Heather stumbles a doubtful smile and mutters thanks. 'How old is she?'

'Eight months.'

Nina leans in close, examining the eyes, the wide white forehead, the silver-blond baby hair. If I'm going to be a doctor, she tells herself, I'm going to have to learn to coo. 'She's gorgeous.'

The baby smiles and Heather shakes her head. 'She certainly knows how to take a compliment.'

Nina leans closer still, sticks out a finger, tickling the palm. 'Are you going to be a violinist like your daddy, then?' she gurgles.

Heather laughs on cue. How many times has she endured this question? 'No. She's going to be a merchant banker – someone's got to pay the bills.'

'What's her name?'

'Louisa. We call her Lou.' Champagne pops behind the bar and everyone turns round. Heather steps from the path of a genteel stampede. Cheerful imperious voices bellow requests across the auditorium and a vigilant Blimp mounts guard against pushers-in. Nina squints through the queue but Heather is nowhere to be seen.

'I guess there isn't going to be an encore, then,' says Lou.

She shakes herself like a wet dog, shedding the music, looks at her watch. 'We might find an off-licence if we're quick.'

'Don't you want to see Philip?'

'I want to get drunk,' she blinks. She won't be serious. There's nothing to talk about. 'You were the one with the full-on crush.'

'I wasn't—'

'You were. *You* go and say hello.' She pushes me. 'Go on. You know you want to.'

I shake my head. Strictly speaking, a gesture is never so bad as an outright lie.

It's warm outside. Concert-goers mill in the semi-dark, discussing the performance and wondering out loud whether to head straight for the pub or try and find somewhere still open for food. They bump into the pleasant silhouettes of colleagues and friends and laugh at coincidences in the faint, municipal gloom. A toothy solicitor gives us directions for Victoria Wine where we choose a half of vodka and a half of whisky which the shop assistant won't sell without ID. Nina flashes her driving licence, grins.

We walk the streets swigging deliciously from paper bags. The sky is brown and moonless. TVs flicker and stream in the corners of uncurtained downstairs rooms. I wonder if anything's happened – an earthquake, perhaps. An explosion. A coup. It's our world now. We're meant to know about stuff like war and politics, we're meant to want to make a difference but Nina and Lou don't care. They stand outside a two-up two-down watching the end of *Inspector*

Morse, then clatter screaming to the end of the road as Nina coughs and a man in an armchair turns his face from screen to window, staring at us through the net. We race to McDonald's, throwing ourselves against the swing door seven full minutes before closing time. The woman behind the counter refuses to serve us all the same. Apple-pies sog in cardboard wallets waiting for the bin and the chip smell makes our stomachs groan.

Nina announces her intention to report the incident to McDonald's HQ and stalks out, waving at us through the glass, the plastic ferns. 'Beth's got a spot,' Lou crows, examining my face in the burger-light. We head back to the boat for tinned custard and toast instead.

By dark the wharf is christmassy, deserted. Naked bulbs shine in seaside necklaces of light staining our faces as we lean against the deck-rail, passing the bottle from mouth to mouth. Our throats are fireproof. Nina watches, hoping for a shooting star, as planes and satellites glint across the hemisphere and the canal cools down. Algae shrinks into itself, a soup of tiny flower-buds, night-shy and folded ready for the next hot afternoon. Fish fly through the diesel spill, splashing back burned and filmy. Coke cans and skip-wood float where Lou imagines crocodile heads.

From nowhere, a narrowboat engine splutters to the head of the lock, slips into neutral. The bow-light throws out a fan of cold rays and a shadow steps onto the towpath. Gears creak and the basin echoes with the sigh of twin cascades. Nina swallows the last few vodka drops. She slips the bottle from its paper bag, holding it to the beam.

'Empty,' Lou murmurs, almost sad. 'Let's chuck it in the canal.' She snatches but Nina has changed hands, teasing, and waves it out of reach. The narrowboat chugs forward softly, its lights sink into darkness again. Low voices smuggle behind the gates.

'Give it me.' Lou leans over Nina, squashing her.

'I'm warning you. Let go or I'll drop it!'

'*I want to throw it in*—' Lou eases her grip, her words are petulant and slurred as Nina stares her down, ready to fight.

'So what were you talking to Heather Allen about?' I ask, distracting them.

'Lou,' says Nina, matter of fact.

'Did she remember me?' Lou's voice changes, she looks away from the bottle in Nina's hand, surprised.

'Not you – the baby. They called their baby Lou.'

'Lou after Lou?' It comes out sharper than I'd meant it to – shrill with sudden, urgent curiosity.

'How should I know?' Nina shrugs. 'Maybe his mum's a Lou.'

An unfamiliar sound slides into the night from somewhere deep inside Lou's chest, a sort of melting, sing-song moan that bubbles and swallows itself, then loops back louder, breathlessly. She hiccups, choking as we watch, amazed, and now I understand that this is laughter. Her eyes crease and her lips mouth silent gibberish. Nina stares at the forgotten vodka bottle, raises her eyebrows, tapping her head with a forefinger as Lou gags, gripping the handrail, doubled up, though surely nothing's as funny as that. We giggle awkwardly, waiting for the tears that never do come, not really, though her eyes are slick. Her cheeks glow and her shoulders shake with silent, heaving sobs. Whole minutes go by. Then, suddenly, she takes a deep breath, straightens her face, quite sober, ready to speak. She looks at us a moment and pauses, struggling to hold the words as laughter surges, stuttering and irresistible once more. The lull breaks. Sliding to the deck, she hugs her knees to her chest, crushes the air from her lungs. Her bones hurt and she bites her wrist and stamps and the noise is hilarious and somehow hollow too.

Nina crouches next to her and stares. 'It's OK,' she soothes, stroking Lou's hand. 'You've got to stop this now. Don't think about anything, just breathe. Nice and slow.'

The fingers twitch. Lou crumples again. 'It's just so — fucking sad,' she stammers.

Nina looks away. The lock is empty and the bottom gate swings open. Lamplight gilds the still canal. 'Calm down, you're getting hysterical,' she says, but Lou doesn't care. She reaches for the whisky, sloshing it over the back of her hand as the cap spins free. Spirits evaporate.

'Don't want to calm down,' she gasps. She swigs. She laughs and laughs and laughs.

Nina packs quietly. I feign sleep but she stands with her back to me all the same, folding unworn sweatshirts, chucking the dirty ones into a Waitrose carrier. Her rolled-up sleeping bag opens like a nylon flower, peeling back against the strings with breath of its own. Her sponge-bag bulges. Sandals lie on the crumpled blanket sole to sole and heel to toe. It's raining but she packs her mum's kagoul, looks round suspiciously as drizzle spatters the glass. I close my eyes. Maybe there'll be a note by the kettle next door. The zips on her rucksack rattle and something brushes my goose-pimpled arm. 'You can stop pretending now. I'm off,' she whispers, hoisting the bag.

I blink at her smooth face, tanned and shadowy against the grey. She doesn't smile. She hasn't dared brush her hair in case breaking the tangles makes too much noise.

'What time's your train?'

'Dunno,' she shrugs.

'I'll walk you.'

She shrugs again. 'Well hurry up. And don't wake Lou.'

Outside the air is cool and slippery. The *Otterburn* shifts as we step up to the shining quay. The cobbles gleam. 'You weren't going to say goodbye,' I shudder, holding the bag as she winds a silk scarf, peasant-style, round her head.

'I knew you were awake.'

'Liar!'

'Your breathing changed.' Our basketball boots squeak on the wet stone and the hems of our jeans splash black. 'It's bloody horrible out here, are you sure you want to come?' she says, threading an arm through mine. She looks around. 'Where is everyone?'

'It's Sunday.' A lorry wheezes past, spraying the gutter. Sheep stare out at us from between the transporter slats, stinking of shit and panic and sweaty wool. Nina wrinkles her nose. She'll always be fastidious like this, I suppose.

'What are you smiling about?'

'Nothing.' My smile extends. 'Do your parents know you're coming then?'

She shakes her head. 'I'll ring from Oxford.'

'What if they're not there?'

'I'll wait.'

'You could come back—'

'I'll wait.'

We follow road signs to the station, a gingerbread house with grimy white eaves and a freshly tarmacked car park in front. The flower shop next door is boarded up. Credit card acceptance stickers curl from the cobwebby glass inside and pigeons murmur on the upstairs window ledge. The pavement is pocked with gum. Someone has ripped the seats from the bus shelter across the road. A skinny boy in stonewashed jeans hops wearily up and down the kerb, kicking his sports bag out of the rain and then hopping some more, so patiently it makes me want to cry. Everything today is dirty and wet and hopeless.

Nina disappears into the ticket office. It smells just like the station at Farham, of lino and electric bars, fag ends, piss and disinfectant. A whiteboard lists the times of Sunday trains. The counter blind is drawn.

'Twenty minutes,' she says, looking up as I walk in. 'That's not too bad.' We stare at the floor. 'I'll ring you in London next week.'

'Yeah.'

'Don't wait with me now – Lou will think we've both jumped ship.'

'Yeah. I'll be getting back.'

'Yeah.'

'OK,' I edge away. 'Lots of love –'

She waves.

An Intercity screams through but I have my back to the station now. I'm headed for the *Otterburn*. Nothing surprises me, nothing can make me flinch or turn. The boy at the bus stop stands in the gutter, head down, staring at his shoes. Suddenly, as I draw near, he bends. Puddle-water splashes his sleeve.

'What have you found?' I ask.

He straightens, looking up from his delighted palm. 'A pound. Just there, under the leaves.'

Trudging into the centre of town again, I make a list,

imagining what you can get for that much money. Washing-up liquid. Bananas from the Caribbean thick with the scent of spiders and pesticide, the fingerprints of farm-workers and grubby English grocers, shelf-stackers in Co-op pinafores. A mug of tea with all the sugar you can dissolve, a chair and table, fifteen minutes' peace and anonymity before the waitress slouches round, kneading her J-cloth. Nearly ten cigarettes. A bus ticket to, I don't know, nowhere very far from here . . .

A van accelerates down the High Street, lurching to a stop, then swerving sharp left just where I'm about to cross. I've seen it before. I recognise the purply rust. The windscreen-wipers rattle and click. The engine isn't sure. Gabriel blinks in the rear-view mirror. Next to him a woman in peroxide dreadlocks traces squiggles in the steamed-up fug, squints at the map on the dashboard, shrugs. The whole world to explore and they're lost already? In three or four years' time that could be me. For a moment I wonder whether to wave. It's not such a coin-cidence. Perhaps they've come to say goodbye. Condensation tears roll down the inside pane and an Alsatian presses its nose to the glass. Sophie's hand scrunches the fur at the back of its neck, tugging a fistful of the warm, loose skin. She looks up, smiles at something Gabriel has said, then kisses the dog. The van reverses, lurching again. A back light indicates. Tyretracks silver and fade along the Sunday-silent road.

Now you can order superb titles directly from Virago

☐	Mummy's Legs	Kate Bingham	£6.99
☐	A Whore in the Kitchen	Amanda Coe	£6.99
☐	The Girl with Brains in her Feet	Jo Hodges	£6.99
☐	The Pleasing Hour	Lily King	£6.99
☐	George Bush: Dark Prince of Love	Lydia Millet	£6.99
☐	Lady Moses	Lucinda Roy	£6.99
☐	Tipping the Velvet	Sarah Waters	£6.99
☐	Affinity	Sarah Waters	£6.99

Please allow for postage and packing: **Free UK delivery.**
Europe: add 25% of retail price; Rest of World: 45% of retail price.

To order any of the above or any other Virago titles, please call
our credit card orderline or fill in this coupon and send/fax it to:

Virago, 250 Western Avenue, London, W3 6XZ, UK.
Fax 020 8324 5678   Telephone 020 8324 5516

☐ I enclose a UK bank cheque made payable to Virago for £ . . . . . .
☐ Please charge £ . . . . . to my Access, Visa, Delta, Switch Card No.

☐☐☐☐☐☐☐☐☐☐☐☐☐☐☐☐☐☐☐☐☐☐☐

Expiry Date ☐☐☐☐   Switch Issue No. ☐☐

NAME (Block letters please) . . . .

ADDRESS . . . .

Postcode . . . . Telephone . . . .

Signature . . . .

Please allow 28 days for delivery within the UK. Offer subject to price and availability.

Please do not send any further mailings from companies carefully selected by Virago ☐